To the Wolves

An Ethan McCormick Novel

Evan Bond

Contents

Chapter 1 7
Chapter 2 14
Chapter 3 22
Chapter 4 36
Chapter 5 46
Chapter 6 57
Chapter 7 64
Chapter 8 73
Chapter 9 80
Chapter 10 88
Chapter 11 94
Chapter 12 100
Chapter 13 108
Chapter 14 121
Chapter 15 129
Chapter 16 137
Chapter 17 142
Chapter 18 151
Chapter 19 162
Chapter 20 168

Chapter 21	178
Chapter 22	184
Chapter 23	193
Chapter 24	205
Chapter 25	222
Chapter 26	232
Chapter 27	243
Chapter 28	254
Chapter 29	271
Chapter 30	290
Chapter 31	296
Chapter 32	306
Chapter 33	318
Chapter 34	333
Epilogue	353
Acknowledgements	355
About the author	357

To the Wolves
By Evan Bond

Copyright © 2015 by Evan Bond

All rights reserved. This book or any portion thereof
may not be reproduced or used in any manner whatsoever
without the express written permission of the publisher
except for the use of brief quotations in a book review.

This is a work of fiction. Any resemblance to actual
people, living or dead, is purely coincidental.

www.booksbybond.com
www.facebook.com/booksbybond

For Melissa, the strongest woman I've ever known.

Chapter 1

A late night storm had passed over the city of Miami leaving the streets drenched. Puddles formed in the roads slowly draining as the night went on. It left behind a smooth shine to the black asphalt. The rain had ceased, but the clouds remained which cloaked the city in a dark and moonless night. A mixture of oil and rain covered the roads making them slick and dangerous. It was late and Miami Beach bustled with nightlife as always. The bright neon colors of hotels and bars cascaded out towards the ocean. Tourists roamed free looking for the best nightclubs. As usual, the city was dark and quiet. Most people were home after a long day's work. Others had migrated to the night scene at the beach.

Officer Ethan McCormick slowed his cruiser to a stop. The traffic light flashed its neon red glow across the white paint of his squad car. Normally he would run the license plates of the vehicles around him. With no other cars around he decided to just relax. Despite popular belief, most cops did not run red lights just because they had the power to do so. Every time the lights flicked on it was logged into an internal database. Later when the officer is dropping off the cruiser at the station he would have to account for every single use. If the battery was dead at the end of the day and there had not been a good reason to use them that officer would be in hot water. Luckily Ethan was not the type of officer to do so.

He was a patient man. Ever since he could remember things seemed to roll right off of him. Girlfriends in his past had always asked how he could always be so calm. Even when facing what seemed to be the most stressful situations. He would only shrug. It was just how he was. Staring at the bright red traffic light his eyelids began to feel heavy. He was on his way back to the station to drop off his cruiser then head home. With the few extra hours, he had worked he could not wait to get some rest.

As the light clicked green Ethan began to go over the details of his day. It had been rather dull. Most days consisted of domestic disputes, drunken fist fights, traffic violations, and more naked people than one could imagine. It surprised Ethan how many times he would show up and someone would be naked, even in the simplest of situations. Once he had arrested a man for breaking into his ex-wife's home. When Ethan arrived the trespasser was naked. He had asked how that had happened but never received a straight answer. That was during his first year on the force. He was happy to have those times behind him.

Ethan's official job was as a detective for the Miami Police Department homicide division. He responded to homicide reports, inspected the scene, and took notes from witnesses. When there was not a homicide Ethan made his rounds just like every other officer. It was nowhere near as exciting as the crime scene shows on television made it look. There was much more paperwork in real life. Still, Ethan loved what he did and tried to do his best every day. The best perk of being a detective was wearing plain clothes. He no longer had to wear the standard blue uniform. Somehow it felt absolutely liberating.

As he rounded a corner he came to another red light. Skidding to a stop Ethan glanced around the intersection. A pearl white Chevrolet Aveo with nearly limousine dark tint rolled slowly through the green light. He was not sure quite what caught his attention, but when Ethan's light changed he stuck close behind the car.

Getting close enough he began to run the plate. A moment later an advisory blinked on screen. The vehicle had been reported stolen the day before. Immediately Ethan flicked on the red and blue lights and increased his speed. The Aveo coasted to the shoulder and came to an abrupt stop. Ethan stopped short just behind the Aveo and shifted the cruiser into park. With the blinding spotlight pointed directly towards the vehicle he could see two silhouettes bouncing nervously back and forth.

Ethan had gathered everything he needed to approach the vehicle and opened his door. As he did the brake lights dimmed and the vehicle tore away. The tires squealed across the pavement. His heart thumped wildly in his chest as he slammed the door shut. Adrenaline coursed fiercely through his veins. Within seconds Ethan was in pursuit.

With his left hand on the wheel, he reached out with his right. Grabbing the receiver he called for backup. He quickly shouted his position and briefly described the situation. Once he received a response he dropped the receiver and placed both hands firmly on the wheel. Above him, the siren wailed noisily through the empty streets. It echoed off the nearby buildings.

The Aveo screeched around a corner with Ethan close on its tail. They would not lose him that easy. They began to swerve back and forth on the slippery road. With each slide, it looked as if they might lose control of the vehicle. Ethan knew they had to bring this chase to a stop before it ended in injury.

Applying more pressure to the accelerator Ethan began to close in on the fleeing vehicle. He was going to try what was known as a P.I.T. maneuver, precision immobilization technique. An officer would attempt to end a dangerous chase by forcing the driver to lose control of the vehicle and stop. This could be accomplished by bumping the suspect's car in the rear bumper slightly off center. If done correctly it would cause the vehicle to slide sideways bringing it to a halt.

Their bumpers collided, but the suspect remained in control of his vehicle. Dropping back Ethan prepared to ram again this time he would apply more force. Before Ethan could try again the car rounded another corner. This time it slid into the opposite lane. If there had been any traffic on the road they would have collided.

Ethan followed closely behind gaining distance. Up ahead on the long stretch of road Ethan spotted several flashing lights. His backup had finally arrived. In a matter of minutes, the fleeing suspects would be cut off and placed in handcuffs. The Aveo slid sideways and skidded to a stop spraying murky brown water across the road.

As two men emerged from the vehicle the other police cruisers slid to a halt. The driver bolted across the street while the passenger dashed to the right down an alleyway. Ethan quickly turned right and ran after the passenger. The other two officers chased after the driver.

Up ahead Ethan could hear the man panting. His shallow breaths echoed through the tight space. His footfalls were loud and accompanied by a splash from the wet concrete. Ethan was forced to push himself faster as the man jutted around a corner. Not wanting to lose the suspect he threw himself around the corner as fast as his legs would allow.

The suspect was several feet ahead of him and gaining distance. The slippery ground was making it difficult for Ethan to keep up. Regardless he pushed himself harder feeling his calves burn. "Stop, now!" He panted when he was only a few feet behind the suspect.

Darting left the man aimed himself toward another alley. Ethan cursed and followed closely behind. His right hand gripped the butt of his Taser as he sprinted. Once he was close enough to the suspect he would take him down.

Ahead of the perpetrator stood a tall wire fence. As the man attempted to climb up Ethan caught up to him. He had only climbed a few feet before Ethan grabbed him by the back of his pants and yanked him back down. As he tumbled to the ground Ethan put himself between the entrance of the alley and the suspect blocking his only escape.

Drawing his Glock Ethan stared down at the man and ordered him to the ground. "Place both hands on the back of your head and get down on your knees, do it now!" The man looked nervous but did not comply. "I am warning you, get down on the ground now."

After the second warning, the man quickly pulled a gun of his own. The reaction had been so fast it startled Ethan. Taking two steps back Ethan began to bark more orders. "Drop the weapon and get on the ground. I won't warn you again."

The man's eyes shifted back and forth nervously. Ethan mentally prepared himself to fire. It was not something he wanted to do but would if left no choice. "He'll kill me if I give up," the perpetrator said as he turned the gun on himself. "It'll be quicker this way." Ethan cried out for him to stop to no avail.

The man squeezed the trigger and for a moment Ethan's ears rang. The smell of gunpowder was thick in the air. Small pieces of skull and brain clung to the chain link fence. A large splatter had erupted onto the side wall. Holstering his weapon Ethan covered his mouth. "Jesus Christ," he cried as the situation sank in. The scene was gruesome. Ethan had never seen so much blood. Even now the man's body slumped over, lying in a puddle, blood gushing from the wound.

Fighting the urge to vomit he spun around and grabbed the radio from his belt. "This is Detective McCormick requesting immediate assistance." He rattled off his general location. Within minutes the two other officers had arrived followed shortly by an ambulance. The paramedics looked at the body and shook their heads. Moments later a coroner was on his way.

One of the other officers turned to Ethan as the coroner scooped up the body and placed it in a black bag. "What the hell happened, Ethan?" At first, Ethan was too shocked to respond. Catching his nerve he turned towards him.

"I had him cornered and he just shot himself. He said it would be quicker. I don't know." A look of horror and disgust spread across the other officer's face.

"Well, at least he didn't try and take you with him, McCormick." Ethan nodded, counting himself lucky.

As the officer patted him on the back he turned and headed back towards his squad car. Ethan did the same. Once behind the wheel, he placed his head back against the headrest. An image of the man's eyes staring into his as he pulled the trigger flashed in his head. It would be near impossible to erase that image from his mind.

Shaking it off the best he could, Ethan put the car in drive. Heading back towards the police department he tried to push the thought of the man out. The image of his lifeless eyes staring back at him seemed to be burned into his retinas.

Chapter 2

After Ethan's traumatic encounter he had taken a few weeks in therapy. It had been mandatory to make sure he did not suffer psychologically over the ordeal. It did bother him, but slowly he began to move on. It had been the lifeless expression plastered on the man's face that had disturbed him the most. He had never watched a person die, much less someone take their own life. The lifelessness behind the eyes had been a haunting image he would not soon forget.

Ethan was convinced he had watched the soul leave the body. It was an eerie feeling. One that he could never explain. It was a cold expression, almost not human. It was that stare that burned into his memory and would not stop tormenting him.

Therapy helped him move forward. He was very grateful for the therapist. She was an older woman who seemed to know everything about him just by listening to him speak. She had recommended he take a vacation and that was exactly what he planned to do.

The Florida Keys were a short drive from Miami. It seemed like the perfect place to unwind. That night after therapy he went home and talked to his girlfriend Sandra Delano. Proposing the idea of taking a week off in the Keys. Instantly she loved it and they began to pack.

Sandra Delano also worked for the Miami Police Department. Her line of work was different from Ethan's, however. She worked for internal affairs in the anti-corruption division. She had always found it depressing that a division such as hers should exist, but ultimately it was necessary.

She had been working for internal affairs for just over two years. She took the job shortly after she and Ethan started dating. Ethan had been on the force for a couple of years, being somewhat new in town. Instantly she was attracted to him. He was a funny and charming man. Hardly ever did he seem to get upset, as if nothing ever bothered him. It was the personality that would put a person in a good mood no matter how they felt.

"You almost ready, babe?" Ethan called from the living room. Sandra was making a few last minute decisions on which items to bring. She picked up her laptop and thought for a moment. Her eyes darted towards the bedroom door.

"Just a second, Ethan." She called back.

Deciding against bringing the laptop she slipped it between the mattress and box spring. Picking up her purse she left the bedroom and met up with Ethan. She kissed him softly as she walked out the front door.

"Let's head out," she said with a hint of excitement in her voice. A week away from everything with Ethan would do her mind good. Work had been stressful lately.

She watched as Ethan locked up the house. Sandra started loading their bags into the trunk of Ethan's 2006 Dodge Stratus. It was dark green with a few scratches here and there, but otherwise still in good shape.

"When are you going to get a new car, honey?" It was a question she had asked him many times before. His answer was always the same.

As he climbed into the driver seat he said, "When this one breaks down." With a giggle, she jumped into the passenger seat.

***

Ethan looked over at Sandra as they drove. Her head rested against the window with her eyelids dropping. Often she would fall asleep on long car rides. Even though Ethan would have preferred her company he decided not to disturb her.

Her long brown-red hair rolled over her face as she slept. He resisted the urge to reach over and brush it away. Trying to keep his eyes on the road he admired her beauty in his head. This trip was going to be wonderful. Ethan had planned a wonderful surprise for Sandra. He knew she would absolutely love it. He could not wait to show her what it was.

Sandra stirred in the seat next to him and sat up. Strands of hair stuck to her forehead. Smiling at Ethan, showing her pearly white and straight teeth, she asked, "We there yet?" Chuckling Ethan told her they were close, but not quite there.

"Sorry for falling asleep on you," she said mimicking a pouty face.

"Sweetheart, it's alright. It gave me time to admire your beauty." Sandra blushed and looked out the window. The ocean on either side of the bridge was a deep blue, nothing like the water in the rest of Florida. Miami was, of course, the exception. There the water was clear and gorgeous. But it was not the deep shade of blue as it was in the keys. There it looked far cooler and refreshing.

Looking back at Ethan Sandra cocked her head and said, "So, when we get there what would you like to do first?" Ethan grinned and looked over at her.

"You," he said putting his eyes back on the road. Smiling she smacked his arm playfully.

"Alright then, after that?"

Ethan shrugged. "I don't know, maybe go down to Key West and enjoy the nightlife. Maybe hit up a bar or two."

Sandra laughed. "You're not much of a drinker, Ethan." Again he shrugged.

"Maybe not, but isn't there a bar there that someone is buried under or something like that?"

"That's right, you've never been to the Keys before, I almost forgot."

"I've only lived down here for a few years, sorry."

"It's fine, I've been there once or twice. I can be your tour guide for the week."

"Can I get the exclusive tour package?"

"And what might that include, Mr. McCormick?"

"A tour of that magnificent body."

Blushing again Sandra looked away.

"I know what's on your mind this morning." Ethan shrugged as if to say can you blame me?

She laughed, "Yes, you get exclusive access to the premium package." Winking at him they both laughed.

After what seemed like hours they finally reached their hotel. Both Ethan and Sandra welcomed the chance to stand up and stretch. The hotel was a beautiful resort on the edge of the water. The lobby was luxurious. After checking in they found their room and slipped inside. It was somewhat small, yet elegant. The tan walls looked almost as if made from bamboo. The far end of the room let out into a small, cozy balcony. Next to the sliding glass door sat a small white sun chair with a large floor to ceiling mirror behind it. It made the room look larger than it was. Directly in the center of the open space rested a large king size bed with a black and white comforter and matching pillows.

Sliding open the glass door Ethan stepped out onto the balcony. The view from the fourth floor was amazing. The deep blue ocean stretched out for miles. Small green islands spotted the horizon. Every so often a jet ski would rip past the coast followed closely by its wake. The ocean breeze swept over his body and he relaxed.

Turning back into the room he looked for Sandra. She was busy admiring the bathroom. It was a large, luxurious room with a stand up shower, no tub. The door that separated the shower from the room was large and glass. It was frosted which would barely show the outline of anyone inside.

Stepping inside the bathroom he watched as Sandra slipped her dress around her ankles. Looking back over her shoulder she locked eyes with Ethan. Her bangs dipped down over her big beautiful eyes.

"Would you like to see your first stop on the premium tour?" She winked at him. Ethan glanced up and down her tight body.

Living in Miami she had spent a lot of time at the beach and it showed. Her skin was lightly tanned, but not too much. It was enough to accent her hair color perfectly. The red panties she wore hugged her butt firmly. Sandra reached back and unsnapped her matching bra and let it fall to the floor.

Covering her chest with her hands she turned around and stared at Ethan. He could no longer contain himself. Rushing over to her he pressed his lips against hers. Her hands worked at his belt buckle as his lips moved to her neck.

Sliding his hands down her back he felt the top of her panties. Sticking his hand inside, he fondled her butt before sliding her panties down. They fell around her ankles and she quickly stepped out of them exposing her naked body.

Ethan ran his hands over her body as if he were admiring a work of art. Sandra slapped his hands away and yanked his pants down. They continued to kiss as she worked on the rest of his clothes. Finally, they found themselves under the water of the rainfall shower head, naked together.

Pressing Sandra up against the wall he stared into her honey brown eyes. "I love you," he whispered as the warm water rained down his back. Brushing aside a wet strand of hair from her face she stared back.

"I love you too, Ethan." They both smiled at each other. It was deep and passionate.

Gripping Sandra's thighs he lifted her into the air and pressed her back against the shower wall. Under the jet of warm falling water, Ethan took her.

***

After their shower, Ethan and Sandra lay naked on the bed holding each other. Ethan brushed his hand through her damp hair. Kissing her lightly on the forehead he said, "Well, should we get moving on our day?" Sandra tilted her head back to look at the alarm clock beside the bed. It was already past noon. She was getting hungry and suggested they go out for lunch.

"The original Margaritaville is here."

"I like Jimmy Buffet."

"There's also a Hard Rock"

"What sounds better to you, Sandra?"

"We have a few days here so we can do either, but if I had to choose I would say Margaritaville. It fits my mood right now."

"Margaritaville it is."

They jumped up and began to get dressed. Ethan gave a playful pout as Sandra slipped her bra and panties back on. "Don't worry, it won't be the last you see of them," she stated playfully. Without responding Ethan slipped his shirt on and sat at the end of the bed to put on his shoes.

When they were both ready to go, Sandra gripped Ethan's hand and pulled him towards the door. Before she let them leave she pulled him close and kissed his lips, grabbing the back of his head. "Thank you," She said as she motioned her head towards the shower.

Ethan smiled, "My pleasure." With that, they slipped out of the door and towards the stairs.

***

The receptionist watched the couple walk out of the lobby. She couldn't help but think what I sweet couple they looked and how cute they were together. Both were in great shape. The woman's hair was long and brownish-red. The man stood tall and proud with his arm wrapped around her. Both of them looked happy and full of love. It opened her heart to see people happy. She smiled and turned around to place some papers on the table behind her.

A ringing broke her concentration. She picked up the phone and answered in a sweet, happy tone. As she spoke with the customer a large, bulky man entered the lobby. Placing his large frame directly in front of her he scowled. Smiling she placed her finger in the air to request a moment. This only seemed to make the man impatient. Letting out a sigh of frustration he leaned against the counter.

Taking a step back she finished her conversation. Once the phone was back on the receiver she smiled at the large man. It was not one of her genuine smiles, this one was forced. This man worried her, but she did not know why.

"Checking in, sir?" The man said nothing, only nodded. She quickly got his information and handed him his electronic key card to his room. Without a word, the man walked away. He did not carry with him any luggage and she noticed he was only staying for one night. It was highly unusual for someone to stay somewhere this nice for only one night and alone. Shrugging it off, she continued on with her duties.

Chapter 3

A beautiful display of greens and blues cascaded from the stage over the main seating area. The large sign read Jimmy Buffet's Margaritaville. The stage was empty now, but they were preparing for what looked like a night performance. Ethan reached to the center of the table and grabbed a handful of nachos. Admiring the colors of the sign he placed the chips on the small plate in front of him.

"It's nice to get away every once in a while," Ethan said taking a bite of nachos.

Sandra watched him and smiled, "I agree and there is no one else I'd rather be away with." Ethan smiled back. Sandra thought she saw a slight blush on his face, but she did not say anything.

The waiter arrived with their meals. Sandra and Ethan ate in silence for a few moments. Finally, Ethan broke it and said, "We should just move down here."

Sandra coughed, nearly choking on her food. "What?" She said completely caught off guard.

"It's so calm and relaxing down here. I could see myself living here I think."

"Ethan, I don't think it's plausible."

"Why's that?"

"What would we do for work?"

"I don't know, there's got to be something we could do."

"Like?"

"Maybe I could be a private investigator."

"A private eye?"

"Yeah, why not? And you always talked about how you wanted to be a marine biologist when you were younger. This place is perfect for that."

"I'd have to go back to school for that, Ethan."

"We could make it work."

Sandra sat for a moment thinking about what Ethan had said. Although she was skeptical the idea did intrigue her somewhat. Marine biology had been her dream job when she was a little girl. She had dreamt of sailing out into the ocean studying whales and sharks first hand. There was so much life in the ocean. So much life yet undiscovered, it was a tempting notion. It would have been a career that would have made her happy beyond belief.

Ethan smiled, watching her think. "Don't worry, I'm kidding. It's nice down here, but it wouldn't work."

Sandra shrugged. "I don't know, I kind of like the idea of you being a private investigator. You could call it McCormick investigators. It has a nice ring to it."

"So the rest of my life I would be chasing down cheating husbands and lost family heirlooms?"

Sandra nodded.

"I think it would suit you well."

The two of them laughed together. It was a laugh that showed they both were semi-serious about the conversation but accepted it would never happen. They both had created lives in Miami and grounded themselves as police officers. It was not something they could easily walk away from.

"Well," Ethan started. "I think my first case is the mystery of the missing waiter. I want the check." Sandra rolled her eyes playfully and giggled. Ethan flagged down the waiter and took the check. They quickly paid for the meal and headed outside.

"So, where to next?" Sandra asked squeezing his hand. Ethan shrugged.

"You tell me. You're my tour guide. Exclusive package, remember?" This time Sandra blushed and led him by the hand down the sidewalk.

"Ok, let's go. You can't go to the keys and not check out the southernmost point. It's the farthest south you can get in the continental United States."

Ethan nodded. "Lead the way."

Sandra gripped Ethan's hand tightly and led him down the street. They passed bars and shops. Most were selling junk, T-shirts, and souvenirs. He didn't mind the occasional souvenir, but he did not like the type of junk sold in most places.

Many of the bars looked interesting and he figured later that night they would check out at least one. As they walked across an intersection Ethan looked to his right. There was a bar with a large tree growing through the middle up through the ceiling. He made a mental note. That would be the bar they would check out. Something about it intrigued him.

Right now he was focused on Sandra at his side. She was holding his hand tightly in hers. He loved her very much and he wanted her to know it. Sitting in his left pants pocket was a small blue box. Inside the box was a surprise he was sure Sandra would be excited for.

Things had been getting very serious between the two of them. Ethan was not surprised. From the moment they met, he had fallen for her. After a few months of being together, he could not imagine his life without her. Keeping that to himself he had quietly waited for the right moment. If a man told a woman he had fallen in love with her after only a handful of months she would run for her life. Instead, Ethan played it cool. He allowed time for his feelings to develop. He was certain she felt the same about him.

With his left hand, he silently patted the pocket which held the ring. He wanted to make sure it was still there. Everything had been planned out perfectly for his proposal. It would happen back at that hotel later that night. The hotel had worked with him to corner off a section of the downstairs bar by the pool. Of course, Ethan had to pay a little extra money for the service, but it would be worth it in the end.

His plan was to go downstairs to the bar area by the pool without Sandra, making something up to go out without her. Then he would help set up the area by the pool bar. A member of the hotel staff would go upstairs and find Sandra. She would be told that she would need to follow him with no explanation. Ethan knew her mind would race and worry. Secretly he was excited about that. He liked giving her a bit of a hard time.

Sandra would be escorted to the pool area to see Ethan sitting by the bar, dressed nicely. Confusion would set in and she would approach. That's when he would pull out the box and drop to one knee. Hopefully, she would say yes. Then they would be spending the rest of the time in the Keys celebrating their engagement. Ethan felt as if the plan was perfect. He knew she would love it. There was no doubt she would say yes.

A smile had formed on his face which Ethan was unaware of. Sandra glanced over at him. "Well, you look excited." For a moment he was nervous, but quickly he relaxed.

"I'm in the most beautiful city in Florida with the most beautiful woman in the world. What's not to be excited about?" For the second time, Sandra blushed.

"We're almost there," she said through a giggle.

Ethan brushed off the close call and focused back on the present. Up ahead he saw a short line of people standing in front of a concrete statue. It was shaped like a buoy with red, black, and yellow stripes. The text painted onto the concrete buoy read southernmost point. Above the writing was a painted triangle with a large conch shell in the center. Around the triangle, it read the conch republic. Ethan was not sure what that meant and made a mental note to look it up later. Or perhaps he would ask Sandra about it later at the bar.

"Here you go," Sandra stated. "This is as far south as you can travel in the continental United states. From here it's only ninety miles to Cuba." Ethan nodded. That was also painted on the concrete buoy. The line of people slowly advanced as people stood in front of the statue getting their pictures taken.

Ethan pulled out his cell phone and pressed the camera application. "Want a picture in front of it?" Sandra nodded and grabbed him by the hand.

She led him to the back of the line where they stood in place. "Let's get one together." Sandra turned to the people behind them, another couple. It did not look like they were there with anyone. "Would you guys mind taking a picture of us together? We can take one for you guys if you want." The couple nodded and smiled. They seemed happy that someone offered.

When it was their turn Ethan and Sandra stood to the side of the sculpture. The couple behind them took their photo. Ethan had his right arm tight around Sandra's waist and a bright smile on his face. He was truly happy. Nothing could have destroyed this moment for him.

***

The man had walked into his hotel room at the end of the hall on the fourth floor. He had nothing with him. No clothes, no luggage, nothing. The truth was he was not planning on staying the night. He had business he had to attend to that night and then would leave the same night. In fact, he had given the receptionist a false name and even paid with a fake credit card.

When he was gone in the morning and his business was done they would no doubt be suspicious. They would try and find him through the name and card he had left, but they would never find him. He had made sure he did not face any security cameras when he walked into the building. The most they would see was the back of his head. It would not be enough to make a positive I.D. Everything had been meticulously planned.

Instructions had been given to him over the phone via a text message. His instructions were clear and concise. The man did not even have to plan for anything. His instructor had told him exactly what to do and how to avoid detection. He even knew the placement of the cameras, telling him how to walk into the lobby without being seen.

It had seemed impossible for a man to know as much as his instructor did, but it was true. He did not know who this person was. He only went by the name Greene. When Greene sent him a text he followed the instructions exactly as they were given.

Tonight's assignment was a different one from anything he had ever been given before. He was not sure if he could go through with it. In the end, he knew that he would. Greene was not a man someone crossed.

The man dropped down onto the bed and checked the time. It was still mid-afternoon. He still had several hours before he had to get to work. Putting his head back against the pillow he shut his eyes. Sleep would help clear his mind, he thought. More rest would keep him focused for his later task.

His cell phone blinked across the room and chirped. It was the phone that had shown up in the mail from Greene. When it went off he had no choice but to read it. Jumping up he raced across the room and checked the screen. Everything is in place. Your assignment continues as planned. He was about to toss the phone back on the desk when it chirped again. Do not fail. He knew a threat when he saw one. It was as clear as day. If he did not kill Sandra Delano he was a dead man.

***

Ethan and Sandra had left the southernmost point and were heading back into Key West. They had taken a detour through an old cemetery. Many of the tombstones had been run down and eroded. Several, however, looked as if they were brand new.

Together they had admired several of the oldest graves wondering who the people had been in life. Despite the erosion on many of the graves, it was a beautiful place. The grounds were kept nice, other than the erosion. Everywhere you turned it felt as if you were surrounded by history.

Together Ethan and Sandra walked passed the graves headed for the exit to the street. Somewhere off to their right something large fell from a tree and landed with a loud bang! Sandra jumped and let out a soft scream. Ethan turned his head to the right in time to see a large iguana skitter past several headstones. He laughed and squeezed Sandra's hand. She punched his arm playfully.

"It's not funny," she gasped. "Scared the shit out of me."

Ethan shrugged. "Were you expecting the undead?"

She shook her head and laughed. "Well, I sure as hell wasn't expecting a damn iguana to fall out of a tree." Ethan laughed and they walked out of the cemetery hand in hand.

"What next?" He asked her.

Sandra thought for a moment then spoke, "How about we check out some of the shops down on Duvall Street?" Ethan glanced at her.

"Sounds good to me."

"Then we can check out Mallory Square. It's where all the street performers are when the sun starts to go down. There's a few more shops down that way too."

"Sounds perfect."

"All right, let's go."

Ethan smiled as they walked on towards Duvall Street. Now they doubled back to Truman Avenue which would lead them to Duvall Street. When they reached Duvall Sandra kept walking straight. "Where are you going, Sandra? This is Duvall Street." He pointed over his shoulder at the street sign.

"The next street over is Ernest Hemingway's house."

"Oh?"

"Your sister is an author right?"

"Yeah, romance novels."

"Well, she'd kill you if you didn't check out the Hemingway house right?"

"Yeah, that's true. All right let's check it out."

Hand in hand Ethan and Sandra headed towards Whitehead Street where the Hemingway house stood on the corner. It was surrounded by plants and trees. A small gate separated the sidewalk from the front yard. Ethan fished a handful of cash from his pocket to pay the entrance fee and they stepped through the gate and into the yard.

Before they went further Ethan stopped Sandra and pulled her close and kissed her hard. She kissed him back and smiled. "What was that for?"

Ethan looked at her and smiled back. "For the nice time I've been having with you."

She leaned close to Ethan's ear and whispered, "Wait until tonight back at the room." She winked at him and took his hand.

***

Pacing in his hotel room the man attempted to formulate a plan. His instructions had been very clear. Sandra's death had to look like an accident or a suicide, murder was out of the question. Greene had been very insistent on that point. If the local police suspected murder in any way everything would be lost. He did not want to imagine what would happen to him if he failed.

Instead, he went over scenario after scenario in his head. It all depended on what happened that night. If the two of them came home drunk she could drown in the bathtub, passed out drunk. Perhaps she could slip over the balcony. It all depended on Ethan McCormick. It would be hard to make Sandra's death look like an accident with Ethan there.

Suicide would be harder to pull off. It would be nearly impossible to force her to kill herself, much less put her in a situation that would kill her. Sticking a gun in someone's face and forcing them into a situation that would kill them was useless. What was the difference? A bullet or a noose? The end game was still the same. His work was cut out for him.

The major point Greene had drilled into him was that it needed to be something which would get people talking. He was not sure why, but Greene wanted to make sure there was plenty of press coverage of her death. A suicide would ensure press coverage. Like vultures, they would eat the story up. An accident would not get as much coverage unless it was something memorable. Lost at sea had been one of his first choices, but Greene also insisted there be a body.

So many rules for the death of one person. He figured it would have been a lot easier if he could have just shot her and went on his way. Greene had been very specific. Guns were out of the question. In fact, he did not even bring his Glock with him. It would have been too tempting to end it all quickly.

He had never killed a person before. When Greene first instructed him he was nervous. He was afraid he would not go through with it and Greene would kill him instead. As the days went by it had become easier to accept. He did not know what they meant, but he did not care. He looked at it like any other job that he had. It was a job he intended to see through to the end. Greene had promised he would be safe. No one would know he had even been there. A strong alibi had already been created for him. All loose ends had been tied.

Now, the only thing he had to worry about was how to complete the task. Ethan would be the biggest roadblock, but he was confident. Before the night was over he knew that Sandra Delano would be dead.

***

Once Ethan and Sandra finished at the Hemingway house they started off towards the hotel. Sandra gripped Ethan's hand tightly. Glancing over at him she smiled. "I like that shirt on you," she stated matter of factly.

"I would think so, you bought it for me."

Sandra shrugged, "Yeah, that's cause I have good taste."

Ethan smiled and kissed her gently, "Yes you do."

"I've got to say," she started. "Those Tommy Bahama shirts work perfectly in this environment."

"Really?"

"Yeah, you look almost like Jimmy Buffet or someone."

"Well, I am just looking for my lost shaker of salt."

Sandra rolled her eyes at Ethan's corny joke, he just shrugged. Ethan basically wore nothing but Tommy Bahama shirts. He had discovered them shortly after moving down to Florida. They were the perfect tropical shirts. One hundred percent silk, most of them, which kept him nice and cool in the hot summer months.

When he wore them on his shift it made him feel like a television detective. He would joke that he and his partner would have to jump in a speed boat and chase down drug dealers. Other officers told him he needed to grow out a mustache and call himself Magnum. It always got a good laugh.

Ethan's sister bought him one almost every year. Either Christmas or his birthday he would receive one from her. He never complained he loved those shirts. Sandra had started to buy him a couple every once in a while, but it was tough for her. Those shirts did not come cheap.

"So, what's planned for tonight, Ethan?" Ethan fingered the box in his pocket and smiled. If you only knew sweetheart, he thought.

"Actually, I thought we would take it easy tonight. Maybe just stay in the hotel. We do have a bit of time left down here. I want to take it slow. Let's not rush through everything in one evening."

Sandra smiled and gave him a curious look. For a moment the sensation of fear engulfed him. He was afraid she had figured him out. Somehow she knew he had a ring in his pocket and planned to ask her to marry him. The surprise was over and everything he had planned was ruined.

"You just want to try and have a repeat of earlier in the shower don't you?" Ethan resisted the urge to let out a sigh of relief.

"Since you're offering."

She laughed and began to blush. "I'm not against it at all."

They continued in silence towards the hotel. Occasionally they would stop at a gift shop and browse, never buying anything. Plenty of people were beginning to pile into the bars. The daylight would soon be slipping away and the night life would soon be upon them.

Before they reached the hotel they jutted left and headed off towards Mallory Square. Sandra had insisted they at least spend a little time there that night. Ethan did not protest. It did not throw a wrench into his plans at all.

Once at Mallory Square, all kinds of street performers prowled around. One kid, who only looked about nineteen, was being wrapped in a strait jacket promising he could escape. Another was juggling batons of fire.

As they passed a break-dancer flinging himself all over the place Ethan spotted another performer. This one stuck out at him. It looked like an old man. He talked with a barely audible French accent. He was surrounded by cages and tables. Inside the cages were cats. They all cried softly as if they wanted to be fed.

The man seemed to be talking to them in his French gibberish. Ethan was utterly confused. He did not know what it was this performer was going to attempt. The only thing that came to his mind was an old Steve Martin movie he watched once upon a time. He turned to Sandra and said, "My god, cat juggling!" He laughed, but she looked at him funny. Her eyes darted back towards the man and they became wide.

"Is that what he's going to do with them?" Ethan shook his head and laughed.

"I have no idea, it's from a movie. Come on, I don't want to know what he does with those poor animals."

With that, they moved on passed the performers and found several shops. Sandra found a few sundresses she thought would be great beach clothes while they were there. Before she could protest Ethan purchased the dresses for her. She smiled and thanked him with a kiss. "You spoil me." Ethan did not say anything. Again he kissed her softly.

***

The man was still pacing back and forth in his hotel room. He was beginning to work up a sweat. There were too many scenarios to plan for. Any little thing could throw everything off. He would have to play it by ear. Too many factors had to be taken into account. All he could do was hope for the best.

He decided he was safe to take the nap he had been thinking about earlier. Jumping down on the bed he closed his eyes. Before he drifted off to sleep he pictured Sandra in his mind. The only regret he had was that he would not be able to have his way with her before the deed was done.

Thinking about her started to drive him wild. He imagined running his hand over her smooth skin, unbuttoning her pants. Her red hair would slip wildly everywhere as he took her. Her sweat would stick it to her face and neck. He began to imagine her struggling to get away and he decided he liked that fantasy the best. Her naked body squirming powerless beneath her until he was finished. For a short moment, he envied Ethan for having such a hot body to come home to every night.

Looking over at the clock he realized he still had plenty of time. He shut his eyes tight and thought about Sandra struggling once again. He played the image over in his mind. He liked it.

Chapter 4

While Ethan and Sandra enjoyed their time off in the Florida Keys the Miami Police Department was hard at work. The driver of the Chevrolet Aveo was still in custody. He was being pressed for information nearly every minute of the day. He remained silent but never asked for a lawyer. With his continued lack of cooperation, it was clear he would not give up any useful information.

Major Derrick White, head of the homicide department, had placed Captain Brad Forester in charge of the interrogation. Brad Forester was an older man with slightly thinning grayish-black hair. He wore thin circle frames over his dark brown eyes. Brad was not a very tall man, standing at only five foot six. Quite often he was dwarfed by Major Derrick White who towered over him at six foot two.

Derrick White used his impressive size to his advantage. Over the years he had packed on pounds of muscle. It made him seem even larger which was exactly what he wanted. His height and size made for the perfect interrogation tool. Before he had been promoted to Major he used to conduct the interrogations. One large palm slapped down on the table was usually enough to make any perpetrator talk. Although he would not have admitted it out loud he loved the effect his size had on people.

Now that Derrick was in charge he left others in charge of the interrogation process. The majority of officers in his department brought in mostly accurate results. There was no doubt this man would give them something. It was only a matter of time. A large collection of fully automatic weapons had been found in his trunk, along with some drugs. He would do time for possession, that was certain. The only issue was the automatic weapons. They wanted to know what his plans had been with them. With as many weapons they had found in his trunk, he could have armed a small militia. Most arms dealers did not keep that many on them. The whole thing was rather suspicious.

Captain Forester had placed one of his better officers on the interrogation. He found himself missing Ethan McCormick. Ethan was usually his go-to guy to get things done. He was a great officer who always did things right the first time. More importantly, he did things properly. Regardless of what movies and television portrayed loose cannon cops were a pain in the ass. They usually created a lot more paperwork than other officers, not to mention property damage. The media and the local government never cared about their results after a shootout on the Venetian causeway. A cop who failed to play by the rules would find himself out of a job rather quickly.

The officer Forester had put in charge of the interrogation came out of the room. "Captain, he's still refusing to talk. He truly thinks we're going to buy he had nothing to do with the guns in his trunk." Forester rolled his eyes.

"All right, Greg, I'll question him for a bit. Maybe a cross-interrogation will reveal something." The officer named Greg nodded and headed off.

Before Brad Forester could enter the interrogation room he was stopped by Derrick White.

Brad stared up at the lumbering man as if he were a skyscraper. Looking down at him his enormous voice boomed, "Has he talked yet?" Brad shook his head.

"No, sir, he keeps insisting the guns weren't his. He claims he didn't know they were in his trunk." Derrick shrugged.

"Can't win them all, I guess." With that, Derrick tore down the hallway. His heavy footsteps echoed in the hall.

As he walked away Brad felt himself remembering a conversation he had with a few of the female officers about Derrick White. Apparently, they found him quite handsome. Many of them said he looked like Idris Elba without the British accent. He kept his black hair shaved close to his head and usually wore nice suits to the office. It was the first time that Brad had seen the resemblance.

Brad had also heard a few jokes about Derrick. Just like any other office many of them disliked their boss. They had found interesting ways to tease him behind his back. The most popular joke was about his ethnicity and the irony of his last name. Brad was quick to reprimand these people. He did not tolerate racism within the department, not even as a joke. It was unacceptable and unprofessional.

Focusing back on the task at hand Brad entered the interrogation room. He did not hold the same presence that Derrick White would have. Many people sitting in that same room before had found him very un-intimidating at first. He never got angry or got in the faces of the perpetrators. Brad used cold hard facts to coherence them into telling truth. It was about the way he delivered it. He refrained from showing any emotion during his interrogation. He would merely speak matter of factly. It gave him a cold and direct demeanor.

Once he had told a perpetrator that if he did not confess the judge presiding over his case would go for the death penalty. He described what it must be like to know the date of your own death. To know what no other person on Earth knew. It had to drive you crazy. Sitting, waiting, and counting down the days. Brad expressed how it must feel to have the needle sticking in your arm waiting for the mix to put you into a sleep you knew you would never wake up from. Had a lawyer been there he probably would have stopped him. And had a lawyer been there Brad would not have received his confession which led to multiple arrests. His cold and calculating method almost always received results.

Brad pulled up a chair from the back of the room and took a seat at the table opposite the man. Unlike in the movies, the room was not a dark area lit only by one small lamp. There was no two-way mirror separating the room from a small group of onlooking officers. It had more in common with a broom closet than the interrogation room from a television show.

With his hands cuffed to the table, the man stared back at Brad. His eyes darted back and forth judging him. Brad knew immediately that he was not intimated, he could see it in his eyes.

"Kyle Matthews, right?" The man opposite him only nodded. "Hello, I'm Captain Brad Forester." Kyle shrugged. "One of my officers tells me that you were unaware of the weapons stowed away in your trunk. Is that correct?" Again Kyle nodded. "Well, we find that a little hard to believe. So, in your own words, could you explain how it is the weapons ended up in your trunk?"

"I don't know."

"Fair enough. I should tell you that the amount of firearms we found in your car, along with the narcotics, is enough to lock you up until your over sixty years old. Let's not forget that your buddy discharged one of the firearms near an officer. Endangering an officer is not something a jury would not take lightly."

"I didn't pull the trigger."

"To the state of Florida, it doesn't matter. The guns were found in your possession which put the life of an officer in jeopardy. You would be held directly accountable."

"That's bullshit!"

"If you admit to weapons belonging to you and tell us what you were doing with them it might show cooperation with a police investigation. It would look a lot better to a jury. We might even be able to make a deal. Perhaps shorten your sentence. If your admission leads to the arrest of a guilty or wanted man you're practically a free man. The only thing standing in your way is a simple explanation."

Brad could see the wheels turning in Kyle's head. He was weighing his options. It was a scenario Kyle obviously had not thought about. He would be more willing to cooperate if he thought there was something in it for him. It was one of the easiest ways to get results.

"I'm telling you the truth, the guns aren't mine." Brad sighed. His technique usually worked. It was upsetting when it did not. Brad had walked in with such confidence sure that he could make this man talk. Now it seemed he was failing. No officer had been able to obtain pertinent information from him. Brad started to wonder if bringing Derrick in would yield better results. His sheer size alone would be enough to get him talking.

Suddenly the man broke the silence, "But I can tell you how they got there." Brad repressed a smile. He knew he should never have doubted himself.

"I'm listening."

"I heard about this guy who was willing to hand over a lot of cash to transport things. I jumped on the option. For a couple weeks, I moved unmarked boxes across town. I never knew what was in them. I didn't ask either. As long as I got paid I didn't care."

"What was this person's name?"

"He only gave his name as Greene."

"What did he look like?"

"No clue, I never met the guy."

"How did you accept the jobs?"

"Through text message mostly."

"He texted you?"

"I was given one of those throwaway phones. I would get texts when there was a job. I don't think he wanted to be found."

"Who gave you the phone?"

"Just some guy on the street."

"Who?"

"No idea. Just some random guy."

"How did you get in contact with this guy Greene without knowing him or meeting with him?"

"Word on the street. There was rumor he was looking for people. I asked around. No one seemed to know him or how to get a hold of him. Eventually, I found a guy who said he had connections."

"And he didn't offer to take you to him?"

"No, he handed me that phone and told me to answer when it rang. That was it. I guess I was his employee after that."

"And you don't know who this person was?"

"Who?"

"The man who gave you the phone."

"Not a damn clue."

"Could you describe him?"

"Hell no, man. It's been months since I saw that guy. I can't remember."

Brad thought for a moment.

"Was your friend connected with Greene too?"

"You mean the guy who blew his head off?"

"Yes."

"I guess so. I received a text that day to bring my car to an alley downtown. That guy was waiting there with a load of drugs and guns."

"Could this guy have been Greene?"

"Fuck if I know. He seemed to be following his own instructions so I don't think so. Like I said I didn't care. I was just after the money."

"Did this guy give you any other information? Where you were headed? What the guns were for? Anything?"

"Nothing, he was reading directions off of his phone. Every few minutes a new direction popped up. I don't think he even knew where we were going."

Brad leaned back and curiosity began to set in. Whoever Greene was had a large operation going. He made a mental note to run all of this by Ethan when he was back from his vacation. He had always valued his input. Ethan was one of the brightest officers on the force. He was constantly thinking outside the box.

Sometimes he was the first to offer up ideas that no one had thought of before.

"All right, Mr. Matthews," Brad said standing up. "You've been very helpful." Without waiting for the man to respond he walked out of the room. He motioned for another officer and explained to him that they were done interrogating the suspect. Brad instructed him to move him back to holding.

Now he was unsure of his next move. Kyle Matthews had not given them any more leads. Unfortunately, the only other man that could have shed any more light on this Greene person was frozen on a slab in the morgue.

Brad began to worry this case would slip into the cold case files. From there it would be filed away for several years. There was a team dedicated to these cases. If an investigation lost all leads the cold case squad would take it over. Most cold cases were never solved. They were doomed to slip out of memory. Before too long there was nothing left to be done.

These cases were considerably harder to investigate. Most of the time the witnesses' memories were unreliable due to the passage of time. They had a difficult time remembering facts and usually were not much help. He did not want to see that happen to this case. When Ethan returned from his trip he was going to put him on it. It was not the normal job for a homicide detective, but something had to be done. Brad had a gut feeling about it. He knew there needed to be a lead and a resolution. He was determined to find it.

Catching up with Derrick White he explained the entire situation. He told him that the suspect did not provide any helpful information. Brad explained the only thing they learned was a man named Greene was most likely behind it. "Greene?" Derrick questioned.

"Yes, sir, that's what Kyle said his name was."

"I've never heard of him."

"I doubt it's really this man's real name."

"You're probably right. What is your next move?"

"When Ethan gets back from his vacation I'm going to have him put on this case."

"McCormick?"

"Yes, sir. Is that all right with you?"

Derrick thought for a moment.

"Brad there wasn't a murder. What do we need with a homicide detective?"

"It's a gut feeling Derrick."

"Crimes are solved by facts, not gut feelings."

"Sir, you know me. I don't waste time and I never fool around. When I have feeling about something I'm usually right. Let me put Ethan on this when he gets back."

"Fine, when Ethan gets back get him caught up. Then put him in charge of it, but if something more important comes up I'm going to pull him away from this case."

"That's fair, thank you, sir."

"Don't mention it. I hope you're right about this. I don't need the chief of police sniffing around here asking why we're wasting valuable time and money on dead end cases."

"He won't, sir, I promise."

"Don't forget, there's been talk about lowering the funding for this division. One of the congressmen is meeting with the mayor about budget cuts."

"I know."

"We can't have that happen. If we waste too much time on dead ends they will be sure to hold it against us."

"I promise sir, this isn't a waste of time."

Derrick Shrugged and walked off leaving Brad to think. It was a serious issue. There had been talk that the Miami Police Department was wasting too much of the tax payer's money. Too many resources were being wasted and too much money was being pumped into the department. There was a rumor that budget cuts and funding cuts would be made. If it happened there might even be downsizing. It was something the force could not afford.

It was a serious issue that had Brad nervous. Nonetheless, he was confident with his decision. Something about this case seemed off. He wanted to get to the bottom of it. With Ethan McCormick leading the case he knew it would be solved quickly and efficiently. "God damnit, Ethan, please don't hurt yourself down in the keys. I need you here." Brad turned around and headed back down the hallway.

Chapter 5

Sandra and Ethan stepped through the threshold of their hotel room. Immediately Sandra kicked off her shoes and made her way passed the bed to drop her shopping bags on the couch. She sat down on the bed and sighed. "My feet ache." Ethan nodded.

"We did a lot of walking today. Maybe I will rub them for you tonight." Sandra smiled and scooted back on the bed.

"I would like that a lot."

Ethan's mind was on the task at hand. His proposal to Sandra would go perfectly, he could feel it. His first task was to come up with an excuse to leave the hotel without her. Simply stating he was going out for a walk would make her suspicious. He needed something concrete.

"So, there was a bar down by the pool I noticed earlier today. I thought I'd grab a quick drink there. Did you want to go with me?" He knew what her answer would be before she spoke.

"Not really. I would kind of just like to relax for a bit." She laid back on the bed and began to slip out of her dress. "I wouldn't want to stop you, though. Go ahead."

Ethan stared at her tight body as the dress slowly slipped down like the curtain of a performance. He had to fight the urge to walk over to her and caress her smooth, beautiful body. He was enticed by the lacy underwear she wore. Almost as if she knew she was drawing him she began to run her fingers up and down her body and squirm back and forth. "Like what you see?" He nodded as he watched her fingers do a delicate dance over her skin.

If he walked out of the room she would know something was going on. There was no chance he would pick having a drink over her. Without hesitation, he headed over to the bed and slipped his hands around her unhooking her bra. Tossing it aside she smiled up at him. Ethan grinned as he slid his hand down towards her panties and pulled them free.

For the second time that day Ethan took Sandra. When they were finished they collapsed in a pool of sweat and exhaustion. "Wow," Sandra muttered not saying another word. The ring was still safely tucked in his pants pocket which had been tossed across the hotel room. For a moment Ethan considered picking them up and giving it to her then, but thought better of it. He held her naked body tight and kissed her hard.

"Well, now I really need something to drink." He smiled and jumped up from the bed slipping his clothes back on. Sandra pulled the bed covers over her body and watched him dress.

"That's fine sweetheart. I'll be here when you get back." He winked at her as he slipped on his shoes and walked out the door.

Sandra laid her head back on the pillow and closed her eyes. A small amount of pleasure still surged through her body. Ethan had been a very generous lover. She always thought he was very good, but tonight seemed different. There seemed to be more passion in his eyes. Her body shivered as she thought about the moment they shared. A few moments went by and she decided to turn on the television. A movie, the name of which she could not remember, was on. She let it play in the background as she stood up to slip on her nightgown.

She admired herself in the mirror. The short, white silk contrasted her dark skin wonderfully. It stuck to her sweaty body in several spots. She let her dark red hair lay untamed thinking it made her look sexier. When Ethan came back to the hotel he would almost want a round three, and she was ready for it.

Sitting down on the bed she watched the movie only half paying attention. Her thoughts were running back to Ethan. She could not get the look of pure passion in his eyes from her mind. He had acted differently all day. Almost as if he were nervous. It reminded her of their first months together. Sandra was unsure of what was going on with him, but she decided she liked it.

On the television, the main character dropped down to his knee and pulled a ring from his pocket. The woman looked down at him and smiled with tears in her eyes. Sandra did not hear the rest. Her eyes lit up and she began to glow. "That's it!" She shouted startling herself. "He's going to propose, that has to be it." It was the only explanation and she knew she was right. It was the reason for the trip. It was the reason for the passion and his nervousness. Excitement pounded through her body and her heart fluttered faster than it had ever moved. Ethan was going to ask her to marry him. Tears welled up in her eyes and she did not wipe them away. She loved Ethan so much and all she wanted was to spend the rest of her life with him. She stared at herself in the mirror and looked at her left hand. Before the night was over she would be engaged. She began to practice saying "Yes!" in the mirror.

A knock on the door interrupted her and she wiped the tears from her eyes. "Yes?" She called out confused.

"Room service," the voice responded. Sandra beamed again. She thought this was all part of Ethan's plan.

"Just a moment," she cried out as she went to the bathroom to grab her robe.

***

Ethan sat at the bar for a moment playing with the ring in his pocket. Staff of the hotel was lighting tiki torches all around the pool. He had worked out a deal with the hotel manager. He agreed to help Ethan with his proposal. Ethan would never have afforded to reserve the entire pool area with his salary. When the hotel manager learned he was a police officer he had made a very generous deal. He had told him his brother was also an officer. Ethan was grateful for the gesture.

The bartender poured Ethan a drink. "Here," she said sliding it across the bar. "This is on the house, for your nerves."

"How do you know I'm nervous?"

"Your hand is shaking."

"Is it natural to be this nervous? She's going to say yes, I'm sure of it."

The bartender looked at him for a moment. "She's a very lucky woman. She has a man that cares a lot about her. Obviously, she is very special to you. The fear of rejection is a strong one, even if the chances are minuscule. Embrace that feeling. It means your love for her is strong and true." Ethan looked at her for a moment. "Like I said, she's a very lucky woman." Ethan smiled at her.

"Thank you," he started. "Not a bad way to earn a very generous tip." The woman smiled and gave him a playful wink.

She turned to the man sitting next to Ethan finishing his drink. "I'm very sorry sir, the pool will be closed for a private event tonight. When you're finished-"

"Of course," he said with a heavy British accent. He turned to look at Ethan whose hands were still shaking. "Getting engaged are you?"

"I hope so," he said sipping his drink.

"Good luck to you. Try not to worry so much. If she's worth keeping she will say yes."

"I suppose. Have any tips?"

"On how to calm the nerves? Not for the situation you've got yourself in, mate. I've done a lot in my life, but marriage was never one. I'm afraid I can't help you there. If you need to know how to escape from a car submerged in water or avoid detection I could help with that."

"What?"

"Never mind," he said as he began to laugh.

Ethan looked at him funny and tossed back the rest of the drink. Without another word the stranger dropped a twenty dollar bill on the counter and walked away. Ethan looked up at the bartender, but she merely shrugged. He pushed the thought from his mind and started planning for his proposal.

The hotel staff finished lighting the pool deck and retreated back to the main lobby. The manager came out to meet with Ethan. "Ah, Mr. McCormick. It's nice to see everything is working out as planned." Ethan nodded. "I will go inside and call your room and have Ms. Delano meet you here at the bar. I hope everything works out to your liking."

Smiling Ethan said, "I think it will. Thank you, Mr. Danes, for all of your help."

As the hotel manager walked away Ethan gulped down the second drink the bartender had poured for him. She pulled the glass away instantly. His heart thumped loudly in his chest. He had never been so nervous and anxious in his life. Everything was going to go perfectly, Ethan could feel it. He turned back to look at the bartender one last time. "Good luck," she said as she went about moving bottles of alcohol around.

The seconds seemed to drag on for Ethan. Never had time moved so slowly in his life. He knew Sandra would say yes, yet he was still nervous. The bartender had put it perfectly. What little chance of rejection there may have been was enough to unsettle him. Everything would go just as he had imagined. He knew there was no reason for fear.

Ethan could not wait to see her face. He was excited to know what she would say and how she would say it. He wondered if there would be tears in her eyes. The more he thought about it the more excited he became. He knew the time was drawing ever closer. Soon Sandra would be heading through the lobby and out towards the pool. He would be waiting for her there alone. The tiki torches would burn all around them. Ethan looked at them as a symbol of their love. She would approach him to ask what was going on. Maybe she would even have a slight idea, but would not ask directly. He would slip down on his knee with the ring in his hand. She would smile and she would say yes. They would have a few drinks to celebrate. Then they would head back to the room and perhaps celebrate again. In his head everything was perfect. He only hoped that it went as smooth as he imagined.

It was not a good sign when he saw the hotel manager come back out to the deck. Ethan was concerned that something had gone wrong. "Mr. McCormick," he called out. "I can't seem to reach her on the phone."

"Did you call again?"

"Yes, sir. I have called three times. She did not answer."

"I hope she didn't fall asleep."

"That is what I was afraid of Mr. McCormick. I can have one of my staff go to the room and knock on the door if you would like. Perhaps it will wake her up."

"I think that would be a good idea. Maybe the phone just isn't loud enough or maybe the TV is too loud."

"It's possible. I will send someone up right away."

Ethan began to shake again. His nerves were getting the better of him. All this sitting and waiting was making him anxious. He was desperate for her to come downstairs.

The manager was nearly back in the lobby when the sound of a woman's blood-curdling scream broke through the air. Ethan jumped and the manager spun on his heel. It only lasted a few seconds before a loud crack reverberated through the silent night. Ethan was frozen in fear for a moment. Something terrible had happened to somebody. Behind him, he heard the bartender mutter something, but he did not listen.

The manager had spun around with a look of pure terror on his face. His thought was the same as Ethan's. A woman had just fallen to her death. Ethan's blood ran cold as he raced off towards the sound. The thought of what he might find filled him with terror. He prayed in his mind that he would not find Sandra there.

He rounded the corner of the building with the hotel manager close on his heels. When he saw the body of the poor woman slumped over in a bloody heap he dropped to his knees. His mouth went instantly dry. He had to hold back the bile in his throat. Fear shuddered throughout his body as tears poured freely down his cheeks. Behind him, the manager let out a terrified gasp.

Lying in a crimson pool was the body of Sandra Delano. She was perfectly still with her eyes wide open in terror facing the sky. Blood pooled away from the body snaking its way over the concrete filling in the cracks as it went.

Ethan crawled on his hands and knees to Sandra's side. He placed a hand on her chest, but it did not rise. Her right arm was extended out with her thumb and pinky tucked away. Only her index, middle and ring finger were extended outwards. Ethan thought it may have meant something, but he did not know what. Gripping her wrist he checked for a pulse. His heart dropped when he felt nothing.

Sandra Delano was dead. Ethan stared at her lifeless body in disbelief. He shut her eyes softly and began to weep. Warm tears gushed down his cheeks like waterfalls. He rocked gently back and forth as he stroked back her soft silky hair.

Ethan turned his head away from her body feeling nauseous again. Instead of puking he spotted something on the ground. A bloody imprint of her three fingers on the concrete. The blood seemed to be compressed tightly on the ground. It had not been a coincidence. Sandra had barely survived the fall. In her last moments, she had pressed her three fingers to the ground as hard as she could. Then she had rolled onto her back and died.

He had no idea what it meant. Moments later he had forgotten all about it when the paramedics arrived. They pulled Ethan away from Sandra's body. He kicked and yelled in protest, but was held down by a large paramedic. They did what they could to revive her, but it was hopeless. They pronounced her dead. Ethan screamed for them to try again. He begged them to help her. The large paramedic holding him back with a firm grip said, "I'm sorry, she's gone. There's nothing more we can do." With that, Ethan collapsed and cried. The paramedic placed a large, comforting hand on his shoulder. "I am very sorry."

With his hands against his head, Ethan laid his back on the ground and stared up at the starry night sky. After a minute he climbed to his feet and watched in misery as the coroner came to collect Sandra's body. As the van drove off down the road he collapsed to his knees once again. Placing his face in his hands he cried again. He had never felt sorrow like this before. The woman he loved, the woman he was about to spend his life with had been taken from him in the blink of an eye. "The night was not supposed to end like this," he whimpered to himself. They were supposed to live happily and grow old together. Ethan felt an anger rise inside of him, but it quickly subsided and turned into depression. It was an odd mixture of feelings he had never felt in his life.

He felt another hand on his shoulder but did not bother to look up. "Mr. McCormick, I am so very sorry." The manager helped him to his feet and walked him away from the pool. He spotted the bartender standing near the bar. She approached him and gave him a large hug.

"Oh my God, I don't even know what to say. I am very sorry." Ethan did not know what it was, but hearing her words set him off again. Silent tears streamed down his face and he gripped her tight. She did not protest. She held him and felt sorry for him. She knew he needed someone to comfort him in this moment. She held him close but said nothing. Ethan continued to cry.

When he had calmed down he pulled away from her slowly. "Thank you for that." She smiled as he pulled away. It was not a happy smile. There was sorrow in her eyes. Ethan could tell she truly cared and it touched him. "I think I need to leave tonight." He whispered. The bartender nodded.

"Do you have family you could call? I don't think you should drive tonight." Ethan nodded.

"I'll call my sister. Thank you again." He turned and walked away from the pool and headed back to his room.

***

Without being seen the man fled the hotel. He was certain Sandra's death would look like a suicide or at the very least an accident. He made sure to cover any evidence of a struggle. In the end, it would look like she threw herself out of the window. There was nothing else to it. He hoped it would be believable. He knew he needed to escape the area as fast as he could.

His car was parked in a small lot across town. He hurried in that direction. Adrenaline coursed through his veins. It was the first time he had ever taken a life. It was like nothing he had ever felt before and it shocked him a little to find it excited him. There was no remorse, nor sadness. He did not feel guilty. Instead, he felt rejuvenated and hyper.

Rounding the corner he nearly ran straight into a large man walking towards him. "Watch yourself, mate," The man called out to him with his British accent. For a moment he stopped, puzzled. He shook his head and kept moving. With the commotion at the hotel far behind him, he headed for his vehicle. Before anyone knew he was there he would be long gone. With a devilish grin on his face, he climbed behind the wheel of his car and tore off down the street. He looked back at the hotel in his mirror and watched it slowly fade from view.

Chapter 6

With his head resting against the glass Ethan watched the road slip away. Ethan's sister, Valerie, and her husband Pierce Masons had arrived as quickly as they could. Pierce now drove his Jeep Grand Cherokee in utter silence.

Valerie followed close behind them in Ethan's car. Barely aware of his surroundings Ethan shut his eyes and took a shallow breath. From the moment they had left the hotel, he had not spoken a word. Pierce knew better than to break the silence. There was nothing Ethan would want to talk about.

When they had first arrived they both offered their condolences, knowing it would not mean much. Ethan had accepted it, but barely. It was apparent he was in shock. Before ushering Ethan into the Jeep, Pierce and Valerie agreed he would have to stay at their place for the night.

As the highway melted away Ethan felt a warm tear roll down his cheek. He wanted to brush it away but found that he could not move. As hard as he tried he could not get his arm to lift. All his strength had left him. In his mind, he saw the lifeless body of Sandra over and over. A quick flash of the blood stained marking on the ground pushed through his mind. Sandra had only moments left to live and she had pressed three of her fingers against the ground. What did it mean? Was it a message? Was she trying to tell Ethan something? Racking his brain he tried desperately to think of the significance of the number three. Nothing came to mind.

Pierce swerved gently to avoid a pot hole causing Ethan to bump his head against the window. Rubbing his forehead he lay back against the head rest. Finally, he closed his eyes and tried to think some more. He thought hard and eventually his head started to ache. Eventually, his mind shut down, followed shortly by his body. Moments later Ethan was asleep.

Looking over he saw Ethan slipping into sleep. He breathed a sigh of relief. Sleep would be good for him. It was not healthy for him to obsess. Pierce had grown to know Ethan very well. He was a very intelligent man. When he put his mind to something he did not give up until he found the answer. It was natural for him, almost as if he had been wired that way. Ever since they had left the hotel Ethan had been trying to figure it all out. Pierce could see it in his eyes. He wanted to know the meaning behind Sandra's death. Pierce did not know how to tell him the truth.

The officers had pulled Valerie and Pierce aside moments before they left. They told them an investigation would be done, but only as a formality. The evidence was pretty clear. It had already been deemed a suicide from the moment the officers saw the body. In the hotel room, there had been no sign of struggle. Nothing was broken, nothing was stolen. If it had been murder there would have been a sign.

At the time telling Ethan was out of the question. He was not in the right frame of mind to hear the news. The officers had thought it best to only inform Valerie and her husband. Once Ethan had slept and was able to process everything better they would sit him down and tell him. No need to overload him. There was no telling how he would react.

Ethan stirred softly in his sleep. Pierce wondered if he was having a bad dream. He prayed he received only happy ones. The next day would be full of nightmares.

***

Behind the wheel of Ethan's Dodge Stratus Valerie cried. She cried for her brother and she cried for the loss of a friend. Ethan had known Sandra for quite a while. They had been together long enough for Valerie to get to know her. Hearing that she was dead was devastating. Seeing how broken her older brother was practically destroyed her.

Her entire life Ethan had been nothing but positive. Even in the hardest of times, he was able to give her hope. She sometimes wondered if they were even related at all. Positivity was not her strong point. It seemed odd that he could always find a silver lining. Valerie thought it was a gift. She admired him for it. When she doubted her writing he was always there to take the thought from her. When a book got a bad review he would put her mind at ease. Somehow he had something special about him. There was always something he could say to take away the stress.

Now, all that positivity was gone. What were once shining, happy eyes were now glazed over in depression and confusion. She knew it was her turn to be the positive one. She needed to for her brother, but she did not have it in her. Trying desperately to think what Ethan would have done broke her down. If the situation had been different. If Pierce had died Ethan would have been right by her side. Somehow he would have helped her through it. He would help her to find the bright side.

She hated herself for not being able to help her brother like she knew she needed to. She felt as if she was failing him. Now she cried for the loss of a friend, for her brother, and for her shortcomings. Valerie wanted to wake up. She wanted more than anything to wake from this terrible dream, that's what it had to be. This could not truly be happening. As much as she wished for it all to be nothing more than a dream she knew it was real.

Her mind now moved to the officers at the hotel. Without telling Ethan they had informed them Sandra's death was already being examined as a suicide. With the evidence presented she could not argue, but something told her they were wrong. They did not know Sandra. She was just like Ethan. When she walked into a room she was always shining, always smiling. Valerie was not sure she was capable of being sad. To think there were demons inside her to make her take her own life made Valerie sick to her stomach. She felt as if she did not know this woman at all.

Quickly her depression turned to anger. If Sandra had truly been depressed why did she not seek help? How could she do this to Ethan? It was not fair. Valerie cursed her for her selfishness. Then she broke down and cried again.

***

After pulling into the driveway they helped Ethan inside. He let his body fall to the couch and was out before he landed. The stabbing pain behind his eyes was too excruciating to keep awake. Exhaustion had taken over him. As he curled up on the couch Valerie stood watching him for a moment.

Wiping tears from her eyes she covered her brother with a throw blanket. As she was about to head upstairs Pierce stopped her. Without saying a word he pulled her close and hugged her. With her hand pressed firmly against his chest Valerie began to sob. Pierce kept quiet. There was too much emotion in the air tonight. Tomorrow they would have a lot to deal with.

Early the next morning Ethan bolted up on the couch. The throw blanket fell silently to the floor. The room was bright and he was confused. He did not know where he was. Looking all around for Sandra he tried to relax. Like a tidal wave, the memories came flooding back. He put his head in his hands and cried.

A soft hand fell on his shoulder. Quickly he wiped the tears away and looked up into his sister's face. She smiled at him, but there was no happiness there. Ethan grabbed her hand and tried to smile back.

Valerie sat down next to him. Wrapping her arms around him she said, "Ethan I am so sorry. I wish there was something I could do." She knew it was not enough, but she had to say something. Ethan rested his head against her shoulder for a moment fighting back the tears.

"Thank you, it means a lot to me. I'm very thankful for you both." In the kitchen, the sound of bacon sizzling filled the air followed by the familiar aroma. It made Ethan sick to his stomach.

Moments later Pierce came out with a few plates of food. "I know you might not be hungry, but I made breakfast." He placed the plate down on the coffee table in front of Ethan. He smiled and thanked him, but did not move.

After sitting in the silence Pierce decided it was time to talk to Ethan. He had calmed down and would be more rational now. "Ethan, he started. "I need to say something and it's going to be hard to hear so just listen, please. The officers think Sandra's death was," he paused gaining his composure. "Suicide, they think she took her own life. Now, they are going to continue investigating, but that's the working theory right now. I know this is hard to hear but…"

Pierce let his words linger in the air. Ethan had shut down again. He did not acknowledge Pierce at all. He glanced over to Valerie who shrugged softly. "Ethan, did you hear me? It's important that you understand."

Quickly wiping a tear from his eye Ethan spoke, "Yeah I get it, suicide. I think I need to be alone for a while. I might head home." With that, Ethan got up and grabbed his keys. "Thanks again for coming to get me." He walked out the front door slamming it shut behind him.

Valerie looked over at Pierce. He could see the confusion on her face. "He needs time to process it, honey. He can't do that here. He will reject it at first, but eventually, he will accept it. Let him grieve in his own time." He gave her a hug and moved back into the kitchen.

***

Once Ethan was inside his home he dropped his keys on the floor. Making his way to the sun room he sat down at a small, round table pushed up against the windows. A wooden chess board sat idly there. Some of the pieces had been moved into different positions from their last unfinished game.

Looking over the pieces he found the queen tucked safely in her starting space. He gently pushed it over and watched it roll around the board. In a sudden burst of anger, he swept his arm across the board. The pieces flew in every direction. Only the queen remained. It rocked gently back and forth.

Across the room, he spotted an end table. A thin layer of dust had settled over the top. Sandra and Ethan had not touched the table in quite some time. He had almost forgotten what was nestled inside. He stood up and walked over to it. Brushing away a bit of the dust he slid open the drawer. Tucked away inside was a 9mm Berretta. He stared at it for several moments before gripping it tightly.

Chapter 7

Over the next few days, Ethan slipped in and out of a depressive state. The Berretta sat out on the side table taunting him. A vision flashed through his mind of the gun pressed to his temple. He wanted so badly to put an end to the suffering, to the sorrow. He could barely stand this torment any longer.

Then the thought of Sandra would fill his mind and he would cry. She would not have wanted this for him. Sandra would have told him to move forward with his life. He did not think he ever could. Ethan slowly walked towards the gun on the table. Running his fingers over the barrel a tear rolled down his face. He knew that he could not do it. He knew that he would not do it. He just wanted more than anything for the pain to stop.

Instead, he turned from the handgun and made his way into the kitchen. As he poured rum into a small glass he remembered a conversation from the day before. Major Derrick White had called him to offer his condolences. He then told Ethan that he would be granting him an extended leave of absence. It would last for six months unless Ethan felt emotionally ready to come back earlier. Major White could not have someone on the force who was emotionally compromised.

The last thing he needed was an officer making a large mistake because of his emotional condition. There was too much at stake in the next few weeks. He had not mentioned it to Ethan, but there was a large vote coming up. There had been talk of cutting funding to the Miami Police Department to save costs for the city of Miami. The bad economy had taken its toll on the great city and cuts needed to be made. Government officials for the state of Florida and Miami would be voting on the budget cuts for major cities. The police department would not be the only department affected, but it was the only one Derrick cared about.

Derrick White was completely opposed to the cuts, but there was nothing he could do. If the votes passed they would suffer. Derrick weighed Ethan as a potential risk to the department. The last thing the department needed now was an officer abusing a citizen due to his emotional state. It would only increase the chances for a vote in favor of cuts. Derrick wished there was something he could do.

Unaware of all of this Ethan accepted the extended leave of absence. He did not want to think about work. He barely even wanted to go near the building. There were too many memories of Sandra there. Before Derrick had hung up he told Ethan that there were some things of Sandra's at the office. Derrick offered to have them dropped off at his house by a fellow officer. Ethan had declined the offer. Instead, he said he would come and get them sometime in the next few days. As much as he hated the thought of walking into the building he knew he needed to get out of his house. He hoped the fresh air would do him some good.

Sitting down at his computer Ethan tossed back the glass gulping down the rum. Pulling up a blank word document he began to type. As he did tears welled up in his eyes.

I cannot take this suffering any longer. It is too much for me to bear. The light of my life has been taken from me and I have nowhere else to turn. This life has nothing in it for me now. What was once a happy home has now become a tomb in which I cannot escape. Everywhere I turn I am reminded of her. The pictures of us on the walls are a depressing reminder of my failure. She is gone now, and I only have myself to blame. I couldn't do enough for her. I wish I could take it all back, but it's over now. I cannot move forward now. I don't wish to leave my family behind, but where I want to go they cannot follow. I am sorry for the pain I have caused.

Ethan saved the document to his desktop and labeled it *suicide note*. He looked at the gun across the room. It seemed to shine as the sunlight broke through the curtains. He shook his head and wiped the tears from his eyes. He had no intentions of taking his own life, of that he was sure. He was just in a depressed state and needed to get the thoughts out of his head. A few days later he would delete the document, but for now, it helped ease his mind.

Somehow he felt better. Writing the letter had almost helped him get the thought out of his mind. His head was now clearer. Shutting down his computer he made his way into the living room. Flopping down on the couch he rolled over and took a nap. When he woke up he would drive down to the station and collect Sandra's belongings. It was about time to get out of the house.

As he slept he did not dream, at least he did not remember them. Every time he shut his eyes he saw Sandra's face. He was terrified of sleep. He did not want to dream of her lifeless body again and again.

Ethan awoke and rolled over. It was just past noon. Stretching he got up from the couch and went to the bedroom to change his clothes. After that, he headed out towards the Police station. He knew there would be a wave of compassion from everyone. They would all offer their condolences. Many would tell them they could not imagine how he felt. Others would say if he ever needed to talk he could call them. It was the normal behavior for when someone had suffered a loss. Ethan almost wished everyone would just ignore his presence there, but it was not human nature.

He pulled off the side of the street alongside the police station. It was a building he knew well. The tan and white building towered over him. The top half slanted outwards as if to form the bottom half of a pyramid. The top half bulged out and the windows slanted downwards as if the officers inside were watching the streets below. Large blue letters on the side spelled out Miami Police Department.

Climbing out of his car Ethan made his way across the street and inside. Quickly he made his way towards Sandra office. He wanted to avoid as many people as he could. Several spotted him and as predicted offered their condolences. Ethan politely accepted them and continued on his journey.

Finally, he reached the internal affairs division. He located the anti-corruption offices and walked towards her desk. Neatly piled in her chair were several personal belongings. Major McKinley, Sandra's boss, had organized everything for him. Snatching everything up he made a final sweep over her desk. The only item he noticed was missing was her firearm. She had not brought it home with her that night. She usually left it at work. Ethan could not find it and wondered where it might be. Perhaps her superior, Major McKinley, had collected it. He shrugged it off and walked away from her desk.

Major McKinley seemed to be absent as well. He would have liked to ask him where the gun was. It would have made him feel better knowing it was not missing. Shrugging, Ethan made his way back out of the building.

As he sat in the car he went through her belongings. He pulled out a small, black photo frame with a picture of them together. It was a photo she had taken with her smartphone on their first date. Ethan tried not to think about it as he put the photo aside. Next was Sandra's jacket. She always complained how cold the office got. She always kept it draped across the back of her chair. It was still rich with her perfume. Ethan pressed it to his nose and inhaled. His eyes watered, but he fought back the tears.

Folding her jacket he placed it on the passenger seat with the photo. Among the other items were desk decorations and a thing of lipstick. A few other personal items littered the pile. Ethan pushed them all aside and started the car. It had been nice to get out of the house, but now it was time to get back home.

The drive home was quiet. His mind was completely blank. He just let himself get lost in his surroundings. Blankly staring ahead he made his way through the traffic until he arrived at his neighborhood. Pulling into his driveway he let out a deep sigh.

Gathering up Sandra's things he carried them carefully inside. Not sure what he was going to do with it all he gently placed them down on the kitchen table. Eventually he would have to go through it all and take care of them, but for now, he did not want to think about it.

Snatching up the jacket he made his way to his bedroom. Curling up in the bed he pulled it close to him.

Holding it tight he pictured Sandra lying there with him. He could still smell her perfume on the jacket and it brought a smile to his face. Ethan imagined her running a hand through his hair and kissing his cheek softly. His eyes grew heavy and he started to drift off to sleep.

His phone beeped loudly startling him awake. Slipping a hand in his pocket he looked at the bright screen. It was an email notification. He did not care to check it and tossed it on the nightstand. Curling back up with the jacket he let himself fall back into a happy place with Sandra. Shortly after he was asleep.

He dreamt of Sandra. They were sitting on a beach together. The ring was nestled on her finger and she stared at it longingly. It sparkled against the sunlight. "Oh Ethan, it's so beautiful," she exclaimed. He smiled at her and they kissed. The ocean lapped at their feet as they lay together in the soft sand. Ethan ran a hand through her silky hair. Again he kissed her soft lips.

"I love you so much." He said as he stared into her sweet, brown eyes. They glimmered in the sunlight back at him. She did not speak, but he knew she loved him. A bag of their things sat closely beside them. Sandra pointed to it and asked Ethan to grab the suntan lotion. With that, she rolled over on her stomach. Ethan spotted his phone inside the bag but pushed it to the side. As he did it lit up and beeped. Ignoring it he grasped the bottle of lotion.

Turning back to Sandra he admired her body. He wanted to run his hands over her and feel her warmth. Behind him, the phone chirped again. Rolling his eyes he squeezed lotion on his hand. As he was about to massage it onto her back the phone buzzed again.

Now he was getting annoyed. Someone would not leave him alone. He just wanted to spend a relaxing day on the beach with the woman he loved. Turning back towards the bag he watched it intently as if it would keep it from ringing.

When it did not ring again he turned back to Sandra. She was no longer on her stomach. She stared up at him with a confused look on her face. He spotted her hand at her side. Three fingers were extended out. Confusion turned to pain. Ethan looked down at the lotion in his hands. It was no longer a creamy white but red like blood. Ethan jumped backward and let out a cry of anger. He saw Sandra lying in a pool of blood, but she still moved. She looked up at Ethan and muttered something.

Getting closer he asked her to repeat it. Softly she whispered in his ear. "Not three." The phone beeped again and Ethan snapped forward. Sweat poured down his face. The dream quickly faded from his memory and he reached over for his phone. Several notifications blinked rapidly indicating new emails. Standing up he walked out of the room with his phone in hand.

He checked the oldest email first.

Ethan, I have some information that may interest you about Sandra. We need to meet right away. I know her death wasn't a suicide. This can't wait, contact me right away. Please meet me at the Venetian Causeway today at 3pm.

Major McKinley

Ethan nearly dropped the phone. He was in shock. Not knowing if he could believe the email he scrolled to the next one.

Ethan, please message me back. This is not a joke. I need you to meet me today. Sandra was murdered and I can help you find out who did it. Please hurry. We may not have a lot of time.

It had come from the same email address, though this one had not been signed by Major McKinley. The next few messages were all the same. They only said Ethan hurry. A chill vibrated up Ethan's spine. He was unsure of what to think or what to do.

From the moment Pierce had told him Sandra's death was ruled a suicide he had been in denial. He knew she would not have taken her own life. There was no chance of it. There was no point arguing the fact. No one would listen. They would merely tell him he had suffered a traumatic experience and was choosing not to accept it. Now it seemed there was some truth to it all. There was a chance to prove she had been murdered. If there was even the slightest chance someone could help him prove that he knew he had to take it. Her true killer could be brought to justice. He could not ignore it. If someone had harmed Sandra he wanted to make them suffer. With every fiber of his being, he wanted them to pay. He wanted to take the person down himself.

Ethan darted his eyes to his wall clock. The second hand ticked wildly away drawing each second closer to three. It was already past two in the afternoon. Major McKinley would be there waiting in less than an hour. Quickly he changed his clothes and put on his shoes. Snatching up the phone again he responded. I'm on my way.

With that, Ethan ran out the door. Peeling out of the driveway he sped off down the road towards the causeway. Blood pumped through his veins. Adrenaline coursed causing him to shake. There were too many emotions running through him to know how he was truly feeling. He wanted more than anything to find Sandra's killer and put a bullet in his head.

Chapter 8

Two blocks ahead of Ethan stood the Venetian causeway. It was a beautiful white bridge lined on either side with tall black lamp posts. The bridge connected the mainland with Miami Beach. It also crossed over a set of manmade islands named The Venetian Islands. Ethan had traversed the bridge several times in his life. Today, however, he did not admire the scenery.

Up ahead he saw a car pulled off to the side of the road. There was no doubt in his mind it was Major McKinley. He pulled over and parked just behind him. Without waiting he climbed out of his own vehicle and approached McKinley's. As Ethan tapped on the passenger window McKinley unlocked the doors. Ethan climbed in and shut the door behind him.

McKinley looked terribly stressed. Ethan did not think he had eaten or even slept the past few nights. His hair was mangled and uncombed, stubble grew across his face, and his clothes looked slept in and grungy. He watched as McKinley looked around as if to check the streets.

"What do you know about Sandra, Major?"

"I shouldn't share this information with you, but I think you need to know. Maybe it can help you find who did this."

"What do you know?"

"Sandra was working on a large case for internal affairs. It may possibly be the biggest case that's ever come through the anti-corruption division. Someone in the Miami Police Department may be dirty."

"How's that so big? There's been dirty cops before."

"We had reason to believe it was someone high up. Someone with a lot of control. Sandra believed someone had been stealing from the evidence room and selling it on the streets. At first, it was a small bag of drugs here, a box of ammo there. We started to get really worried when guns disappeared. I'm not talking small pistols either. Fully automatic weapons went unaccounted for."

"How could the chief of police not find out that much evidence was missing?"

"Whoever it is has been covering their tracks, covering them very well."

A car drove by and McKinley spun in his seat to face it. Ethan first thought he was being paranoid, then realized he had every reason to be. Sandra may have been killed for the information she knew. It would not take long before they came for McKinley.

"You should come in with me. I can keep you safe. We can gather a few officers that I trust and figure this thing out. Major Derrick White can…"

"Ethan, it's not safe at the department. Think about it? Who do you think could be covering their tracks so well?"

"I don't know, but…"

"Ethan, Sandra thought it was Major White."

"Oh, shit."

"Now you see the problem. We can't just stroll in and arrest him under suspicion. It would be a major scandal in the city, citizens wouldn't feel safe. If he turned out to be innocent it would destroy the department. We need hard evidence. That's what Sandra was working on. She must have got too close."

"Wait a moment. He's stealing from the department, presumably making extra money on the side. It's illegal, but not worth killing over."

"You're right, there's more to it."

"What do you mean?"

"Something's happening, something big. We don't know what it is. Unfortunately, Sandra had more information on that before she was killed."

"How big?"

"We're not sure. Maybe domesticated terrorism, maybe gangland takeovers, it's unclear."

"You're saying there's a pattern?"

"Exactly. We picked up a couple people off the streets. One of them told us something was coming, that they were planning something big. It would 'change the city.' All we learned was a man named Greene was in charge."

"Greene?"

"Yeah, just Greene. People are pretty scared of him."

"Any idea who he is?"

"No clue, Sandra seemed just as stumped about this. Whoever the dirty cop is might just be working with Greene."

"If we find whoever this Greene person is we can find the dirty cop?"

"Exactly my thinking. It's the safest way."

"Is there anything else?"

"I'm sorry, that's all I know. I wish I knew who killed her. I want to see the bastard pay. She was a wonderful officer. I am very sorry for your loss Ethan."

He placed a firm hand on his shoulder squeezing it. Ethan fought back tears. Looking out the window he regained his composure. "Just one more question," he asked, but was interrupted. Small holes burst in the windshield as something struck McKinley's chest. He convulsed several times and blood splattered over the steering wheel.

Without hesitation, Ethan removed his sidearm and flung himself out of the car. As he lay on the ground he tried to get a sight on the target's feet. Before he had a chance to reposition he felt the barrel of a gun press into his back. In the car to his left McKinley groaned.

"On your feet, Ethan," a voice demanded. Ethan did as he was told. His gun was yanked from his palm. Again McKinley groaned in agony. Another shot rang out. This time the bullet ruptured his skull just above his right eye. Blood poured down his cheek as he slouched against the side window.

With great force, Ethan was spun around and pressed against the back door. He was now staring eye to eye with fellow officer Geoffrey Hunt. "Hello, Ethan," he said sticking the barrel of his gun in his face. Wrapped around the grip was a small, white towel.

Geoffrey leaned over and looked inside the car. The seats and wheel were stained with blood. McKinley was propped against the door motionless, his eyes stuck open. He shook his head and looked back at Ethan.

"What have you done, Ethan?"

"What the hell are you talking about?"

"You killed Major McKinley in cold blood."

"Are you out of your mind?"

"I saw you do it. Got in his car and shot him in the head. Then you climbed out and put several rounds through the windshield."

"What do you want?"

Geoffrey grinned wide. "It's not what I want, Ethan, it's what Greene wants."

"Who is Greene?"

"Don't concern yourself with that, Ethan, you have bigger problems."

"You son of a bitch, no one will believe you once I talk to them."

"Yeah, that's why you're not going to talk to anyone."

"Going to kill me too?"

"Nope, you're going to leave."

Ethan was stunned. He did not know what Geoffrey was getting at. He had just gunned down Major McKinley in cold blood. Now he wanted him to run? It did not make any sense.

"Here's the deal Ethan. I know who killed Sandra. I can give you that information, but you have to leave here."

"I'm not going anywhere."

"Then you die right here as a cop killer, Sandra's killer goes free, and I pay your lovely sister and her husband a visit."

Ethan thought it over. There was no chance he could risk his sister's safety. He also needed to know who killed Sandra. The man needed to be brought to justice, no matter what. If Geoffrey killed him now no one would ever know who did it. The investigation was closed. The killer would be free and he could not allow that.

"Fine, what do you want me to do?"

"Well, you see this gun here? This was Sandra's. It has your prints all over it. It's going to stay here. You're going to go on the run."

"You want me to take the fall for McKinley's murder?"

"Finally, you get it."

"Why?"

Ignoring his question Geoffrey spoke on. "You take the heat for his death and get out of town. Then I will give you the information you're looking for." Ethan got the strong feeling it was all a bluff. He did not know who killed Sandra. Ethan was nothing more than a pawn. Someone needed him gone. Framing him for murder would discredit anything he said in the future. He would be deemed guilty before there was even a trial if he ever made it to trial. Officers trigger fingers got real itchy when it came to cop killers.

Sirens blared in the distance as Ethan considered telling Geoffrey to take his deal and shove it. "Oh, looks like times running out, Ethan. Run or bullet in the head? Your call." The sirens were approaching now. Geoffrey cocked the hammer back and pressed the barrel against his forehead.

"All right, all right, I'll do it. Just stay the hell away from my family."

"Good choice."

"I'm going to find you when this is all over. You're going to give me the information I want one way or another."

Geoffrey tossed Sandra's gun in front of McKinley's car and kept Ethan's gun trained on him. He slowly started to back away. "Yeah, good luck with that. Oh and one more thing, leave the car."

The sirens were closer now. Any moment they would turn the corner. Ethan took off running at a full sprint towards the nearest side street. Just as he turned the corner two police cruisers skidded around the corner and screeched to a halt at the scene. Both had come to a dead stop behind Ethan's Dodge Stratus. Each officer exited their vehicles at the same time with weapons drawn.

Geoffrey was gone. He had run back to his own car and drove down the opposite street Ethan had taken. A few moments after the two other officers exited their vehicles he drove back around the corner and on the scene. Like the others, he drew his sidearm as he jumped out.

He greeted the two other officers with a nod as they checked the car. "Oh shit," the other officer yelled. "That's Major McKinley, internal affairs." Geoffrey acted surprised as he turned to the other officer.

"Holy shit." The other officer walked back towards Ethan's car and wrote down the license plate number. Pretty soon he would run the plate and find that it belonged to Ethan McCormick. Then the prints on Sandra's gun would come back his. Before long there would be a massive man-hunt for him. Everything was working out just as Greene had expected. With a smile, Geoffrey holstered his pistol.

Chapter 9

Hiding in the bushes Ethan was unaware his shirt was coated in blood. At some point during his escape, he had spread a large amount to his face. If he was caught there would be no denying he had been at the scene. There was no other choice now. He had to keep going. He had to do what Geoffrey told him to do. If he wanted to find Sandra's killer he had no choice. More than anything he wanted to find her killer.

Just after leaving the scene of the shooting he began to think it was a bad option. Running would only make him look guilty. It was probably what Geoffrey wanted. He had been so caught up in finding out who killed Sandra and why he had not thought clearly. Then there had been the mention of his sister and her husband. There was no telling if the threat was real, but he did not want to take the chance.

Had he waited for the police he might have been able to explain the situation. He might have had a tough time going to court to prove his innocence, but in the end, he thought he would have won. It was what the justice system was for after all. Then he remembered what McKinley had told him. Major Derrick White might be corrupt. If McKinley was correct Ethan may not have stood a chance on trial.

Looking back Ethan knew none of it mattered now. He had to see it through to the end. He had run from the scene of the crime. He would be the first suspect. Soon there would be a massive search for him. Ethan knew his time was short. He had to get out of town and fast. Though he knew he had to be very careful. If he left the state the FBI might be called. He did not want them on his tail.

Still crouched in the bushes he looked up at the house of the only two people he now trusted. All he could hope for was for them to believe him. He also hoped they would help him. As much as he hated the thought of involving them he knew he needed their help. There was nowhere else to turn and he hated himself for it.

Once the street looked clear he darted to the front door. Without hesitation, he pounded on it with his fist. Moments later it swung wide open. Valerie stood in the threshold. At first, she looked surprised and excited to see her brother. Her face suddenly changed to a look of horror when she spied the blood. Without a word, she dragged him inside.

"Ethan, Jesus Christ, what happened to you? Are you all right?"

Ethan wanted to answer, but the words would not come out. Pierce stopped halfway down the stairs when he spotted Ethan. He looked wild and crazed. His eyes were wide and he was covered in blood.

"Holy shit, Valerie what happened?"

"I don't know, he just showed up like this. He hasn't said a word."

He nearly pushed Valerie aside as he approached Ethan.

"Hey, man, are you okay?"

Ethan looked up at Pierce and back at Valerie. Slowly he found the nerve to speak as he realized they were looking at his face in horror. His hand sprung to his face and he felt something warm and wet. When he pulled it away he nearly fell over as he spotted the blood.

As he looked down he saw his shirt was covered as well. Now he understood why they were so frantic.

Looking back up he finally spoke, "It's not mine, I'm fine." It did not seem to put either of them at ease. With a quick glance towards Valerie Pierce decided to step in.

"Who's blood is it Ethan? What happened?"

Ethan took in a large gulp of air as he readied to tell his story. He told them all about Major McKinley's email and about the meeting with him. How Geoffrey Hunt had shown up and killed McKinley. Ethan omitted the part about Geoffrey threatening to kill her and Pierce. There was no chance he was about to put his sister into a panic. Tears filled Valerie's eyes as he explained his only option was to do exactly as Geoffrey had told him. There was nothing else he could have done.

Without hesitation, Pierce and Valerie believed his story. They knew he would not lie to them. Ethan had always been a straight forward, good man. Valerie trusted him without question.

"I'm sorry I came here. I didn't know where else to go. They're going to be looking for me soon. I can't be here when they do."

Valerie looked at him and nearly cried. "We'll help you whatever it takes."

"I hate to ask this, but I need to borrow some cash and a car."

Both of them nodded in response.

"When the police arrive you say I showed up with a gun and stole it all from you."

"There is no way I'm going to say that!"

"Valerie, there's no choice. If they think you've helped me you'll end up in jail."

"He's right, honey. As much as I hate it we don't have a choice."

Ethan nodded at Pierce as a thank you. Valerie still looked unhappy. She started to cry and threw herself down on the couch. Ethan went to comfort her, but Pierce stopped him. With a firm grip on his arm, he pulled him aside. He began to whisper.

"Ethan, listen, I don't want Valerie to hear what I'm about to say. The less people who know the better. I want you to take the keys to my car, but I also want you to take my credit card and some cash. Go to Miami international and buy a plane ticket somewhere far from here."

"They will trace the card and..."

"Listen, after that leave the airport and head west."

Pierce fished out his keys and pulled a copper key off the ring. "Take this key. It's for a condo in Indian Rock's Beach on the other coast. It belongs to my cousin. She lives up north, sometimes uses it around summer. She shouldn't be using it this year so you will have it to yourself. Go there and lay low until we can figure all of this out."

Ethan grabbed the key and slipped it into his pocket. Pierce also handed him a wad of cash with his credit card hidden inside. "Thank you, Pierce, I don't know what to say."

"Just stay safe, we'll figure this out."

"One more thing, keep Valerie and yourself safe. Both of you might be in danger."

"Don't worry, I'll keep us safe."

With that, they both headed back towards Valerie. She was still weeping on the couch, a pillow pulled firmly up to her chin. Pierce disappeared for a moment and came back with a new shirt for Ethan. He quickly changed and used the old one to wipe the blood from his face.

Once he was cleaned up Valerie threw her arms around him. "I love you so much, Ethan." She cried on his shoulder. Ethan gripped his sister tight in his arms and held her for a moment. He told her that he loved her too and she let go.

"I have to get out of here now. The second I'm down the street I want you to call the police. If you don't it will look suspicious. They are already going to think you've helped me."

Before Valerie could protest Pierce told him they would. Ethan and Pierce's eyes locked for a moment. Ethan tried as hard as he could to show his thanks. Somehow he could see it in his eyes that he understood. With a quick handshake, he ran out to their garage.

Nestled in the dark garage was Pierce's Jeep Grand Cherokee. Ethan jumped behind the wheel and opened the garage door. He knew the police would be there any moment. Valerie and Pierce would call the police, but only to protect their innocents. They would be nearly to their house when the call was made. The last thing he wanted was for them to be pulled down with him. They needed to look innocent of everything.

As he drove down the road towards the airport a rage built inside of him. It boiled under his skin like nothing else he had ever felt before. He had never been an angry person. Usually, he could keep his calm, but this was different. Someone had killed Sandra, now someone was threatening him and his family. He found himself daydreaming about beating Geoffrey to death with his bare hands. He wanted it more than anything. He hoped he would soon get the chance.

Now he focused on driving to the airport. He would follow Pierce's plan. It was a good one. It would throw the heat off his trail for a while. It would not last forever and Ethan knew it. Eventually, they would find him. He could not hide forever. But he thought it might just give him enough time to figure out who was behind it all. He did not know how he would do it, but he had to try.

There were not many clues for him to go off of. McKinley had told him that Derrick White may have been dirty. If that were true he may have been the one to have McKinley killed as well. He may have been behind Sandra's death too. Ethan could not help but wonder if Geoffrey had killed Sandra. Somewhere deep down he believed it was true. If so he would pay with his life.

If Geoffrey was a dirty cop and working with Major White then there had to be others. Did Derrick have a small group of dirty officers doing his work for him? How many did he have? What were they up to? What was the big picture? There had to be an end game. There always was.

He wondered about Greene. It sounded as if the man was a ghost, which was not possible. If he existed there had to be some trail to follow. It sounded as if Greene was some sort of crime boss on the streets. Several criminals were afraid of him. As far as Ethan could recall there were no outstanding warrants for a man named Greene. The name had never come up before. Was he perhaps the mastermind behind everything? Perhaps he was blackmailing Major Derrick White and pulling his strings.

The more he thought about it all the more he did not understand. There was no chance it was all about making money on the side selling weapons and narcotics. It was impossible. Theft and illegal distribution were nothing compared to murder. Why would someone murder to cover it up? Ethan knew something bigger was going on.

McKinley had spoken about something being planned, something big. Ethan could not imagine what that had been about. Whatever it was Sandra had been the key to it all. She knew more than McKinley thought she did, of that Ethan was sure. She stumbled across something big and she had been killed for it.

He wondered how much she had known. How much could she have proven? Ethan figured she could not prove much since she never made a move. Someone got nervous and had her killed. She had been on the right track. Somehow he had to finish her trail for her. Ethan wished he could speak to her. If only she had left something behind. If only she had given him a clue.

His mind flashed back to the night she died. He thought he might be sick. The image of her body sprawled over the pool deck flashed in his mind. With tears welling up he shook his head trying to erase the image. Recalling the odd position of her hand he wondered if she had been trying to tell him something. He remembered her three fingers had been pressed against the ground. Three bloody fingerprints were left behind. He wondered what about the number three was significant. What did it point to? Ethan could see no correlation with the number to her death. Was she counting the number of killers? That did not make sense.

Ethan racked his brain for an explanation but came up empty.

He swore to himself that he would figure it all out. He would bring whoever was responsible to justice. Sandra's death would be avenged one way or another. Her work would be finished, whatever it took. Even if he had to do it outside of the law, it would be done.

Turning into Miami International Airport he headed for the long term parking. He knew the officers would check for Pierce's Jeep there. When they found it and the purchase of a plane ticket they would believe he was gone. Of course, it would not fool them forever.

There was only one problem with this plan. He did not know how to get to the other coast. Renting a car would be too risky. They would need a credit card. Sitting in the Jeep for a moment he looked around as if the answer would show itself. No ideas came to mind. Just as he was about to give in and rent a car his answer came.

Chapter 10

As Ethan pulled into the long-term parking at the airport the police arrived at Pierce and Valerie's home. They had briefly discussed what they would tell them. It was very straight forward. Ethan showed up stating that he needed to borrow the car. When they asked why he had snatched his keys and a few other items. Before Pierce could stop him he was out the door with his car. It was not a foolproof lie, but they might buy it.

Outside three police cruisers parked in the driveway. The first two officers climbed out and waited for the third. Valerie peered out the window and traced their steps as they approached the front door.

Pierce pulled open the door the same moment they knocked. Staring back at him was Ethan's superior Major Derrick White. Without hesitation, Pierce motioned for them to come inside. The two officers stood beside the door as Derrick White approached Pierce and Valerie.

"I am so sorry to be here like this," he said reaching out his hand. Pierce shook it. Derrick turned towards Valerie and opened his arms to her and she hugged him. "Valerie, I'm sorry. I wish there was something I could say to you to make it all better."

When Valerie did not respond Derrick let out a sigh looking at the two other officers. "Well, I suppose we should get down to it. What happened exactly?"

Before Valerie had a chance to speak Pierce stepped in. "He showed up on our doorstep, blood on his face. I let him in thinking he was hurt. He cleaned up and I gave him a change of clothes. We asked him what happened, but he didn't give us a straight answer. Then he asked to borrow my car. When I asked why he grabbed my keys and wallet off the table. I didn't have a chance to stop him before he got to my Jeep. Then he was gone." Pierce pulled his wallet from his back pocket. "At least I got this back. He tossed it on the ground when he ran. Took my credit card, though. I don't know what's going on with him, but we just want to make sure he's all right."

Derrick thought for a moment. One of the officers by the door was scribbling in a small, black notebook. The other officer stood opposite him. He seemed disinterested in the whole situation. Something about him made Pierce uneasy. He did not know why, but he did not trust him.

"Derrick," Valerie started. "What happened? What's going on?"

With a sigh, Derrick stepped closer to Valerie. With his booming voice, he said, "I don't really know how to say this so I guess I'll just come out with it. Ethan is the prime suspect in the murder of another officer. His car was found at the crime scene as well as a weapon with his prints."

Valerie's eyes welled with tears. Although she had already heard it from Ethan it still upset her. Somehow hearing from another officer set it in reality for her. Derrick reached out to comfort her, but she retreated to the living room. Dropping down on the couch she began to cry again. Pierce was unsure if she was acting or if the emotions had become too much to bear again.

"I hate to have to ask this, but who will if I don't? You're absolutely sure he didn't say where he was going? There isn't something you're not telling us, right?"

Pierce did his best to look genuinely offended. "It's all we know. If I knew anything that would help bring Ethan back safely I would tell you." Pierce looked at the other two officers. The first still wrote away in his notebook. Something about the other officer still seemed off. Their eyes locked. Pierce could not be sure, but he thought he detected the hint of a smirk. It angered him, but he kept silent. No good would come from harassing one of the officers. Especially when Valerie would need him for emotional support. Not to mention Ethan was out there alone. When he got where he was going he might contact Pierce. If that happened he needed to be there to help in any way he could. Ethan might not have been blood, but he was still family and Pierce never turned his back on family.

As the officers were about to leave Valerie stood up. "Promise me one thing," Derrick gave her a nod. "Bring him back safe. Don't let anything happen to my brother." Again Derrick nodded looking her in the eyes.

"I promise, your brother will be just fine," He said as they headed out the front door. Valerie and Pierce watched out the window as the three officers stood talking for a few minutes in the driveway. Pierce still could not place what was off about the man. It was almost as if he knew more than everyone else in the room, but had not shared. He had tried to read his name tag, but never got a good look at it. He shook it from his mind and turned to Valerie. He threw his arms around her as she began to cry.

"He's going to get through this, I promise. Your brother is smart. He didn't do what they say he did, we know that. He will figure out what's going on. I'm sure of it."

Valerie did not speak. She pressed her face into his shoulder and cried.

***

Officer Fidel Sanchez pocketed his cell phone and stood up from his desk. The building seemed fairly empty now. Whatever officers were not at the scene of the shooting had been deployed around the city trying to catch the killer. It had been quite a shock to hear Ethan McCormick was the prime suspect. He did not know him personally, but he knew of him. It seemed odd he would be wanted in the murder of an officer.

Then again his girlfriend had just killed herself while they were on vacation. Witnessing something like that could really screw with a person's head. Maybe it had knocked a few screws loose. He could have suffered a sort of mental breakdown and had lost touch with reality.

Fidel shrugged it off and headed away from his desk. He and only a handful of others had been told to "hold down the fort" in case Ethan came back to the station. It was unlikely, but it did not matter. Fidel had work to do and he was happy he had been left behind.

Quickly he made his way to the holding area and slipped in unnoticed. Slowly he made his way towards cell number three. He stopped just in front of Kyle Matthews's room. The holding cell was more or less a glorified broom closet. The door was made of thick, heavy metal to ensure no one broke in or out. It was mostly used to keep offenders locked up until they could be transferred to the right location. Or they were used to hold those arrested for DUI. It was where they would "sleep it off."

Fidel slid the door open quietly. The man was sitting on the bed staring at the wall. When Fidel pulled the door shut behind him he looked up with a puzzled look on his face. Before he could ask any questions Fidel lunged at him and put him in a headlock. Kyle choked as he tried to push him off. Slowly Kyle began to lose consciousness. When he was out Fidel let him slip to the floor. He landed with a hard thud!

He turned to the bed and snatched up all of the sheets and pillow cases. He ripped them in half and began to furiously wrap them together. Eventually, he was able to turn the sheets into a makeshift noose which tied nicely to the light fixture on the ceiling. Fidel pulled with all his weight to ensure its strength. Once he was satisfied he looked down at Kyle's unconscious body. He untied the noose and slipped it over Kyle's neck. It took all of his strength to hoist the man over his shoulder, but he managed. He was able to tie the rope back to the light fixture and slowly let Kyle's body slip from his shoulder.

The roped fastened its grip around Kyle's neck and his eyelids snapped open. A few seconds later they began to bulge. As his fingers clawed at the rope he stared down at Fidel with fear and confusion.

"Greene sends his regards," Fidel said as he watched the life slip from his eyes. When Kyle's feet finally stopped twitching he snuck out of the holding cell and made his way back to his desk. Several hours later someone would find his body strung up to the ceiling.

They would believe he had hung himself. Fidel had done exactly as Greene had instructed him to.

Chapter 11

Shortly after leaving Pierce and Valerie's house Derrick made a phone call to Brad Forester. He explained what had happened at Valerie's home. Ethan had stolen their car and Pierce's credit card at least that was their story. Derrick did not want to say it to Brad, but he was skeptical.

For a moment Brad was silent. "Took his credit card?" Derrick told him that was correct. After another long pause, Brad spoke up again. "We need to send officers to the airport. I think he might be trying to fly out of state." Derrick agreed and told him to make it happen. He also told Brad to set up roadblocks on the major highways leading out of the city. If Ethan was driving they would catch him. If he was flying they would know where. Either way, they would have him in custody before the day was over.

"Derrick, one last thing. I think we need to keep the media out of this one as long as possible."

"Why's that, Brad?"

"Guilty or not Ethan was a good officer, one of our best in fact. The media will tear him apart. Think about it, being accused of killing a cop? They will run that story into the ground. I think, for now, it's best that we keep it under wraps. I would prefer a fair, just, and unbiased trial."

"Of course, you're right. Make sure you advise all officers of that when you make the call. I'm going to head to the airport myself. Meet me there."

With that, Derrick hung up and slipped the phone back in his pocket. After explaining to the other two officers their new tasks he jumped behind the wheel of his cruiser. With his lights blaring, he sped off towards Miami International Airport.

As he powered through a red light he heard a voice break over the radio. Brad was making the call explaining for all officers in the area of the airport to head there immediately and for all remaining officers to head off major roads and set up road blocks.

"We are looking for Officer Ethan McCormick. He is wanted for the murder of Major McKinley. Remember, he is only a suspect and is innocent until proven guilty. Please treat him as such. Let's do our best to keep this quiet. Anyone asks what the road blocks are for only tell them a suspect is at large. You are not at liberty to discuss it further. Keep your eyes open out there."

Derrick imagined many officers would be surprised by the call. Ethan McCormick had been a great officer, never did anything wrong. He was always one to follow protocol and never caused any problems. Something must have snapped after Sandra died. The man was stricken with grief and that does strange things to people. He wished it had not worked out the way it did. Unfortunately, there was nothing else that could be done. He had no other choice.

As he drove, Derrick was hit with a powerful headache. He started to feel nauseous. He nearly had to pull over thinking he might vomit. He put one hand to his temple and applied as much pressure as he could. After a few minutes, the headache let up. Shaking it off he continued towards the airport.

When he reached the airport he slid to a stop in the drop off lane as his lights strobed wildly. Seconds later Brad arrived in an unmarked black sedan followed by three police cruisers. Derrick ordered two of the officers to start sweeping the parking lot starting with short term. The third officer went with Brad and Derrick. The manager of security came running up to meet the officers with a worried look on his face.

"Officers, what can I do for you?"

"We have a man using a stolen credit card who might be trying to board one of these planes. He is the prime suspect in a murder investigation. We need you to run a search in your system for the credit card information." Derrick said.

The security manager said he would be glad to help and asked for all the information he needed. Derrick explained the credit card information would be under Pierce Mason. The head of security ran off towards his office to run the trace.

Brad turned to the other officer and instructed him to start searching the airport as best he could. When other officers arrived they would be instructed to do the same. After he walked away Brad turned back to Derrick.

"Keep me updated with what the manager says. I'm going to take a look around. Maybe stumble across some clues. If Ethan made a mistake here we'll find it." Derrick nodded and Brad walked away.

A short moment later the security manager reappeared. "There was a match. It seems this man bought a plane ticket to Iowa a short while ago. There's just one problem, sir."

"What is it?"

"That plane already departed."

Derrick was furious, but he kept his cool. Lashing out at this man would not do him any good. If Ethan had made it aboard the plane he would have to call ahead to airport security in Iowa and have them detain Ethan. At least they knew where he was going. He would not be free much longer. Before he could instruct the security officer to make the call a better idea formed in his head.

"Call the pilot and have him turn the plane around. It can't possibly be that far from here by now."

The manager shook his head. "Sorry, that won't be possible. We'd have to get clearance from the FAA to allow the plane to turn around. By the time the call was made and the clearance went through the plane would be nearer to its destination than here. I will contact airport security in Des Moines and have them apprehend your man when the plane lands. Officers will be standing by as well. He won't get away."

Derrick shook his head and rubbed his temples. He told the manager that would be acceptable and gave him Ethan's name and description. After he was done speaking with this man he would call the police station in Des Moines and talk to someone directly. He wanted to make sure this was done correctly. If he had made it over the state border and the local police in Iowa were unable to apprehend him the FBI would have to get involved. Brad did not want that to happen and neither did he.

***

Brad Forester walked towards the security checkpoint. He watched as people removed their shoes and belts. After placing them in the bins he watched them walk through the scanners. His phone began to ring.

It was Derrick. He explained everything he had learned from the security manager. Derrick went on to explain that he would contact Des Moines and have officers standing by to arrest Ethan. Brad hung up with Derrick and continued to watch the security checkpoint.

He doubted Ethan had made it through security so quickly. There was no chance he had had enough time. Then his thoughts turned to Derrick. He sounded more frantic than he should have. Something was going on with him and Brad did not know what it was. There was tremendous pressure on him to find Ethan before the media found out, of course. If it leaked that a corrupt cop and accused murderer managed to escape they would have a nightmare on their hands. Yet Brad did not think that was all it was. He could not place what it was, but lately, Derrick had been off.

Brad decided to update the other officers via radio but advised them to continue to sweep the parking lot. He wanted to make sure nothing was missed, at least on his end. Turning on his heel he headed towards the bathroom.

Staring in the mirror for a few moments he splashed a little water on his face. Snatching up some paper towels he quickly dried his face. He was just about to toss the used towels in the trash when something caught his eye. Something gold protruded from under the used towels in the trash bin. Shoving them aside Brad found a badge. He knew right away it belonged to Ethan. He recognized the badge number of four hundred ten. For some reason, he had tossed it in the trash.

Brad snatched it up quickly. A small piece of paper was tucked under the clip. He removed the paper and slid the badge into his pocket. He unfolded the paper and nearly stumbled backward. Written was only three words, but they said enough. Written on the paper were the words Greene, White, and Hunt. Brad knew exactly what Ethan was trying to say.

Ethan was lucky Brad had stumbled across his clue. Quickly he pushed the note into his pocket and walked out of the bathroom. The note did not prove to Brad that Ethan was innocent, but he believed in seeing all angles. He did not want to tarnish Ethan's reputation if something bigger was going on.

Derrick's name had been written on the note and Brad knew it had to mean something. He had had a bad feeling about Derrick for some time now, but could not quite place it. Maybe there was something there. Brad wished he could talk with Ethan somehow. If only he had not run. If he was innocent why would he run? He thought. It did not make any sense. If a person was innocent running from the police was the last intelligent option. It only solidified the conception of guilt.

Not everything was adding up and Brad was determined to bring it all together. He decided he would keep the note to himself and see what else he could find. Then Brad had an idea. He was going to pay Ethan's sister Valerie a visit. Maybe she and her husband knew something that would help him. Brad did not want to admit it, but deep down he could not shake the thought that Ethan was truly innocent.

Chapter 12

Before Ethan had dropped his badge in the restroom trash can he had sat in his car trying to formulate a plan. He could not use Pierce's car to drive to the other coast, he would be caught very quickly. He needed a completely different one. The answer had driven in and parked next to him. A flustered looking woman had climbed out of her Chevrolet Volt. With her luggage dragging behind her she headed towards the airport.

Ethan quickly went into action. As fast as he could walk without drawing attention he attempted to cut her off. When he was perfectly in line he darted towards her at a brisk walking pace. The two of them collided with great force. The woman's purse fell and spilled out over the parking lot.

"Oh my God, I am so sorry ma'am. Let me help with that." Ethan did his best to sound apologetic. The woman was not pleased with all. As Ethan helped her scoop up the contents of her purse she swore and glared at him. Mostly she mumbled under her breath, but she complained several times about being late and missing her flight.

Doing his best to ignore her complaints he had scooped the last bit of her things into her purse and handed it to her. With a smile he held it out to her, apologizing. The woman snatched the bag and took off in a half jog towards the airport. Ethan heard her call back out to him as she drifted away. He could not be sure, but he thought she called him an asshole.

Ethan looked down at his hand and grinned. It had worked perfectly. He now had the keys to her car. He felt bad about stealing it but tried his best to get passed it. It made him feel better knowing she had parked in long term parking. She at least would not know she had been robbed for a while. As he headed into the airport he made a silent promise that he would somehow return the car to the woman.

After Ethan had bought the ticket and made a detour in the restroom he had run back out to the stolen Volt. Without hesitation, he drove out of the lot and made his way out of Miami. He was already several miles down the Tamiami trail when Derrick was arriving at the airport. Any road blocks would be too late, although Ethan was still a bit on edge. He would not feel better until the four and half hour trip was behind him. At least then he would feel he was slightly safer.

Now he had been on the road for just over an hour. It would be getting dark soon. Ethan welcomed it. He was not sure what the Miami police were planning at that very moment. It all depended on how they wanted to handle it. If they wanted to keep things quiet there would not be an all-out manhunt. If the media caught wind of the story there would be one. He hoped for the former option.

With around three hours of driving ahead of him, Ethan struggled to keep his mind occupied. The last thing he wanted to do was think about Sandra. For now, he would have to put her out of his mind. It would only be a dangerous distraction. Her memory might get him killed or cause him to make rash decisions. It was best to keep things simple.

Ethan decided to plan out his next step. He did not want to take a stolen vehicle directly to the condo he would be staying at. If it was reported stolen sooner than he hoped it would lead the local police right to his doorstep. It was attention he could not afford. He did not know the Tampa Bay area very well, but he knew there were a couple of large airports there. First was the Tampa International Airport. Then there was the St. Petersburg, Clearwater Airport.

He was slightly more familiar with the latter. Pierce Masons, Valerie's husband, worked for the Coast Guard. The St. Petersburg, Clearwater Airport doubled as a Coast Guard base. Pierce used to run rescue missions from the base in his younger years. Ethan had received a tour of it while Pierce was still there. It seemed like a fitting place for Ethan to make his next move.

In his mind, he planned to stop at the Clearwater airport and leave the stolen Volt in the long term parking. It was the perfect hiding spot for a stolen car. It would look natural sitting in the long-term parking at an airport. It would essentially be hiding in plain sight. Then from there he would take a cab to the Indian Rocks Beach area, but not all the way to the condo. In case the cab driver was questioned by police he did not want him to know exactly where he was. He had the cash he got from Pierce in his wallet which he would use to pay the fare.

After the cab ride, it would be a nice walk to the condo. If all went well Ethan would arrive just before midnight. He imagined he would curl up in the bed, or the couch, and sleep first thing. In the morning he would get started on what was next. At this moment there was no point planning any further ahead. He could only focus on what was right in front of him.

As the sun slipped behind the horizon Ethan let out a sigh of relief. He felt safer now and with Miami falling farther behind him the feeling of security only increased. He felt horrible about leaving his sister behind knowing she could be in danger if Geoffrey Hunt got to her, but Pierce was there. Ethan was confident he would keep her safe. But if anything happened to either of them while he was gone Ethan knew he would never forgive himself.

With around two hours left of his drive, Ethan started to grow tired. He started to wish he had taken a less fuel efficient vehicle. Maybe then he would have had an excuse to pull over somewhere and stretch his legs. With the Volt, he would make it to the St. Petersburg International Airport with plenty of fuel to spare. He supposed it was a positive, but it still would have been nice to pull over.

Out of boredom Ethan turned the radio on and played a CD that was in the player. A few seconds of loading went by before some horrible pop singer blasted through the speakers. Ethan could not understand what the woman was saying and it sounded terrible. He did not understand why anyone liked that kind of music. He switched it off. He sunk down in the chair and prepared for a long and boring two hours.

Ethan surprised himself by keeping awake over the next hour, but now he was terrified. The traffic ahead was coming to a halt. Further, up he could see flashing blue and red lights. He could not tell if it was a road block or an accident. Either way, he had to keep moving forward. Backtracking would take too long, as well as draw attention to himself. Gripping the wheel tightly he pressed on.

For nearly thirty minutes the traffic was stop and go. The police lights drifted closer. Ethan tried to see which it was, but could not see around the other vehicles. He hoped he was being paranoid, but realized that he could not blame himself for being so.

The final push came. The police officer was standing outside of his car on the shoulder of the highway. Two cars were crumpled together against the guard rail. Ethan counted himself lucky that it was not a road block and picked up speed with the other drivers.

Once they were completely free of the accident the roads cleared up again. This time there were no disturbances the rest of the way. He pulled into the long-term parking at the airport and found a nice spot in the corner to leave the stolen Volt. With a last minute thought, Ethan crammed the car keys into the glove box. If the car was found and returned to the owner she would still have her keys. He hoped everything was over by the time that happened. He decided to make another promise to himself. If he got through this alive and was found innocent he would make it a point to see if the car was still there. If it was he would pick it up and bring it back to Miami. It was a promise he would not keep.

Now he climbed out of the car and headed towards the entrance to the airport. It was nearly ten at night and the airport was hardly busy. He lucked out when he spotted a taxi waiting out front. Waving his hand out the taxi driver pulled up in front of him. He quickly climbed in the backseat and greeted the driver.

"Where to?"
"Indian Rocks Beach please."
"You got an address for me?"

"Actually I'm visiting some family of mine. I know they live in a condo on the beach, but I forgot the address. And of course, they're not picking up their phone. It's ok. I think I know which one it is. I can point it out to you when we get there."

"All right, buddy."

With that, they headed off towards the beach. Ethan took the time to admire how the traffic here was not so hectic. Back in Miami traffic was always hectic. Over the years he had grown accustomed to it, but he forgot how relaxing a nice drive could be. Especially when he was not the one behind the wheel.

He tried to put his head back and relax, but the driver started up a conversation. "So you say you were here visiting family?" Ethan simply stated yes in reply. "I can't help but notice you don't have any luggage." Ethan was not ready for the question and a rush of fear engulfed his body. "You flew in without even a carry-on?"

"Yeah, I like to travel as light as I can. Save some money. Plus, it helps that my family insists on buying me all new clothes every time I come down to visit. Helps having rich family."

"Very generous of them."

"Yes, it is. They usually have to buy me a suitcase so I can take home everything they bought me. One of these days I'll have to tell them to just keep a closet full of clothes just for me."

"Wish I had rich family like that. When I stay with family for the holidays they try and charge me rent."

The cab driver erupted into a laughter and Ethan followed suit. He was happy the driver had believed his story. He did not want to raise any attention to himself. Not that he was afraid the cab driver would find him all that suspicious. Driving strangers around he must have come across others who were more worthy of the suspicious title. If the cab driver had a scale of weird people he had driven Ethan would hardly have made the list. He would be another nobody to the driver by the following morning. For that, Ethan would be thankful.

He stared out the window as the buildings went by. Most places were closed at this hour except for the occasional bar or restaurant. It seemed like a nice area. Ethan found himself drawn to the quiet of it all. Compared to Miami the Clearwater area was practically empty.

A small park passed by on his left called Largo Central Park. It seemed like a nice little park which families would take walks or where kids would skip school. There were probably plenty of places for teens to hide and make out, perhaps even more. Ethan caught himself reminiscing about his high school days but quickly snapped out of it.

They came up on a bridge that connected Indian Rocks Beach with mainland Pinellas County. When they were nearly over the driver called out to Ethan asking if it was a right or a left. He was not completely sure which so he said right. If it was wrong he would just have to walk further.

Luckily they seemed to be heading in the right direction. Down the road a ways Ethan recognized the building. It was the condo he was looking for. Another condo was coming up on the left. He instructed the driver to pull over into the parking lot. The cab driver pulled into the lot and stopped the meter. Ethan paid what he owed, tipped him well, and wished the driver a good night. With that, the driver was gone.

He waited about five minutes in the parking lot before he continued down the street, just in case the driver was still in the area. That would have been very suspicious if he was spotted walking away. Lucky for Ethan the cab driver was long gone and no longer thinking about him anymore.

The walk only took him about fifteen minutes. After a short elevator ride and a brief walk down the hallway, Ethan had arrived at the condo. He was dying to kick off his shoes and fall fast asleep. In the morning he would get a good look at the place and take a look at the surrounding area. He would need to plan out escape routes in case the police came for him, but that would be tomorrow's work. Now it was nearly midnight and he was exhausted.

Turning the key he stepped inside. Flipping on the light he called out to see if anyone was home. Pierce had told him his cousin would most likely not be there, but he wanted to be sure. When no one replied he checked the bedroom. The bed looked as if it had not been slept in all year.

He kicked off his shoes and laid on the perfectly made bed. Without even slipping under the covers Ethan passed out. The weight of the day had finally got to him. For now, he would get a good night's sleep. In the morning his work would be cut out for him. But for the moment he dreamt sweet dreams of Sandra.

Chapter 13

The plane to Des Moines approached its destination while Ethan was still on the road. The pilots were not given any special instructions nor were they notified anything was abnormal. The airport, however, was fully aware of who might be on board. The local police were standing by with orders to arrest Ethan McCormick on site. They were also instructed to be as discreet as possible.

Now two security guards stood outside the terminal with three police officers at their side. If Ethan was onboard the plane they would grab him quickly. There would not be enough time for him to escape before they spotted him. Just in case there were two other officers waiting in the cruisers just outside the airport. All of them confident he would be caught.

As they waited impatiently the plane landed safely. The radio blared on the security guard's shoulder. They were being told the plane was taxiing across the tarmac. About ten minutes later the passengers would be unloading.

Finally, the plane came to a stop at its gate. Minutes later people began to stream out. The two guards and the police officers fanned out. They formed a U-shape around the gate exit. There would be no missing Ethan McCormick.

The security manager on site sat in front of the security monitors. He eagerly watched the video feed from the gate. As the officers searched he intently watched those who walked by them. If somehow he made it past them he would spot him.

The plane was virtually empty now. Ethan still had not been spotted and the officers were getting anxious. If he had made it past them they would be ashamed. When the last of the passengers were off the plane they knew they had made a mistake. The officers instructed the security guards to make their way towards the entrance of the airport while they advanced to the plane. Perhaps Ethan was hiding out onboard.

Once the plane had been thoroughly searched they knew he had somehow slipped passed them. Cursing themselves they radioed the other officers. "Not sure how, but he made it passed us. Everyone be on high alert." With that, they headed off to the airport to sweep every possible area.

Still sitting in the security booth the manager sighed. Somehow they had missed him, but how? If he was onboard the plane they would have seen him. He checked every face that came across the monitor. He had never been onboard. He decided to find the officer in charge and tell him. They would be wasting their time searching the airport and the parking lot. The man they were looking for was not on the plane. He was not even in the state. It was the only possible explanation.

Thirty minutes later Derrick White received a phone called from the Des Moines police department. They apologized but did not think that Ethan was ever onboard the plane. They theorized he must have missed the plane or intentionally deceived them.

Derrick was outraged. It had been their only lead. How could he not be on the plane? He bought the plane ticket to Des Moines. Why would he buy a ticket if he was not planning to fly? Then it dawned on him. It had all been a diversion. Ethan had bought a plane ticket to waste their time. They put all their effort into the plane. It gave Ethan plenty of time to escape. By now he could have been anywhere. It would be impossible for them to track him down.

He decided to make another phone call to the airport security. He would have them search for any suspicious plane tickets bought or even any others bought with Pierce's credit card. He would also have them check the security cameras. They could watch Ethan and maybe get a better idea of where he went. Ethan may have managed to duck by them, but he would not stay hidden forever. Soon they would find him, of that he was sure. It would only be a matter of time.

***

The next morning Geoffrey Hunt awoke in his bed. The cell phone on his nightstand was flashing. A text had come through while he slept. With a loud yawn, he swung himself out of bed. Before he looked at his phone he figured he would go to the bathroom. Whatever it was could wait another minute or two.

When he was done he snatched up the phone and headed towards the kitchen. He read the text message as he started the coffee machine.

The police are keeping things from the media. It's time they find out. Throw Mr. McCormick to the wolves.

It was from Greene. It was obvious what he wanted him to do. After breakfast, he would make an anonymous call to the local news station. They would report on Major McKinley's death. Then they would speculate that the killer was former officer Ethan McCormick.

They would go on to explain his recent loss. Sandra's death would be linked to the cause of his unstable behavior. Perhaps Ethan blamed McKinley for her death. Maybe she was being overworked and could not handle the stress. Ethan would be looked at as the villain no matter which way the media turned it. He had, as far as they knew, killed a fellow officer. They eventual might go as far as blaming him for Sandra's death. Maybe even downright murder.

When everything was blamed on McCormick he would have to be dealt with. If Ethan was allowed to live there would eventually be a trial. Although the trial might be biased thanks to media involvement he might still get a very good lawyer. If that happened he might just make it out. Even if he did not get off he would bring up things that Geoffrey and others did not want talked about. Geoffrey knew the call to take care of Ethan would come through soon enough and he was happy about that. He just wanted to get it over with.

Greene would be safe even if Geoffrey was sent to prison for murder and conspiracy. The two of them had never met. It would be impossible to take Greene down with him. There was hardly any evidence he even existed. Geoffrey obviously did not want to go to prison. He would be happy once Ethan was dead. Once he was everything would be fine. Greene had explained they only needed a scapegoat. The media needed to focus their attention away for a while. The manhunt for Ethan was sure to get everyone's attention.

Eventually, new evidence would be "discovered" that linked Ethan to the theft of high-powered weapons from the Miami Police Department. Once the evidence came forward it would be obvious that Ethan murdered Sandra to keep it quiet. She was internal affairs and she was investigating him, at least that is what he would make everyone think. The only other person to know what Sandra was up to was her superior McKinley. He would not be talking to anyone either. Now Geoffrey looked forward to receiving the call. After Ethan was dead he would be home free.

Geoffrey sat down and enjoyed his bacon and pancakes. When he was finished he dropped the dirty dishes in the sink on top of several others. He made a mental note to wash the dishes that night but knew he would forget. He found a new set of clothes and changed.

He would need to find a public phone to call the news station. There could be no chance of tracing it back to him or suspicion would arise. That would be easy enough. There were not many pay phones left in the city, but he knew where some would be.

Heading down the road he decided to travel to Miami International airport. There would be a payphone bank there. It seemed fitting to toss Ethan to the press from the same location he evaded the police.

***

After the call came from Iowa explaining Ethan was never onboard the plane Derrick had contacted the head of security at Miami International. He gave them clear instructions to pull Ethan up on the security cameras purchasing the plane ticket. From there they needed to follow Ethan everywhere he went. After barking at them to have a compilation made up and emailed to him directly within the hour he hung up.

Another terrible headache was brewing so he took a couple ibuprofen. He hoped it would settle down before it got bad. "How the hell could he have slipped by us?" He said aloud. Sitting alone in his office he felt crazy for talking to himself.

When the video arrived he would take a careful look at it. Hopefully, it provided clues as to where Ethan went. He did not board the plane and he did not rent a car. Where could he have gone? Clearly, he did not stay in Miami. It would have been a mistake on his end. Derrick knew he was not stupid. He had left town, there was no doubt about it. Now he was certain he had not left the state. So he was somewhere in Florida. The question was where?

Derrick decided to give Brad Forester a call. He was with several officers conducting a search of Ethan's home. He wanted an update on what, if anything, was found.

"This is Brad."

"Brad, it's Derrick."

"Yep?"

"Any news at the McCormick house?"

"Not much yet. We found Ethan's personal computer. We'll be bringing that in. We confiscated a Beretta and any ammunition we could find. It seemed to be the only firearm in the house."

"What's on the computer?"

"I'll have someone take a look at it once we bring everything in."

"All right, keep me posted if you find anything else."

"You got it."

They hung up and Derrick massaged his temples. Despite the ibuprofen, the headache was growing stronger. He hoped there would be something on the laptop that would incriminate Ethan otherwise it was another dead end. He could not bear another one, not today.

An email sprang up on his computer. It was from airport security. Attached was a video file. Derrick sat back and pressed play. It showed Ethan walk up to the counter and purchase a ticket and head towards security. Instead of stepping in line for security he veered off into the bathroom. The time stamp advanced several minutes before Ethan reappeared.

From there the video tracked Ethan as he made his way back out of the airport and towards long term parking. At first, it looked like he was heading back towards Pierce's stolen Jeep, which was currently impounded, but then he darted to the left. He climbed into a small white car and drove off. Derrick played the last part again and paid closer attention. It was a Chevrolet Volt. He had no clue where he got the keys to the car from. Derrick wondered if he had met with someone in the bathroom who gave him the keys. Was someone working with Ethan? He wrote down the tag number and made a phone call.

***

Brad Forester swept over Ethan's home one last time. The note he had found at the airport was safely hidden at his own home along with the badge. If he found something similar at Ethan's it would be nearly impossible to pocket. Police were in every possible room checking every single corner. They looked like ants devouring a meal.

One of the officers was in Ethan's bedroom. He turned over the mattress and called out that he found something. Brad rushed into the room. "Sir, I found another laptop. Not sure who it belongs to."

"Let's bag it and bring it in. We'll have forensic check for prints and power it up. If there's anything worth finding on it they will." Brad watched as the officer placed the laptop in a forensic bag.

They did not find much at Ethan's house. So far nothing pointed to Ethan being a dirty cop. Brad was not surprised, but he kept the thought to himself. When he was satisfied there was nothing more to find he ordered the officers to pack it up. He then instructed them to take the evidence to the station and have forensics look at it. Shortly after he climbed into his car.

Brad waited for the officers to leave before driving off. He thought maybe he was being a bit paranoid, but he did not want any of them knowing which direction he was headed. There was something he needed to do that could not wait. He was going to have to talk to Pierce and Valerie Masons. If there was any information they could give to help him he would get it out of them. Brad knew it would not be easy, but they would come around. He just needed them to understand he was their ally in this. Brad did not want to see Ethan hurt or killed. He did not want to see him behind bars either. If there was information that pointed to him being innocent he needed it, for Ethan's sake. As long as the press stayed out of the situation they would be able to take care of everything nice and quiet. For that Brad was thankful.

The drive to their home was quiet and the traffic was light. He pulled into their driveway and slid into park. With a deep breath to gain his composure, he exited the car. With a heavy knock on the front door, he waited nearly a minute for a response. Pierce cracked the door enough to barely see his face.

"Who are you?" He demanded. Brad cleared his throat and explained. He asked if he could come in and have a word with them about Ethan. Against his better judgment, Pierce agreed. Valerie came down the stairs after the door shut behind them.

"Who's this?" She asked.

"This is Brad Forester. He worked with your brother. He just wanted to ask us some questions."

"We already told you guys everything we know. What more could you want?"

"Mrs. Masons, you misunderstand. I'm not here as an officer of the law, but as a friend of your brother's."

"He never talked about you."

"Well, maybe friend is too strong a word. Nonetheless, I am not here to cross-examine you or accuse you of anything. I'm not even here to accuse Ethan of anything."

"Then why are you here?" Pierce said.

"I was hoping there was any information you could give me that might explain what happened to Ethan. If he contacted you and told you anything I would love to know. Even the smallest detail might help paint a picture for me."

"I thought you weren't here to blame my brother for anything. It sounds like you still think he's guilty."

"Not at all Mrs. Masons. Let me be honest, I think something is going on. I don't know what it is, but something seems wrong. I don't know if Ethan is part of it or not, but I am going to find out. I don't want to bring your brother in to drag him through a long embarrassing trial. If he's found innocent it will still ruin his career. I want to keep this as quiet as possible. I believe Ethan is still innocent until proven guilty."

Brad could see a minuscule amount of trust in Valerie's eyes. He also sensed she was holding something back. He could not blame her. She wanted to protect her brother. Valerie did not fully understand Brad wanted nothing more than to protect him too. The best way to protect him would be to bring him in. An investigation would be done and most likely a trial. Brad would see to it that it was fair and quick. If Ethan was innocent everything would work out for him.

With a deep sigh, Valerie walked into the living room and sat on the couch and faced the television. The local news was on, but the volume was too low to hear. Brad pushed up his glasses, rubbed the bridge of his nose and looked up at Pierce.

"I have instructed the Miami police to keep everything as quiet as possible right now. We are keeping the news out of this. The last thing I wanted was for Ethan's face to be plastered all over the news calling him a murderer. I'm trying to protect him as best I can, but I still have to bring him in. Like I said, I'm not here to ask you if you know where he is or where he might be going. I just want to know if there is anything unusual you can tell me."

For a moment it looked as if Pierce had something to say, but he was interrupted. In the other room, Valerie let out a startled cry. Pierce and Brad both rushed in as she turned up the television volume.

A picture of Ethan was in the upper right-hand corner of the screen with a news anchor just to the left. The headline below the anchor read Manhunt for Miami Killer Cop. Brad was too enraged to listen to the report. He swore loudly as he snatched out his cell phone. "I told them to keep this quiet. How the hell did this happen?" He cried as he dialed Derrick's number.

When Derrick answered Brad began yelling, "What the hell happened Derrick?"

"What's wrong Brad?"

"We agreed not to get the media involved in this."

"My officers were under clear instructions not to."

"Then why am I looking at Ethan's face plastered all over the damn local news?"

"Shit."

"I know. It gets better. They've already labeled him a killer cop. Damnit Derrick this is going to cause a panic."

"I know."

"Goddamnit, I wanted to keep this quiet. This is going to ruin Ethan and the department. What the hell do we do now?"

"Well, I guess there isn't much we can do. It's already out there. I can't get up and make a statement that it's false."

"No, but we can make a statement stating it isn't as bad as it sounds."

"How so?"

"Let's not label him the prime suspect. Ethan was merely the last person to see McKinley alive. We can run with that. His disappearance doesn't make him guilty. Perhaps it makes him a victim."

"Damn, that's good."

"We are looking out for Ethan's well-being. We are trying to bring him in to keep him safe. After all, that is the truth."

"Do you think the people will buy that?"

"It doesn't matter if they do or not. It looks better than killer cop on the loose."

"That's true. Damn, this is going to really affect the vote in the next few days. They were already talking about budget cuts. This won't make us look good. It will probably be used against us."

"Ever the more reason to make it happen, Derrick."

"All right, I'll get started writing a speech. Get back here as soon as you can. I'll need your help."

Brad hung up the phone and turned back to Pierce and Valerie. Valerie's face was buried in Pierce's chest and muffled sobs rose through the air. Pierce stared at the television holding back tears. He knew exactly what this meant for Ethan. It would only be a matter of time before this news went national. When it did there would be no safe place for Ethan to lay low.

Brad told the Masons he had to go and promised he would fix the problem. Before he walked out the door he called back to them saying he would talk to them about Ethan soon. Behind the wheel of his car, he sped towards the police station still furious over the entire situation. If Derrick was behind the media leak he would make him pay. Everything was becoming more complicated.

Chapter 14

He woke to the warm morning sun breaching through the window in the bedroom. Somewhere in the distance, a seagull squealed as it fluttered through the air. Ethan stretched his limbs as far as he could and slowly sat up in the foreign bed. The comforter was still neatly draped across the bed with only a few wrinkles. In his morning grogginess, Ethan had forgotten about everything that had happened. For just a moment he was free of his stress.

Then it all flooded back in one giant tidal wave of emotion. The thought of Sandra, the gun in the end table, Major McKinley, and being framed for murder. It all had pounced on Ethan's consciousness at once. He pressed his hands to his temples and did everything in his power to keep himself from collapsing to the floor.

He fought back the stress and emotion. There would be time when it was all over. All Ethan could do now was focus on making his way through the day.

With the fear and sorrow nagging at the back of his mind, Ethan wandered out into the condominium. To his left, just beyond the kitchen, a balcony stretched away from the building. The view of the ocean from this height was magnificent. Although the ocean was not as clear and blue as back home it was still a wondrous sight.

Seagulls flew through the air as people gathered on the white sandy beach preparing for their day. Ethan watched them from the window beside the dining room. A family was setting up their beach umbrella, chairs, and cooler. Their two children ran around kicking up sand at their heels. Several boats ran up and down the coast causing larger waves to break across the shoreline.

He could tell it was going to be a perfect day for the beach. The sky was a rich blue with barely any clouds. Couples would walk over the sand together hand in hand. Families would swim and build sand castles. Others would collect seashells or search with metal detectors.

Ethan pressed his head against the glass and sighed. He could only watch as the people on the beach enjoyed their lives without care. All of them were oblivious to the man several stories up watching them. All of them oblivious to his situation. Soon the news would flash pictures of his face. Everyone would know what he looked like. Police stations all across the state would memorize his photo. They would all be on the lookout. He was a "cop killer" and there was nothing cops hated more.

Leaving the thought behind him Ethan made his way into the kitchen. Browsing through the fridge he decided to make himself some eggs. He did not have much of an appetite, but he knew his body needed the fuel. Whether he liked it or not he would force himself to eat.

As he prepared the kitchen he spotted the television remote on the kitchen counter. He decided some noise might help his mind keep from drifting. The flat screen in the living room powered on. The local news station mumbled on in the distance as he cracked the first of two eggs. As he cracked the second one he thought he heard his name.

He dropped the shells into the pan with the rest of the eggs and clambered to the living room. The sixty-inch flat screen television was mounted on the wall opposite a tan leather couch and matching recliner. The room was very inviting, but Ethan hardly noticed. His full attention was now on the anchorwoman sitting behind the desk. A picture of himself hung just left of her face as she spoke.

Ethan fumbled with the remote trying to turn up the volume. When he finally did he heard her say "If you have any tips on his whereabouts please call the tip line. The Miami Police Department has advised that he may have fled north, but have warned all major cities in Florida. A statewide search will surely be conducted by the local police departments."

The two anchors began to talk back and forth about the story, but Ethan did not hear it. All he could hear was the rapid beating of his own heart. He felt as if he were having a panic attack. His breathing became labored and his thoughts started to race. It would not take long for word to spread. Soon he would not be able to show his face. There would be no escape.

He knew it would hit the news eventually, but he had hoped for a little more time. The police department more than likely wanted to keep the entire ordeal as quiet as possible. An accused dirty cop and a dead officer made for bad press.

There was nothing he could do about it now. The story was out there. Once it hit major news networks, which would be soon, he would be doomed. Ethan changed the station to CNN. They were in the process of covering some political story as normal. He had a little bit more time.

He needed to find out who had Sandra killed and why. Whoever Greene was had to be the person who had her killed. But it was only an alias. There had to be a trail back to him. There was only one lead for him and that was Geoffrey Hunt. It was impossible for him to question Geoffrey. Somehow Ethan had to figure out who was behind it all without access to evidence or clues.

Ethan started to wonder if drawing Geoffrey to him was a good idea. If he came to him Valerie and Pierce might be safe. If Ethan was able to get the upper hand on Geoffrey he might just be able to make him talk. Geoffrey was more than likely connected with Greene in some way. There would be a way to hunt him down.

Ethan then realized that an attempt to draw Geoffrey out would make him a target for local law enforcement. He might be able to evade them for a while, but eventually they would catch him. He knew he could not run forever. There was another scenario that kept him from acting. Geoffrey was back in Miami with his sister. He had been told to run or Valerie would die. If Geoffrey caught on he might just kill Valerie and Pierce. With the cold and heartless way, he had killed Major McKinley he had no doubt of his seriousness.

There had to be something he could do. Pierce would be willing to help him back home, but he could never contact him. Using his cell phone would get him caught. A payphone might work, though, it would be tough to find one. If he did manage to find one they would be able to trace the call easy enough. That was if they were watching Pierce and Valerie. There was always the chance that they were not.

Ethan decided against trying to contact Pierce. There would be no inconspicuous way of doing it. Every option would cause him to show his face in public. Eventually, someone would recognize him. He had no choice but to stay hidden in the condo until he could formulate a plan.

He went back to making his breakfast while the news continued on scaring the public with the latest terror threat. It was merely white noise in the background for Ethan as he fished the bits of eggshell from his breakfast.

When it was all done he sat at the table next to the window which overlooked the beach. He chewed softly on the overcooked eggs not tasting it. It was merely a form of energy for him now.

He gulped down his eggs and again he pressed his head against the window. As he watched the beach goers prepare for their day he let out a sigh. For a moment the glass fogged over. He wiped it away and stood up from the table.

The plate from his breakfast stayed on the table as he walked around the condo. In another room he found a desk neatly clean and organized. A yellow legal pad was neatly pushed to the side with a pen placed on top. He thought it would be a great way to organize his thoughts.

Ethan snatched it up he headed towards the balcony. He left the sliding glass door open so he could hear the news in the background. If the story about him made major news network he wanted to be aware of it.

Currently, he was safe. They had taken to criticizing the current president. "I'm just saying it's not presidential of him. It makes our country look weak," one of the women on the news stated.

"Being sick makes him and our country weak? How do you figure that?" The other woman bit back.

"The world should always believe that our government is ready for anything. Making a public statement that the President of the United States of America is in bed with the flu is like shooting a flare gun into the sky. The world knows we are weaker now. It leaves us open for a terrorist attack."

"The world knows the country is not run by one man-"

He ignored the continuing debate and he stared at the blank legal pad for nearly five minutes unsure of where to start. There was not a lot of information to work with. He rapped the pen against the pad before he wrote Major Derrick White's name. Major McKinley had mentioned a possibility of his involvement. Ethan could not believe he was a key player in whatever conspiracy there was. With a dash next to his name, he scribbled the word involved?

The next name on his list was Geoffrey Hunt. The word Ethan wrote next to his name was much more direct, guilty. Below Geoffrey, he wrote the name, Greene. This was more complicated. Next to the name he wrote involved, who, and why?

A few lines down he wrote DECEASED. Underneath it, he wrote Sandra Delano with care. He lingered for a moment on her name still in a sort of denial she was no longer alive. Below Sandra went Major McKinley. He wrote the same description next to each, Internal Affairs. He followed this up with motive.

Ethan knew they had both been killed for their investigation into the Miami Police Department. One of the officers there was guilty of something. It had to be something horrible it is was enough to kill for. There was no doubt Geoffrey Hunt was guilty of murder, but Ethan was convinced he was not the mastermind. Whoever was behind everything would avoid doing the heavy lifting.

This, unfortunately, would point to Major Derrick White of the homicide division. White would want to avoid getting his hands dirty. That's where Geoffrey came in. He was possibly using Geoffrey to take out anyone in his way. The question remained, what was his end game?

Ethan thought this over for a moment then decided it could not be right. It if was then Ethan would have been killed along with McKinley. If Derrick was involved there would be no way he would risk letting Ethan get away. Letting Ethan go free would only allow him time to find proof of Derrick's involvement. If Derrick truly was the "mastermind" he would have been too paranoid of what Ethan knew to let him live.

Ethan decided that if Derrick was involved he had to be a pawn, either willing or unwilling. The real mastermind behind everything had to be Greene. Part of his plan was obvious. Ethan would take the fall for the murders. It would draw attention away from whatever Greene was up to. His plans, whatever they may be, would go by without any resistance. It could be the only reason Ethan was still alive. There needed to be a scapegoat for the time being. Once Greene finalized his plans Ethan would be killed and he knew it. There was limited time to work with. Unfortunately for Ethan, there was no guessing how much time he had left.

Frustrated he tossed the pad on the concrete floor. He stood up and walked back into the kitchen. The news still blared in the other room. Ethan paid no attention. He cracked open the fridge and shuffled items aside as he looked for a drink. Unfortunately, it was not very well stocked. Pierce's cousin only came down a couple times a year, if that. There would be no reason for her to keep it fully stocked.

This presented another problem Ethan had yet to think about. What would he do for food? Water from the tap would be fine, but the food was a separate issue. There was no telling when it would be safe for him to show his face again. But eventually, he would need to eat something. There was a small ration of food between the fridge and pantry, but it would not last more than a week.

Ethan decided food would be the least of his worries. If he made it a week without attracting the attention of the local authorities it would be a miracle. Ethan thought he would not be there long enough to worry about it.

Alcohol was not his normal drink of preference. Very seldom would he have a beer. At a barbecue with family or out to dinner with a handful of friends were about the only times he drank. Water always won the battle for his thirst. With a few beers hidden in the back of the fridge, he opted for one. With a quick twist of the bottle cap, he tossed his head back and gulped half of it down.

Ethan headed back out to the balcony with the bottle in hand. Something creaked on the opposite side of the condominium and he froze. For a moment he assumed it had come from the television. He spun around and stared at the front door. He watched in horror as the knob jiggled back and forth. The unmistakable sound of a key disengaging the lock reverberated in his ears. The door swung open with no time for him to hide.

Chapter 15

The sun shimmered on the tin roof of a small shed. Inside a man sat alone braving the scolding heat. He diligently fiddled away with an item in front of him. Sweat poured from his brow and down his face. The humidity was nearly unbearable as sweat soaked through his shirt. He would wipe the excess sweat away with a towel but in a matter of minutes it returned.

A small metal contraption sat on the table in front of him. Carefully he connected the wires and small pieces. Once it was finished he grabbed the backpack off the floor and carefully slid the contraption inside. It fit well. It was not so small that it flopped around inside, nor was it stretching the fabric of the bag. Anyone who looked straight at the pack would see nothing wrong. It had been done exactly as instructed.

Now the man tucked the backpack in the corner of the shed and covered it with a damp brown tarp. He made sure to move around some large items to hide the tarp from view. He finally received the look he wanted. It resembled a naturally cluttered shed.

He stepped through the tin doors and slid them shut with an ear piercing squeal. A light breeze parted his wet hair. The cool air felt invigorating on his hot skin. Despite what he had become involved in he felt good. It was the feeling of belonging to something bigger than himself. Those had been the exact words used when it had been explained to him.

The cell phone in his pocket buzzed to life. He read the text carefully. It asked if his task had been finished. He quickly replied that it was and it was well hidden. Good, I will contact you with further instructions, the reply said. The man pocketed the cell phone and headed back inside his home.

It had been nearly two weeks since he had first been contacted. A man who called himself Greene had sent him a text message. There had never been a moment when he spoke to the man directly. The communication was strictly through texts.

The first text was short and simple, but it had filled him with more fear than anything before. It had only read, I know what happened. He tried to play innocent and pretended not to know what it meant. He had merely replied asking who they were and what they wanted. When the reply came it was cold. Your wife doesn't know, but I do. Do as I ask and it stays quiet. This time he barely denied it. He only told the man to leave him alone but was only harassed more. The next couple days he was relentlessly harassed. Finally, Greene told him it was his last chance before he emailed photos and records to his wife. Finally, he caved and did exactly as he was told.

He wondered how Greene could possibly have known his darkest secret. Several years ago Greg had cheated on his wife, but she never knew. He had been out at the bar alone when a beautiful woman sat next down next to him. She was stunning with a smart haircut and slender body full of curves. The short black skirt fitted tightly across her legs which seemed to shine under the lights. Her face was warm and inviting and he felt an instant attraction to her, albeit only sexual. They talked and shared several drinks. As they laughed he ordered more. Once those were tossed back she excused herself to the restroom. While she was away Greg dropped a small pill into her drink. It dissolved just before she came back. When she was firmly seated next to him they finished their drinks.

Less than an hour later she complained of being dizzy and lightheaded. Greg offered to drive her home so she would be safe. Not completely in her right mind, she agreed. He held her arm all the way to the front door to help keep her balance. He waited impatiently as she fumbled with the keys. They slipped from her hand twice before she managed to open the door. Without hesitation, Greg shoved her inside and she stumbled to the floor. The skirt had been pushed up to her mid-thigh revealing her bright pink underwear. Being half conscious she did not have the strength to push him away. That night he had his way with her on her living room floor.

Greg left her passed out on the floor with her blouse undone and his seed seeping down her thighs. He was certain he would never get caught. She had thrown back too many drinks, not to mention the drug he had slipped her. When she woke up she would assume it had been a one-night stand. She could not possibly believe she had been raped.

Still, the terrible feeling started to set in. He began to think of everything he had done wrong. Greg had never done anything like it before and was unsure what to expect. In his lust filled rage, he had forgotten to clean up the scene. At the very least he should have washed her thighs. He hoped she would wash in the morning and wash away the evidence. If not and she went to the police he was ruined. Then he started to relax. She had hit on him all night. She had wanted it. She will wake up and remember it as consensual if she remembered it all. Sure she would wake up feeling used and maybe a bit disgusting, but that was all. He was certain he was in the clear.

In the morning she had woke to her blouse torn open and the residue on her thighs. The skirt was pulled up around her waist and underwear pushed aside. Right away she knew what had happened and she cried. She did not have a clear memory of what had happened, but to her it was clear.

For two hours she stood in the shower. She stood until the water became ice cold. She scrubbed at her thighs until they were raw. The constant stream of water continually washed away her tears. Eventually, she fell to her knees and cried into her hands. When she was finished she wrapped herself in blankets and cried on the bed. Several times she jumped up to vomit in the trash can in her bathroom.

For the rest of the day, she scoured her mind for any sort of clue. She could remember his face, but not his name. Refusing to accept defeat she went back to the bar she had been picked up at. After a few conversations, she finally got one of the bartenders to give her something useful. It turned out he had tried to hit on one of the bartenders the same night. He asked to buy her a drink. She denied him saying she was working and could not accept drinks on the job. She was unaware of how lucky she was.

With his name she had received from the bartender, she scoured the internet. A few minutes of online research brought her Greg's home address and his cell phone number. Several weeks went by before she decided something had to be done.

Many times she struggled with the thought of involving the police. Ultimately she decided she wanted to keep this a secret as much as this man probably did. If her mother ever learned of the incident she would have likely died of a heart attack. Not to mention the pain and embarrassment would all but destroy her life. She did not think she could handle it. It had to be kept a secret for her mother's health and her sanity.

At first, she decided she would just forget the whole ordeal. It no longer seemed worth it. There was no telling what would happen if she confronted him. Would he rape her again? Would he kill her? Would he beat her? Her imagination drew up wild conclusions and she was terrified.

The final straw came when she was late for her period. She took one test, then another, then another. They all came back the same. She was pregnant. A doctor's visit confirmed her fear. Then came another conflict. She wanted more than anything to kill the unborn child. She did not want the spawn of a disgusting rapist inside of her.

She had always been passionately against abortion yet the idea stuck in her mind like a tumor. She fought with herself several times. When she finally worked up the resolve to drive to the clinic she stopped half way there. It was then she knew she could not go through with it. On the way home, she cried until her head pounded. She was keeping the child, for better or for worse.

When courage finally hit her she decided something needed to be done. Several months had gone by and she was sure nothing could be done through the legal system. With no proof, it would be her word against his. In the end, she decided to take matters into her own hands. For nearly a week she dug up any information about him as she could. She even staked out his house for a few nights. When she was ready she followed him to work and stopped him just outside the front door.

At first, he did not recognize her and tried to brush passed, but she would not allow him to. "My name is Jessica, I'm the girl you raped months ago." The look of terror that broke over his face deeply satisfied her. He made a valiant effort to lure her away from the office building, but she refused to budge.

"I'm carrying your unborn child you disgusting excuse for a human being. You think you get to just fuck and forget? You'll rot in hell for what you did!"

Greg became frantic. With no other options, he begged her to lower her voice. She said she would and leave the police out of it under several conditions. Without question, he said he would agree to all of them. It would take a large sum of money to ensure she stayed quiet. Along with this, he would have to pay child support every month until he was eighteen. The moment the money stopped she would show up at his front door with a child that looked just like him. She would tell his wife everything. There would be a blood test and a trial and she would see to it he spent his life in prison for what he did.

Greg agreed without a second thought. He would be able to set money aside each week and transfer it to her without his wife knowing, as well as pay her off. But Jessica was not finished. She had one final demand she referred to as the deal breaker.

"You will go to the doctor this weekend and get snipped. I want you to be less of a man. I don't want you to rape another poor woman and force her to raise your bastard child!"

He had no choice but to agree. He would make up some lie to his wife to explain why he was doing it. In the end, it might destroy his marriage, but he might be safe from jail. After that day he never cheated on his wife again. He hardly even looked at another woman. When he had familiar urges he would just think of Jessica. It would scare him straight.

The man who called himself Greene had somehow learned all of this information and used it to blackmail him. At first, Greg thought it was the woman attempting to harm him further. He was going to refuse and tell her he had done enough for her. Eventually, he realized it could not possibly be her as it was all too elaborate. Why would she go through the trouble of it all? Perhaps it was someone working for her, but there was no way to prove it. In the end, he had no choice but to cave in.

Greene had compiled a list of items he needed to gather covertly. It had been made extremely clear he had to be quiet about it. With a look at the list and all the different items he needed he could not tell what they were for. Without question, he went about searching for all the right materials. Slowly he gathered them and stored them away in his shed.

Once everything was collected he was sent an anonymous email with explicit instructions how to assemble the pieces. When it was finished it was to be placed in a backpack and hidden until needed. About half way through the process Greg began to see what he was building. When it was finally finished he thought he knew exactly what it was. He assumed he had helped Greene build a bomb.

Chapter 16

Geoffrey Hunt sat at his kitchen table with a beer in his hand. Sleep had been brief the night before. Unable to sleep through the night he decided to stay up and drink. When he was ready to pass out he made it to the couch and collapsed.

In the morning he continued with the half empty and now warm beer on the table. Now with a fresh one in hand, he began to think of all he had done. He tried to lie to himself about everything. He tried hard to convince himself none of it bothered him, but he knew better.

He had killed Sandra Delano and Major McKinley in cold blood. Geoffrey tried to tell himself Greene had forced his hand and left him no choice, though he knew better. The choice to follow through had been his. The feeling of taking another life had left him feeling sick and miserable. At first, the adrenaline had led him to believe it was exhilarating. When it all wore off it left him feeling empty.

Before it all, he had been attracted to the idea. He thought there may have been a certain excitement to it. There was a certain attraction about being the one to blow out the flame of another human being. Now he no longer shared the feeling. Thinking back on it all almost forced him to vomit, but he kept his cool.

Greene had ordered him to kill Sandra and McKinley. It was only a matter of time before he was told to kill Ethan as well. He would regret the instruction, but he would do it all the same. Besides Ethan was different. Killing Ethan would be in his best interest. Ethan knew what he had done. He watched him gun down McKinley. Killing him would be a sort of self-defense. He wondered if he would acquire the taste for it after doing it enough. For now, the alcohol helped to calm his scattered mind.

Months ago he had received a cryptic text message from a man who called himself Greene. It said, there's blood on your hands Geoffrey. That night Geoffrey had cried himself to sleep. Like a child, he had curled into a ball and cried all night. He ignored the text for days. It only made it worse. The messages would pile up the longer he waited. He was haunted nearly every waking moment by his phone.

Finally, he shut off the phone and tossed it under his bed. It only gave him a day of silence. His E-mail inbox started to flood. When they started to show up on his work computer he knew he had no choice but to answer. Each message was exactly the same, which disturbed him further. They all read bloody hands.

Geoffrey had known the meaning of this message from the moment he had laid eyes on it. He had hoped no one would ever find out about it. Several years had gone by and he thought it had become a distant memory. To his horror, it had become a source of blackmail for someone else.

Years before Geoffrey had been investigating an armed robbery. A high-end home somewhere in the Venetian islands had been robbed. Thanks to a security camera installed in the home Geoffrey was able to obtain the man's identity. He confronted the man at his home slapping the handcuffs on his wrists. It was then he had been offered a deal he should have ignored.

The man had pleaded with him to not arrest him. He said he would be killed in jail. If he lived through his sentence he would be killed when he got out. The trust would be lost with the people he was associated with.

At first, Geoffrey acted disinterested, but then the numbers dropped. He could no longer remember the total amount, but it had been more than he made in a year. In fact, it was more than he made in a few.

Geoffrey caved and accepted the money. The temptation had been too great. He released the man and took the money. He was certain he would never get caught. The perpetrator was not going to run his mouth. He made sure not to spend any of the money right away. That was the best way to get caught. Instead, he stashed the money away in a safe at his home for a long time. Slowly he would start to spend the money only after he knew it was safe.

Days later the same man had committed another robbery. This time an officer had made it to the scene. The suspect was shot and killed, but only after he had fatally wounded the officer. Geoffrey was flung into the worst panic of his life. He knew he was to blame for the officer's death. Because of him, that man was still on the streets. He was directly responsible by not doing his sworn duty. There was no doubt the Miami Police Department would have seen it the same way.

An investigation was opened, but no one ever came for him. He was never even questioned. With relief, he felt as if he were off the hook. There had been nothing to tie him with the shooter. He thanked his lucky stars and moved on with his life.

From that day on he had been hiding from the truth. He wanted to keep his secret buried. He tried as hard as he could to forget about it. Alcohol was the only medicine. Some days were better than others. Eventually, he had all but forgotten. Then the message had come. It had dragged him back down into relentless turmoil.

Geoffrey had to obey his instructions or the whole department would learn his secret. Geoffrey knew he should have stood his ground and asked for proof, but he was too terrified. He did not want to push his luck. In the end, he thought it would not be worth the risk.

Ultimately he agreed to follow Greene's instructions. He was told to keep his phone on him at all times. When his first assignment was ready he would receive a text message with his instructions.

The first handful of tasks were easy. He was instructed to obtain weapons from evidence at the police department. From there he would distribute them as told. Local gangs, weapons dealers, and other shady characters. Geoffrey soon learned he was able to make quick cash by selling some of them for himself. Then later the police would arrest the men with the stolen weapons. The guns would go back into evidence and he would start the whole process over again. In the meantime, he made a nice profit. Greene did not seem to mind this. As long he did exactly as he was told there were no issues.

Then came the first large assignment. The text had been short, but eerily clear. Sandra Delano is in the way. It was obvious he meant for her to die. Geoffrey thought of every possibility. He despised the idea of taking her life. Once he even thought about rejecting the job and turning himself in. Then he realized what he had been up to lately. Now he had racked up his list of crimes and the punishment would be far worse. His only option was to play Greene's game. If Greene shared his information his life would be over. He would be put away forever. A cop in jail did not last long, even a dirty one.

Finally, he came to terms with it and tried to pump himself up for it. There was a certain adrenaline rush that came along with planning the death of another human being. It got his heart racing and his adrenaline pumping. He thought he enjoyed it. He forced himself to enjoy it.

When the moment came he hated it. He nearly vomited as he ran away. It was the worst feeling he had ever felt in his life. Before his hands had been indirectly covered with another man's blood. Now his hands were dripping with it.

As he threw back the last bit of beer he stood up. Before he could make it to the kitchen for another the cell phone on the table buzzed. For a moment he stood motionless. Then in a fit of rage, he threw the beer bottle at the wall screaming at the top of his lungs.

With his shoulders slouched and his head down he walked back to the phone. As before the message was short, but obvious. It's Ethan's turn. Find him. He was being told to end another life. This time it would be Ethan McCormick.

Ethan had seen him kill McKinley, which made this kill personal. He wanted Ethan dead. He promised himself after Ethan was gone he would find Greene. Greene would be his last. Then his problems would be over. Ethan was one of the last hurdles to finally cleansing himself.

Chapter 17

"I'm calling the police," the woman in the doorway sneered. Ethan stood mesmerized for a moment. As the door had swung open he had been unsure of what would happen. His worst fear had been the police. Instead in the threshold stood a beautiful woman with a can of mace firmly gripped in her hand. He knew he had to be careful.

With luck, it would be Caroline West, Pierce's cousin who owned the condo. Although he was not sure if it would truly be lucky, but anything was better than the police. If it was Caroline he wondered what would be best, truth or lie. The truth sounded incredible and, unfortunately for Ethan, unbelievable. To avoid her turning him over to the authorities he had to win her over. A lie would make that nearly impossible.

Ethan decided he had to take the chance with a lie. He could not risk everything trying to be honest. Everything would be over. Valerie and Pierce might be killed. He could not risk putting them in danger no matter the cost. He needed more time to figure out a plan.

"Please, wait, don't do that. Caroline right?"

The woman froze and pulled the mace closer. The stranger in her living room knew who she was and it caused her to panic.

"I'm sorry for being here. I'm a friend of Pierce, your cousin right?"

"Yeah, Pierce is my cousin. What the hell are you doing in my condo?"

Ethan thought one last time about the truth. Again he decided it was not the best course of action, not yet at least. Perhaps if he gained her trust he could coax her to call Pierce herself and he could explain everything to her.

"I am so sorry, Pierce said you probably wouldn't be here. Still, I thought he would have given you a heads up. My name's Ethan. I'm having some, uh, family troubles. Pierce said I could stay here for a few days while things sort out."

It was not a total lie, but nor was it the truth. Ethan could live with it. But the question was would she buy it.

Caroline loosened the grip on the mace, but only slightly. She slipped her cell phone back in her pocket. Ethan assumed it was a good sign. Now he just needed to make her trust him completely.

"I can leave right away if you would like. I really don't want to impose. I didn't think you'd be coming here so soon."

"No, it's all right. You can stay for a couple days. If you're a friend of Pierce's you must be all right." She still did not put the can down. Slowly he was gaining her trust. It was all he could hope for.

"I'm actually a police officer back in Miami."

He hoped it would put her mind at ease. It seemed to have some effect, but not much. She glanced over at the television. The news station still had not mentioned his name. He was grateful for his luck. Eventually, the major networks would catch wind of it. He knew he needed to change the channel and fast.

"What brings you down here so early?" He asked as he searched for the remote.

Caroline sighed as she placed the can of mace back in her purse. It now sat on a table next to the door. Ethan's muscles relaxed as she stepped away from it. It would not be long before she started to relax too.

"Just taking a little break from work. It gets busy there. Sometimes I like to just take a break and come down here. It helps clear the mind. I think it might be the sea breeze."

They both shared an uncomfortable laugh. After there was a strong silence Ethan was desperate to break. Anxiously he scanned the room for the remote while trying to not seem nervous. He saw it sitting on the kitchen counter next to the sink. Now he remembered leaving it there while he had made breakfast.

"Here, let me change it to something a bit more uplifting." He said as he picked up the remote. She sat down on the couch and told him not to bother.

"Leave it on, I need to catch up with current events. Been too busy lately to take notice."

She sat back and put her feet up on the coffee table. Ethan started to sweat now. He dreaded the breaking news scroll to pop up on the television. Once that happened it was all over. The trust between them would be broken. She would call the police and he would fail. He needed to convince her to call Pierce before that happened. If he was too pushy she would become suspicious, but he had to act fast.

"Maybe you should call Pierce and let him know you're here. He might want to apologize for not warning you I'd be here."

"That's fine. Like I said if you're his friend you must be alright. Pierce has always had a talent for judging people's character. Besides you seem a nice enough guy."

"Yeah, that's true about Pierce. He did marry my sister."

She spun around on the couch and looked at him.

"Wait, you're Valerie's brother?"

"That's me," he said plastering a large smile on his face.

"Oh my God, he talks about her all the time. Well, at least when we do talk she's all he talks about."

"That's very sweet of him."

"Yes, he is. Always has been since we were kids."

"How long has it been since you talked with him?"

"It's been a while, almost a year maybe."

"You should probably catch up with him then."

"You seem a bit anxious for me to call him."

"I was just saying-"

A large red banner scrolled across the television screen followed by a loud chime. Ethan's blood ran cold when he read the words Breaking News. He said a silent prayer it was not about him. There was no doubt, though, that his luck had finally run out.

"Breaking news, the Miami Police Department has issued a warrant for the arrest of an officer wanted for the murder of two fellow officers. The names of the victims have not been released yet as they are still part of the investigation. The suspect is Ethan McCormick who worked as an officer in the homicide division-"

The remainder of the bulletin was drowned out by Caroline. She leaped off of the couch and ran towards her purse. Ethan yelled out for her to wait, but she did not listen. She ignored her purse and did not go for the mace. Caroline pulled open a drawer and removed a small revolver. Ethan nearly toppled to the floor when she pointed it at him.

He tried to plead for her to listen, but she told him to shut his mouth. With a mixed look of fear and anger in her eyes, she snatched her cell phone from her pocket and looked down at the screen. There was no time left. If she dialed those three numbers his life and his sister's was over.

Without thinking, he dropped to his knees and put his hands in the air. Unexpectedly a tear rolled down his cheek.

"Please don't call the police. I can explain everything. No, call Pierce he can explain it."

"I don't care what you have to say."

"You have to trust me, please."

"You murdered two cops!"

"I did not do what they say."

"I don't care."

She was about to dial when Ethan tried one last time.

"If you call the police you will have to shoot me. I can't live to watch them kill Valerie and Pierce."

Caroline paused and looked at him questioningly. There was a look of intrigue and distrust in her eyes. Ethan could not blame her. If he were in her situation he would not have trusted the person on the floor.

"I won't shoot you unless you make me."

"If you dial that number I will make you. I will be killed if I'm caught, but not before they make me watch my sister die."

"You're lying!"

"Call Pierce, he will tell you the truth. Please, just call him. If talking to him doesn't satisfy you then call the police. I won't try to stop you then."

Ethan could almost see the wheels turning in her mind. Everything was happening so quickly. She knew the right move was to call the police. For some reason, she was compelled to trust this man cowering on her condominium floor. Maybe he was just a good actor. She considered his proposal to call Pierce. He seemed very confident he would vouch for him. Finally, she decided it was worth a try.

"All right, I'll call Pierce. If you move even an inch I will shoot you. If I don't believe your story after talking to him I will call the police."

"Thank you."

He watched as she pressed her fingers against the touch screen display. It had been more than three numbers. He let out a sigh of relief. The few seconds it took for Pierce to answer had been the longest of his life. He knew everything was riding on this call. If he did not answer she might just call the police and let them sort everything out.

Finally, he heard Piece's voice from across the room, although it was faint. His mind was racing faster than he ever thought possible. Caroline's voice became nothing but a faint echo in his head. The floor seemed to spin around him and he felt nauseous.

Pierce had to vouch for him, he knew he would. If he did not convince his cousin everything would be over. Valerie would die, Pierce would die, Ethan would die, and Sandra's killer would be free. There was no chance Ethan would allow it to happen.

As her voice echoed in the distance Ethan began to plan. He could not allow himself to fail. An anger he had not felt before began to boil inside. He could feel it deep in his gut. If Caroline hung up the phone and still did not believe him he would have no choice. Ethan knew he would have to keep her from calling the police at all costs. This woman would not bring harm to those he loved. The only people left in his life worth saving. He would defend them to the death. He began to wonder if he could kill her to protect them. Would he go that far? Could he go that far? He considered the thought. He began to believe there were no other options.

Caroline slammed her phone down on the table and lowered the gun. Ethan was snapped out of his trance and the anger seemed to subside. She looked down at him with tears in her eyes. He knew instantly she believed him.

"I'm so sorry for everything Ethan."

"You believed him then?"

"Pierce wouldn't lie to me, not about this."

"I appreciate that, really I do."

"Don't get too comfortable yet, I'm not. I still don't know you. I'm still keeping my eye on you."

"That's understandable."

Ethan picked himself off the floor and nodded at her. She returned the gesture, but still gripped the handgun tightly. He knew eventually he would earn her full trust. He rubbed his temples as he sat down on the couch. His head was hurting, but he felt better.

"So, what is your plan now? Are you just laying low until this all blows over or what?"

Ethan thought about it for a moment. He really had no clue what he should do next. He needed to figure out why he had been set up and who was behind Sandra's death. If Derrick White was involved he needed to know why. Then there was Greene. He needed his identity. None of that would happen while he was hiding. What he really needed was a way to get back to Miami. It would be the only way to investigate everything.

Going home would be impossible and he knew it. If he went back he would be putting Valerie and Pierce in mortal danger. The only way to get back home was to learn who Greene was and isolate Geoffrey Hunt. He was stuck in a loop. There was no way back home and no way to clear his name without going home. Then an idea struck him.

"Do you think you could do something for me?"

"I hardly know you and still not one hundred percent on the whole trust issue and you want a favor?"

"It's a small one, I promise nothing major."

"Maybe."

"I need you to get me one of those pay as you go phones. Can you do that?"

"I guess that would be fine. Why, though?"

"I need to communicate with Pierce, but it can't be traceable back to me."

"All right, I will go to the store today and get you one. I need to stock this place with a little food anyway."

"Thank you, Caroline. That will be a huge help."

"I'm taking the gun with me, though."

He did not tell her that he would have preferred she left it. He understood why she wanted it with her. Ethan admired her intelligence. It was something he would have done had he been in her shoes. Although he really wished he had a firearm. There was no telling if Geoffrey would catch up to him and try to take him out.

The thought had been on his mind since his drive from Miami. Whoever was behind all of this was not going to let him live. If he lived to make it to a trial there would be an opportunity to bring others down with him. An investigation into the deaths of Sandra Delano and Major McKinley would be reopened. It was something they clearly did not want. Eventually, Geoffrey would come for him, he was sure of it.

"No problem, Caroline."

Without responding, she slipped the gun into her purse and headed out the door. He let out a sigh of relief and collapsed sideways on the couch. Minutes later he was fast asleep. It was still mid-morning, but the stress had taken its toll.

Chapter 18

Together Valerie and Pierce watched the morning news. They huddled closely on the couch. Derrick White stood tall at a podium covered in microphones. By this time all the major news networks had showed up. The Miami Police department had advised they would issue a statement about the officers' deaths as well as Ethan McCormick.

"The death of this excellent officer is a great tragedy to the police force and to the city of Miami. His killer will be brought to justice."

Derrick cleared his throat.

"Fellow officer Ethan McCormick was the last known person to see Major McKinley alive. This does make him one of the suspects in his death. We are doing everything in our power to locate McCormick. However, his disappearance does not prove his involvement in the death of Major McKinley. We are currently running this as a missing person's case. Right now we are trying to locate McCormick for his own safety. Once he has been located we can allow the justice system to do what it does best. No one should be treated as guilty until it has been proven so in a court of law.

We will be asking several police departments around the state to help in our search for Ethan McCormick. If you see this man please report it to the police right away. I will not be taking any questions, thank you."

As Derrick walked away from the podium a murmur erupted from the reporters. They tried to ask questions regardless of what he said. They began to quiet down as he walked back inside the doors of the police station.

The camera feed cut back to the anchors in the studio. Both had stern looks on their faces. "Well, you heard it here everybody. The search for alleged killer Ethan McCormick is still underway. He has been labeled one of the prime suspects in the death of fellow Major Doug McKinley. Scary isn't it Deborah?"

Before his co-anchor could answer Pierce muted the television. Valerie sat next to him with tears in her eyes. At first, she did not speak or even move. She just stared straight ahead as if in a trance. Pierce decided not to interrupt her. He would let her take a moment to soak it all in. What she was going through now he could not even imagine. Instead, he wrapped his arms around her and held her tight.

Minutes later she broke out of her trance and looked over at him. She looked more miserable than she had ever looked in her life. The image nearly broke his heart. Valerie threw her arms around him and cried on his chest. As she did he stroked her hair gently. There was nothing he could say at the moment to make her feel better, so he stayed silent.

Eventually, she began to calm down. With her head still buried in his chest, she said only one word, "Why?"

"Why what Sweetheart?"

She pulled away from him and wiped the remaining tears away. Now she looked him straight in the eye and no longer looked sad. Instead, she looked angrier than he had ever seen her before.

"Why would they still say that?"

"Who?"

"The news! They are still labeling him as the prime suspect. The whole press conference was called to tell everyone not to jump to conclusions. Why would they still do it? That isn't fair!"

"They're afraid, Valerie. When people get scared they will point the finger at anything to make themselves feel better. That's all it is. Eventually, this will all blow over and everything will be back to normal. We know he isn't guilty and any jury will see that too."

"I'm not worried about him being found guilty or not. I'm worried some overzealous cop or idiot with a gun might shoot him. They've made him out to be a cop killer. Do you think if he's found by someone out there they are going to believe he's innocent?"

"They might."

"But they might not. All it takes is for the wrong person to find him and it's all over. I don't want to see that happen."

"Honey, I will do everything in my power to help your brother where I can."

"How? What can you do?"

"I don't know, but when I figure that out I will be damn sure I do my best."

Valerie stood up and walked to the kitchen. After she poured herself a glass of water she sat down at the kitchen table. All she could think about was her brother. Her worst fear was getting the news he had been shot and killed while "on the run." Just the thought was enough to drive her crazy.

He was the only family she really had left, except for Pierce. She could not stand to lose him. When she and Pierce started having kids she wanted them to know their uncle. He would be great with them and she knew he would always be there for all of them.

She gulped down the water and placed the glass in the sink. With a throbbing head, she made her way back into the living room and lay on the couch with her head in Pierce's lap. Neither of them spoke. Valerie shut her eyes as Pierce began to rub her head softly. She fought the urge to cry again. Her eyes could not handle any more tears. They were already raw and puffy. Instead, she turned over on her side and tried to sleep. Pierce continued to stroke her head as she drifted off.

Pierce sat in complete silence stroking a hand through Valerie's hair. The television still flashed on the opposite side of the room. The remote control sat on the coffee table just out of his reach. He no longer wanted to watch the news. With Valerie asleep in his lap, he decided to deal with it.

He sat and watched the news flash back and forth about Ethan McCormick and the Miami Police Department. It looked as if they were showing the press conference on a loop. They would cut to a group of people sitting around a table discussing the events. Eventually, his eyes grew heavy and he placed his head back against the couch. With a soft sigh, he began to drift off to sleep.

When the sound of glass shattering woke Pierce from his nap he was up on his feet in seconds. Valerie barely had time to sit up before he had turned around and told her to stay quiet. He waited for a moment before he heard the soft crunch of a shoe on broken glass. Someone was in the house.

"Valerie, get upstairs and call the police." He barked at her, but it was too late. A man rushed around the corner with a pistol in hand. It was pointed directly at the two of them with the hammer secured back. The intruder wore a black ski mask over his face and a brown leather jacket. Pierce thought he would sweat to death in the summer heat.

Pierce's eyes shifted to the stairs wishing he could get to his safe and grab his gun. Now he was defenseless in his own home. The fact that Valerie was in danger was worse. There was nothing he could do, they were trapped.

"Get down on your knees, both of you." The stranger ordered. Quickly they both did as they were told. The man began to approach and stuck the firearm in their faces trying to intimidate them. Valerie looked scared but held her gaze forward. She was not giving the man the satisfaction of tormenting her. Pierce found a whole new admiration for her.

"Just take whatever you want and leave. No one has to get hurt."

The invader let out a chuckle that made him sound psychotic. He looked Pierce in the eye and delivered a firm fist to his stomach. As Pierce doubled over in pain Valerie screamed out. She looked up at the man now standing over Pierce with his gun in front of him.

"What the hell do you want you bastard?"

The man crouched down and put a firm knee on the back of Pierce's neck holding him down. He waved the gun wildly in her face, but she did not flinch. Her heart was beating so fast she thought it might tear clean out of her chest. A cold sweat had broken out over her body, but still, she remained as calm as she could.

"Where is Ethan?" He grumbled. "If you tell me where he is no one has to die." He pulled his knee off of Pierce and pulled him to his feet. Pierce panted as the gun was shoved in his face. Valerie screamed that they did not know where Ethan was. Pierce knew she was actually telling the truth. She did not know where he was. Right now he was very thankful for being so careful.

The man hit Pierce in the face with the pistol and rammed it under his chin. He glared into his eyes as he yelled, "One more chance. Where is Ethan?" Again Valerie begged him to believe her, but he ignored her. Instead, he kept his eyes focused on Pierce. He stared directly into his eyes as if he could read the truth in them. It seemed as if the man knew Pierce had the answer. Pierce made a silent vow that he would let this man shoot him before he gave up Ethan.

To Pierce's horror, the intruder decided to change his interrogation tactic. He pushed Pierce aside and snatched up Valerie by the hair. She screamed as she was pulled to her feet. He jammed the gun into the side of her neck as she tried to pull away. Tears welled up in Pierce's eyes as he begged him to let her go. He may have been willing to give up his life, but he could not let anything happen to Valerie. He could not live with himself and knew Ethan would never forgive him.

A shot rang up and Pierce recoiled in horror. Instinctively his hands covered his ears as they rang. The man had fired a shot into the kitchen. Something in the distance shattered. With his eyes still focused on Pierce he placed the barrel against her temple.

"That was a warning shot. Next one goes in her skull."

"Let her go, please."

"Tell me where Ethan is or I will make sure the last thing you ever see is your wife's brains scattered over your dining room floor. Do not test me!"

He finally broke down and nearly dropped to his knees. He had to give up Ethan's location. There was no way out of it. There was no option, but to keep her safe. Somehow he would have to reach out to Ethan and warn him someone was coming to kill him.

"I will tell you where he is if you let her go."

"After you tell me we have a deal."

"How do I know that you won't kill us after I tell you?"

"Well, I could kill her now and force the information out of you if you'd like?"

"Fine, Ethan is on the other coast."

"More specific jackass," he said as he pushed the gun harder into her neck.

"All right! He's in Indian Rocks Beach staying in a condo. I can give you the exact address just leave her alone!"

"See, now was that so hard?"

Pierce cursed the man under his breath. He knew he had to do something. He could not let him leave and go after Ethan. Once the man stepped away from Valerie he would take him down. He could not risk making his move until after she was out of harm's way.

"Write down his address on a piece of paper and slip it in my jacket pocket."

Pierce did exactly as he was told. Before he pulled away from Valerie he checked the note to make sure it was an address. He looked satisfied and stuffed it back in. With the gun still pressed to Valerie's neck, he began to back up slowly. As he did he kept his eyes on Pierce.

"Since I can't trust that the address is correct I am going to have to take her with me."

"You son of-"

"Shut your mouth or I'll shoot her now. If the address is good I will bring her back to you. If not she dies."

The man paused for a moment waiting to see if Pierce would change the address. When he made no move he nodded. "I suppose you didn't lie then. Either way, I need insurance. She comes with me."

Now Valerie began to protest, but it was useless. She was still being dragged towards the back of the house. When Pierce tried to advance towards him the man jammed the gun harder in her neck causing her to cry out. He was forced to stand by and watch as his wife was dragged down the hallway.

Without warning, the man's foot slid out from under him abruptly. The empty shell from the round he had fired into the kitchen shot out across the floor and his foot slipped backward. It had not been enough to make him fall, but Valerie was quick to react.

She rammed her elbow into the man's face. The momentum sent him tumbling backward. Without hesitation, Pierce charged at full speed. Before he could regain his balance and aim his gun Pierce had tackled him to the floor.

They wrestled over the gun in the narrow hallway. Both were rammed against the wall several times. Valerie wasted no time running into the kitchen to find a weapon. As she did the gun flew out of his hands and further down the hallway. Pierce was able to drag the man to his feet. With all of his strength, he pushed the man towards the living room.

Now he was between him and the gun. The man closed the gap between them quickly and threw his fist at Pierce. He ducked just missing a hard hit to the jaw. He quickly rammed his fist into the man's side and he stumbled sideways.

They exchanged punches in the living room until the intruder gained the upper hand. He placed Pierce in a firm headlock and began to squeeze. Pierce gasped for air and began to choke. Valerie darted around the corner with a butcher knife in her hand. She slashed wildly at the man opening a large gash in his arm. He dropped Pierce and stumbled backward clutching his wounded arm.

Before Pierce or Valerie could follow him he bolted down the hallway. There was just enough time for him to snatch his gun and escape. Pierce was still on the floor choking for air. Valerie dropped the knife and wrapped her arms around him. Finally, he caught his breath and hugged her back. He managed to whisper thank you as he pulled himself to his feet.

Though many parts of his body ached from being punched he knew he would be fine. He ran to the back of the house. There he saw the broken glass strewn about the floor. He had broken a window to enter and now the back door was wide open. Glancing outside he saw a short trail of footprints leading away from the house.

Satisfied the man had actually left he made his way back to Valerie. He tried his best to calm her down, but now she was shaking. Shock had finally set in. He grabbed the phone and started to dial the police when Valerie stopped him. "What are you doing?" She snapped.

"I'm calling the police. Someone just tried to kill us."

"But they'll want to know what he was after."

"I would assume so, yes."

"If you tell them he wanted to know where Ethan is what would you tell them?"

Pierce had not thought this far ahead. He knew he could not tell them Ethan's location. If he did not tell the police then Ethan's life would be in danger. Somehow he had to contact Ethan and warn him. He decided he would have to lie to the police and figure out how to help Ethan before it was too late. There were still a few hours before the intruder made it to the other coast. It would give him plenty of time.

Pierce told her what he planned to do before he called the police. A unit was dispatched to their home immediately. Pierce decided to ask for Brad Forrester personally. He seemed like a very trustworthy man and would feel better about receiving his help.

He hung up with the police and instructed Valerie not to touch anything. There was a small puddle of blood on the floor from where the knife had struck the assailant. Forensics would be able to test the blood and determine the man's identity. The empty shell on the floor would most likely have a fingerprint. Either way, they would learn his identity.

Letting out a sigh he collapsed on the couch. Finally, his heartbeat was returning to normal. The adrenaline which had been coursing through his veins finally subsided. He started to relax when his cell phone interrupted the silence. Confusion swept over him when he saw it was his cousin. What could her reason for calling be? They had never been the type to just call each other out of the blue. Then it hit him. She must have come down to her condo. If it was the case it meant she found Ethan. He hoped to God everything had gone all right. He slid his finger across the screen to answer the phone. As he did so he pulled the phone to his ear and prayed everything was fine.

Chapter 19

In one phone call, all his prayers had been answered. His cousin had called to explain she came down to her condo and found a man there. He said his name was Ethan McCormick and had told her he was a friend of Pierce Masons'. Caroline wanted to verify if he actually knew this man. With a mixture of emotions running through his body, he explained that he did.

She began to explain the wild story that Ethan had described to her. Hearing it from someone else he understood how unbelievable it sounded. Regardless he explained to Caroline that everything he had told her was the truth. Pierce explained how much trouble Ethan was in as well as Valerie. He knew it would be a lot to ask her, but he needed her trust. He also needed her cooperation.

Pierce explained as best he could while leaving out some details, what Ethan had been caught up in. When he was finished he knew Caroline believed him, though she still seemed skeptical. That he could understand. She did come home to a strange man wanted by the police in her condo. He would have surely reacted the same way, if not worse.

He avoided telling her about the man who had just attempted to kill them. There was no reason to tell her. It was something he would mention to Ethan when he talked to him but now was not the time. Now that he knew Caroline was there with him it would be easier to contact Ethan.

After he hung up with Caroline he thought for a moment. It was probably not a good idea to be making many phone calls to her. If the police received a warrant to search their phone records they would be led right to him. If he was going to stay in contact with Ethan it would have to be untraceable.

He decided he would deal with it later. Right now he needed to focus on comforting his wife. She was still very shaken up from their ordeal. He turned around and saw her collapsed on the couch still shaking. Her hands were upon her head caressing her temples.

Not knowing where to start he walked over and threw his arms around her. There was nothing he could say in this moment that would make her feel better. He could tell her it was all right. He could say that everything would be okay, but he barely believed it himself. As he held her he realized that he was terrified. Everything was out of his control. From where he was he could not help Ethan as much as he would have liked. He had barely been able to protect his home and his wife. Nothing seemed all right and nothing seemed as if it would be fine.

He gripped Valerie tighter to hide a tear from her. It was not something he wanted her to see. Right now she needed someone to be strong. Her brother was out there in trouble. Now it had only become worse. Whoever had broken into their home and threatened them was on his way to find her brother. Understandably she was an emotional wreck. There was nothing to do now but keep her calm.

For the next twenty minutes, they sat huddled on the couch together not saying at word. Valerie buried her face into his neck but did not cry. Pierce sat with his arms around her. Neither of them moved, neither of them cried, and neither of them spoke.

A police cruiser pulled into the driveway followed by an unmarked car. Moments later the crime scene investigators showed up. Pierce let go of Valerie and ushered the detectives inside. He spent several moments speaking to a man in a brown suit explaining the ordeal many times.

Cameras flashed all over the house and several items were bagged as evidence. Their home bustled with the noise of everyone talking in unison. It was overwhelming, but Pierce did his best to keep calm. The whole time he was worried for Valerie. She still sat motionless on the couch hardly speaking a word. When an officer did ask her to make a statement she simply declined.

As the bullet casing was collected and a sample of the blood had been scooped up Brad Forrester walked through the door. He surveyed the scene for a moment and pulled Pierce aside. With a hand on his shoulder, he said, "I'm sorry this has happened. Tell me everything?"

Once again Pierce went over the details. He made sure to once again omit the part about Ethan. Brad might have been looking out for Ethan's best interest, but he still could not trust him. Ethan told him some of the officers may have been corrupt. Brad may have been one of them, although Pierce's gut told him that was wrong. He decided to play it safe.

"We will find the person who did this. They left us a shoe print in the dirt, possibly a fingerprint on the empty shell, and thanks to your fast acting wife, their DNA. They won't get far, I promise."

"Thank you, Brad."

"Don't mention it, Pierce. Just doing my job. I'm very sorry this has all happened like this. First Ethan now this. Would you like me to have a guard stationed outside your house for the next few days?"

"That's not necessary. I'd be willing to bet it was merely an isolated incident. Probably someone thinking they could take advantage of us."

"Yeah, that could be it." There seemed a strange change in his tone as if he knew more than he let on. Pierce tried to ignore, but the suspicion nagged at him. He did his best to shake off the feeling and shook Brad's hand.

"Thanks again for everything. Please let me know if you find anything."

"Of course."

With that, Brad left. Less than an hour later the crime scene had been cleaned up and all the officers dispersed. A thick piece of plywood had been drilled over the broken window courtesy of the police department. The kitchen knife had been taken as evidence and the blood no longer pooled on the floor. The detective had told him it could take up to a week to get a match from the blood sample. They would do their best to get the results faster, but could not promise anything. If there was a finger print on the shell they could have the identity within eight hours.

Pierce knew he needed the identity of the man to properly warn Ethan. He could call and tell him someone was coming after him, but without the identity, that person could be anyone. The tip would not be much help. Ethan would not know who to look out for. The best option would be for him to leave the condominium. He had no choice but to find somewhere else to stay. Caroline would have to go with him. If she stayed behind it would only make her a target. Pierce had no clue where they could go. With his face plastered all over television, Ethan would be left with very few options. Someone would recognize him for sure.

With a sigh, Pierce collapsed on the couch next to Valerie. She still sat in silence. Pierce thought about holding her again but figured it would not help. Now was the time to talk to her. He turned towards her and looked straight into her eyes. She continued to stare off at the wall. Her eyes seemed glazed over as if she had shut down completely. Pierce had never witnessed his wife act that way before. The stress was clearly becoming too much for her to bear.

"Valerie, sweetheart, would you like to talk?"

She shook her head slowly. It was not much, but it was movement.

"I know I can't sit here and tell you that everything is going to be okay. I wish I could. I do know one thing for sure. Your brother is tough. He can handle himself. He will get through this no matter what." Now Valerie nodded her head slowly. "I am going to do whatever I can to help him. I will call Caroline back and warn Ethan that someone is coming for him. That will give them plenty of time to get out and find a new place to hide. We can figure out the rest after that."

"You knew where he was the whole time?"

"I did sweetheart, I'm sorry. He wanted you to be able to truthfully say you did not know where he was. It was smart to think ahead like that."

"You shouldn't have told him anything."

"Valerie, he was going to kill you."

"Better me than Ethan!"

"No, that's not true. There's time to warn him. There wasn't time for you. If something happened to you your brother would be devastated, I would be devastated. I had no choice."

Valerie sat quietly for a whole minute before she spoke again, "I know, I'm sorry. I'm scared Pierce. I don't know what to do. I want him to be safe, but there's nothing I can do. I keep expecting this to all be a terrible nightmare. That I will wake up in my bed and none of it will have happened."

Pierce did not say anything. Instead, he pulled his wife close to him and wrapped his arms around her. He stared deep into her eyes before giving her a passion filled kiss. They both held on to each other for a moment before pushing back. Neither spoke a word. Instead, they relaxed and found comfort in each other.

Chapter 20

When Caroline returned from the store Ethan was relieved. There was still a part of him that thought she would turn him in. He was thankful when she handed him the pay by the minute phone. He ripped open the packaging and activated the minutes. A few moments later he was dialing Pierce's number. It rang for what seemed an eternity. He began to worry Pierce would never answer.

"Hello," the familiar voice on the other end said. Except it did not sound like Pierce's normal perky voice. He sounded miserable and solemn. Ethan was instantly worried. All of his worst fears came flooding into his mind at once.

"Pierce, what's going on?" He asked and was answered with a large sigh. He braced himself for the bad news he knew was coming.

"Ethan, Valerie and I are both fine, but something happened not too long ago. A man broke into our home with a gun. He threatened both of us."

"Jesus!"

"We're all right, though, I promise. I need to tell you something, Ethan."

"Yeah?"

"Whoever it was that attacked us was looking for you."

"Did you tell him where I was?"

"I had no choice. He stuck a gun in Valerie's face. There was nothing I could do." Ethan could tell he was holding back tears.

"It's all right, Pierce. I don't blame you for that. As long as you two are all right. I can find a new place to lay low. Do you know who it was?"

"No clue. The police were here a while ago. We have a sample of his blood so they should be able to do a DNA test. Hopefully, they will know soon."

"All right, this is what I want you to do…"

Ethan explained he wanted him and Valerie to head to his house once they hung up. The detectives more than likely cleaned the place out, but Sandra was smart. If she had anything worth hiding she would have hid it well. It was possible she had stashed something where they would never have found it. She would have known all their protocols and every place they would have checked. Ethan told him to look for anything she may have kept notes on, a flash drive, an external, or even a notebook.

He also informed Pierce about his new phone. He told him to call that number directly. It would help them communicate without bringing attention to his location. "Once we hang up I will try and find a new location to stay. I don't know where I will go yet, but I will figure it out. Tell Valerie that I'm all right and let her know I'm thinking of her." Pierce said he would and they hung up.

With a sigh, Ethan slipped the phone into his pocket. It was then he realized Caroline was staring at him from the other side of the room. Her eyes had gone wide. At first, he was confused and nervous. Then he realized she must have heard the conversation. He could only guess her thoughts were on her own safety, which he understood.

"Something wrong?" He asked her knowing the answer. For a moment she stood motionless. Finally, she seemed to work up the courage to speak.

"Did Pierce say that someone's coming for you?"

"Yes, he did."

"What does that mean?"

"I don't know. Someone broke into their home and threatened them. I can only assume it's no one we want to meet."

"So what do we do?"

It was then he realized wherever he went she would have to follow. If she stayed behind she would only be hurt by the unknown assailant. She would be an easy target with potential information about him. He could not leave her in harm's way. Too many people had been hurt on his account. There was no other option. Caroline had to tag along.

"Do you have any friends nearby that you can stay with?"

"I don't, not around here."

"Then we have to get a hotel."

She looked at him as if he had suggested they sleep together. "Separate rooms," she said as she glared down at him. Ethan shook his head and rubbed his temples.

"The room would have to be in your name. I can't use my card or the card I got from Pierce. If you rent two rooms it would look suspicious."

"Fine, one room, but it will be two queens."

"Caroline," he said as he stood up and looked her in the eyes. "I'm really sorry you got roped up in this. It would be in your best interest to head back home until all of this blows over. You've helped me out more than you know with the phone. I can't ask any more of you. I need to do this alone."

For a moment Caroline was quiet. It seemed as if she would walk out the door at any second. If she did Ethan would not have stopped her nor blamed her. It was not fair she had been caught up in everything because he was hiding out in her condo. The less people involved the better. He could never live with himself if someone else got hurt because of him.

"I'm staying," she said finally. "Like I said, Pierce vouched for you. He must have a good reason. I wouldn't feel right just abandoning you like that. Plus you said you can't rent a hotel without me. If I left I would be putting you in danger. I can't let that happen."

"Thank you, Caroline, I mean that sincerely."

She smiled but did not respond. Quickly Ethan instructed her to pack some clothes and whatever essential items she would need. As she did he took a step back out onto the balcony and took in a deep breath. The sea salt in the air was thick but comforting. It reminded him of home. Again he watched the people on the beach as they swam, walked, and played. He envied them. As they went about their daily lives he was being hunted like an animal.

Once Caroline was packed they left the condo and headed downstairs. Although it was only a short walk to the car Ethan was still nervous to show his face in public. When they were safely inside her vehicle he would feel a lot safer. Though he knew they were not out of harm's way yet.

***

As Caroline and Ethan left the condo Piece and Valerie packed into her car. Pierce found himself missing his Jeep. He hoped Ethan had stashed it somewhere safe. When everything was over he wanted to be able to get it back. He immediately felt ashamed for the thought and swept it from his mind. He still missed his Jeep as he climbed into the passenger seat of Valerie's Chrysler Sebring Cabrio. It was lower to the ground than he was used to. His Jeep Grand Cherokee towered over her small car. He did not truly hate her car. They had some great times in it, especially when no one was around.

Pierce smiled and quickly wiped it from his face. He knew it was not the time to be fooling around. Ethan needed his help and he refused to let him down.

While they drove they hardly spoke to each other. Both were too worried to talk. Valerie was worried about her brother finding a place to stay and the same thought was on Pierce's mind. He wanted desperately to call Ethan to ask if he had left yet. The uncertainty was driving him crazy.

When they reached Sandra and Ethan's home they did not find it a warm and inviting place as it used to be. Now it seemed dismal and sad. A grayish hue seemed to hang over the entire building as if the property itself had been robbed of its glow. The windows which had once radiated with light were now engulfed by darkness. Pierce and Valerie were unsure if it truly looked miserable or if their own feelings had left an impression upon it. Regardless they headed for the front door.

Valerie retrieved her copy of the house key from her purse. Ethan had once given it to her so she could bring in the mail while he was on vacation. Afterward, he had never asked for it back. He told her she was welcome anytime. With a heavy heart, she opened the door. The afternoon sun cascaded through the windows illuminating the house. Pierce switched the light on anyway. Everything was eerily still and quiet throughout the house. The memories they had both shared here flooded their minds as they walked. All the game nights, dinner parties and barbecues they had attended sprang up in the forefront of their thoughts. It felt as if those times were lost forever. With Sandra gone they knew it would never be like it was. It was a depressing feeling.

Pierce decided they needed to move quickly and instructed Valerie to start searching. They needed to find anything Sandra may have used to hide information. As Ethan had said it might have been a notebook, a flash drive, or an external hard drive. Pierce thought an SD card could be another option. He realized they could be looking for anything. Their chances were very slim.

As Valerie searched the living room Pierce took the bedroom. The mattress no longer rested on the bed frame. Instead, it was up on its side leaning against the wall. It almost looked as if someone had ransacked the room. Pierce figured the police had torn the place apart looking for evidence. He hoped they were not wasting their time and the police had everything of value.

He started with the closet. He pulled the shoes out one at a time checking inside each pair as he did. When he was finished sorting through Sandra's shoes he went through Ethan's. He did not think he would find anything, but he had to start somewhere.

When the shoes were free from the closet and strewn about the room he crawled inside to check every corner. There was nothing on the floor and there were no hollow spots in the wall. He stood up and started going through the shelves just above the hanging clothes. As he sorted through the boxes he found one with items he wished he had not seen. Other than Sandra's intimate belongings he found nothing. He placed everything back in the closet and turned around and got a good look at the room.

There were the obvious places such as the nightstand and jewelry box. He was almost certain there would be nothing in either of them, but he needed to check either way. As he thought they were empty of anything valuable. A few batteries and a television remote were all he found. It was the same with the dresser drawers. As he brushed Sandra's underwear aside to check the drawer he got an eerie feeling as if she was there watching him. It was uncomfortable and he finished rummaging through the drawer as fast as he could.

Pierce was certain he would find nothing in their bedroom. Whatever he was searching for may have been under the mattress. If so it had been found and they were wasting their time. He refused to believe that was true. Sandra was smarter than that. If she had something to hide it would have been hidden better. There was no chance she would have left something important in such an obvious location.

While Pierce searched the rest of the bedroom Valerie perused over the living room. She checked under every couch cushion and inside every drawer. There was nothing under the couches and nothing inside the entertainment center. She even checked each lamp thoroughly making sure nothing was taped under the lampshades. Everything came up clean. If there was something there for them to find Sandra had hidden it well.

Pierce continued his search in the second room at the back of the house. It had been turned into an office space rather than a bedroom. A large oak desk sat under the window against the far wall. Opposite this wall stood a tall, cherry finished bookshelf crammed full of books. He figured it was a good place to start.

He removed a few books on each shelf and stuck his arm behind the others. There was nothing behind them. He decided he had not been completely thorough. Instead, he took every book off of the shelf and stacked them nicely on the floor. He looked back at the shelf in defeat. There was absolutely nothing left behind, not even a bookmark.

He quickly placed the books back on the shelf as neatly as he could. Next, he decided to check the desk. Each drawer was filled with pens, paper, paperclips, and other random items. To Pierce's surprise, there was not a single flash drive. If he was going to find one he figured it would have been there, though it would have been too obvious.

Continuing on he searched the entire room just as he had done before. He treated the closet the same. This time the shelves were loaded with board games and cards. Pierce pulled each down and opened every box. It was a lot of work, but he felt it was necessary.

Valerie was getting frustrated having searched the kitchen, living room, and dining room. She was giving up hope they would find anything at all. Before she joined Pierce in the study she took a quick sweep of the bathroom. Just as she suspected she found nothing of importance. It utterly demoralized her. They were not going to find anything helpful here. The whole house had been thoroughly searched by the detectives. Whatever it was they hoped to find had already been taken. The search was a complete waste of time.

She stepped into the office and watched as Pierce stacked the board games back in the closet. He looked over at her with a questioning looking on his face. She only responded with a shrug of her shoulders. They both believed their efforts were fruitless.

"I guess that's it," Pierce said as he shut the closet door. He propped himself against the wall to the left of the bookshelf. Valerie sighed and sat down in the computer chair. She spun it around so she could face Pierce.

"Is there something that we're missing? Did you thoroughly check the bedroom?"

"Like a comb, babe."

"Do you think the police found it first?"

"I don't know. I don't even know for sure what we're looking for. For all I know, I found it, but didn't even notice."

Valerie did not respond. She shared his disappointment. They could not be certain what they were looking for. If it had been one of the items Ethan had listed they were sure they would have noticed it. As she combed over the house in her mind she stared up at the bookshelf. After a few minutes, she stood up and walked closer.

"Pierce do you notice something off about these books?"

"Not really, no. Why?"

"I mean the types of books. They're mostly thrillers and romance. Maybe the occasional horror."

"Yeah? What's your point?"

"One of these doesn't belong."

She pointed to the spine of a dark gray book with a wrinkled cover. The spine read The Story of Edgar Sawtelle. She looked at it for a moment before looking at Pierce. "I know this book, it does not seem like the kind of story Ethan or Sandra would read."

"Why, what's wrong with it?"

"Well, nothing. It just doesn't strike me as their taste."

"All right, so what's that mean?"

Valerie grabbed the book off of the shelf and held it in her hands. It had the normal weight of a book and it looked completely natural. She opened the cover to the first page and flipped through the next few. After about ten pages she smiled. She was staring at a hollowed out section. Inside rested an external hard drive which seemed to shine back at her. She snatched it out and placed the book back on the shelf.

"It's a faux book!" She nearly screamed as she turned to face Pierce. His eyes were wide with amazement as he stared at her.

"That's amazing Valerie. I can't believe it."

"I think this might be what we're looking for."

Quickly they rushed out of the house and began to head for home. They were anxious and excited to see what was on the hard drive. They were hopeful the contents would provide enough information to clear Ethan's name.

Chapter 21

The sun sank behind the horizon as the black Hummer H3 pulled into an empty parking space. An ivory colored building towered over him. The peach colored sky reflected in each of the condo's windows. Geoffrey climbed out of his car and stared straight up at the building. He shielded his eyes as he made his way towards the entrance.

Once inside he climbed the stairs as quietly as he could and as quickly as he dared. Several times he had to slow his pace to catch his breath. With labored breath, he opened the hallway door at the top floor. The dim hall light splashed a muted gray color against the walls. It took a moment for his eyes to adjust. As he walked he checked each number on the door until he found the one he was looking for.

Before he got to work he glanced over each shoulder to make sure he was alone. Then he dropped to one knee and whipped out his lock pick set. After he inserted the small pins into the knob it only took about forty seconds to unlock. A professional could have picked the lock in under thirty seconds, but he was proud of his time. He then went to work on the deadbolt. A minute passed before each pin had been popped into place.

Slowly he swung the door open and stepped into the quiet darkness. The condo was entirely cast in shadow. The sinking sun had slipped behind the horizon offering no light inside. From the doorway, Geoffrey could see out the back windows. A blanket of darkness began to shroud across the horizon only contested by the small remainder of sunlight.

When Geoffrey was safely inside he slipped his sidearm from his pants. The Berretta M9 was equipped with a suppressor. It doubled the pistol in length and weighed it down some. Even so, Geoffrey could not contain his grin. He had seen several movies use the suppressor and he always wanted to wield one. It was his first opportunity to use one and he was anxious to do so.

This particular suppressor had been obtained from the evidence lock-up room. Ethan McCormick was the one to thank. The two men he had busted before one killed himself, had been loaded with weapons. Among them were suppressors for a myriad of weapons. With glee, he had borrowed the suppressor for his M9. He had taken proper steps to cover his trail. No one would know it was missing. He thought he might keep it when it was all over. No one would miss it.

With light steps, he began to search the condo. If Ethan was there he would find him. After he found him he would put one bullet in his chest and the other in his stomach. The idea was to make it look unlike a professional had killed him. Geoffrey wanted it to look like an altercation. Afterward, he would drop his body in a random dumpster and phone in an anonymous tip. It could not be traced back to the Miami Police Department or Greene and he was confident he would be successful.

In the dark, it was hard to make out the finer details. However, he could see the living room furniture and part of the kitchen. Opposite the kitchen appliances stood a large island counter. It started after the carpet from the living room ended and ran several feet through the kitchen, creating a sort of pathway through the kitchen. Beyond the bar sat the actual dining room with what looked like oak wood tables.

Just left of the table Geoffrey spotted the sliding glass door which led to the balcony. He decided it might be a good spot for Ethan to hide. Quietly he made his way there. He slid the door open as silently as the metal track would allow. Finally, he stepped out into the night air.

For a moment he was distracted by the view. The curtain of darkness seemed to grow thicker. He traced the shoreline with his eyes. A few miles from the coast he could not see a thing. It was like a thicket of black fog. It was not something he was used to and stared at it for over a minute before moving on.

He stepped back inside the condo and decided to quickly check the remaining rooms. He was frustrated when he found no sign of Ethan. Moving back to the kitchen he inspected the sink. Several dirty dishes sat with breakfast residue. Someone had been there earlier in the day. Geoffrey wondered if Ethan had found a new place to lay low. If so he wondered why? Did he know he was coming and how could he have? Then he realized Pierce or Valerie must have warned him. He cursed himself for not grabbing Valerie like he had planned.

There was no time for regrets. He shook the thought from his mind and walked into the living room. He stood still absorbing the silence for a moment. There had to be a way to find where he went. There had to be a clue. It would be nearly impossible to show his face around town. More than likely he had help. If he did, from whom? Geoffrey assumed it was the person who owned the condo. He somehow had coaxed them into helping. Now he had to track down two people. He was upset that plans had changed, but he would adapt. More than anything he wanted to get this over with. The moment Ethan and whoever he was partnered with were dead he would find Greene. Once they were all dead he would finally be free to live his life in peace.

A noise from the outside hallway startled him. In his excitement to take out Ethan, he had forgotten to shut the door. He ducked behind the bar and watched as a dark figure shuffled across the threshold. He hoped the stranger would leave before he was forced to add him to the ever-growing list of deceased. The figure moved slowly into the condo not bothering with the light. Geoffrey could hear feet shuffle across the carpet.

Finally, the voice of an old man broke the silence. "Caroline, are you home? Your door was wide open. Is everything all right? Caroline?" His voice grew louder as he approached the kitchen. Geoffrey held his breath hoping the man would leave. He hated the idea of adding him to the body count.

The shuffling continued onto the tile just on the other side of the bar. The old man stopped there and Geoffrey could hear him breathe. "Caroline? I'm going to call the police. I think someone broke in." He said to himself. Geoffrey had had enough. He popped up from behind the bar and found himself looking at the back of the man's head. His forefinger wrapped around the trigger, but he held his stance.

A combination of thoughts raced through his mind. He had no desire to kill the old man, but the old man had talked about calling the police. He could not allow that to happen, not yet. The last thing he needed right now was for the police to arrive while he was in the building.

He slowly pulled the trigger back until the Beretta fired. There was a spray of red mist before the old man slumped down on the other side of the bar. The suppressor had been louder than he had been expecting, but it had been quiet enough. It had sounded closer to a nail gun than an actual firearm. It was definitely not like in the movies.

As he walked around the counter he was filled with a familiar rush. His heart raced in his chest and could almost feel the blood pump through his veins. It was the familiar feeling of excitement, an excitement that he only seemed to achieve while taking a life. It was a rush that made him feel like nothing else could. Before taking a life he despised the action and even the thought. After he felt like a whole new person. He savored the moment as he stared down at the lifeless body.

After several minutes the feeling dulled. Now he realized there was work to be done. First, he collected his empty shell and slipped it in his pocket. Next, he took a towel from the kitchen and began to wipe down any surfaces he may have touched. The sliding glass door, the kitchen counter, and door knob were his main focus. When he was finished he stuffed the towel in his pants pocket.

He looked down at the slumped body. Bits of brain hung out of the small hole in his forehead. A river of thick blood flowed from the wound pooling on the tile floor. It looked almost black in the darkness. Blood poured from both wounds soaking the floor. He did not know it was possible for the head to bleed as much as it was. It looked as if it would never cease.

There was no reason to move the body. Right, where it was would be fine. He looked back into the kitchen sink at the dirty dishes. He hoped they were filthy with Ethan's prints. It would be all the evidence the local police would need to connect him with the murder.

When he was certain he left nothing behind he headed for the door. If he had done his job right there would be no trace of him for the police to find. From his car, which he would park a few blocks away, he would monitor the police band. Whatever clues they gave up he would pick up on. Pretty soon he would be led straight to Ethan.

He promised himself when he found him he would make his death slow and painful. He had caused him quite a bit of stress. Chasing him all over the state was driving him crazy. Ultimately he knew Greene was to blame and in the end he would suffer. For now, he had to find Ethan and take his anger out on him.

Chapter 22

As Ethan slumped over in the front of Caroline's rental car she argued with the clerk in the hotel lobby. She demanded a room with two queen beds. The woman shook her head and apologized. Only two rooms were available and both included king size beds. She mumbled a curse and forked over her credit card. The woman behind the counter refrained from asking why it was so important. Instead, she smiled and accepted the card.

Once she signed her receipt and collected the two key cards she made her way back to the car. She scowled and barely spoke a word. Ethan decided it was better not to ask. He remained slouched as Caroline parked the car. There was a second entrance around the corner from the main one. Ethan pointed to it and told her they would enter through it. It would be too risky to walk through the main lobby. A lot of hotels keep the local news on the lobby televisions. There was a good chance his face was plastered on one.

Caroline nodded her head as they climbed out of the car. They rushed across the parking lot as fast as they could without looking suspicious. Caroline had to scan the key card in order to unlock the entrance. It took three tries before it clicked open.

There was an elevator just inside the hotel and Caroline called for it. Their room was on the fourth floor. High enough for Ethan to feel safe to open the curtains and look around. If they were any lower opening the windows would be too much of a risk. Now he would be able to keep an eye on his surroundings. If anyone came for him, including the police, he might be able to spot them first.

The elevator doors slid open and they shuffled inside. They were both relieved to be the only passengers. Caroline pressed the fourth floor and it lit up red. Seconds later the elevator quickly rose towards their floor. A fear gripped Ethan tight as he imagined someone waiting for the elevator to arrive. There was a chance they would recognize him from the news. Once they reached their room he knew his anxiety would finally subside.

No one was waiting for the elevator when the doors creaked open. They made it down the hallway and to their room with no trace of another person. As Caroline swiped the key card Ethan decided to ask why she was scowling.

She flung open the door and flipped on the light. "That's why," she said as she shut the door behind Ethan. One king size bed sat in the middle of the room. Other than the dresser and the desk it was the only piece of furniture in the room. There was not even a couch for him to sleep on. He accepted that he would be sleeping on the floor.

"Apparently they did not have any other rooms available, at least not one with two beds. We are not sleeping in the same bed."

"It's all right. I will take a pillow and sleep on the floor."

Caroline did not speak. She sat down on the bed and stared at Ethan. He took no notice of her as he collected a pillow and tossed it on the floor. He sat in the desk chair and took a deep breath. He watched as

Caroline grabbed her suitcase. She tossed it on the bed and began to unpack her clothes.

"I didn't know how long we were going to be here so I packed as much as I could."

He smiled at her and told her it was good thinking. She placed herself back on the bed and grabbed the remote. When the flat screen television in front of the bed came to life Ethan decided to head to the bathroom. He told her he needed to shower and would be out soon. She nodded as she rested her head against the pillow.

Ethan stepped into the small bathroom and shut the door. There was no mirror or sink. Both were outside the bathroom door. It was only a shower and a toilet. After he used the toilet he began to remove his clothes. He folded them up and placed them in a neat pile on the towel rack. The shower head spurted to life, raining room temperature water. He stepped inside and stood under the water for almost ten minutes before he began to clean himself.

While he showered Caroline lay in bed and flipped through the channels. There was nothing interesting on. Eventually, she left it on a random channel and she walked over to the window. The sun was already well beyond the horizon casting the world in shadow. The lights in the parking lot poured out a bright artificial white. She could see the main highway from their room. The view was terrible. Under normal circumstances, it would have annoyed her. Tonight she did not care.

She turned her back on the window. The faint sound of cars veering down highway nineteen could still be heard. The shower still echoed from the bathroom. Quickly she closed the curtains and began to undress. Her heart raced as she stepped out of her clothes. Now she was naked standing in the middle of their hotel room. She knew that any moment Ethan would shut off the shower and burst out of the bathroom to see her standing there. Fumbling through the drawers she found a nightgown that was longer than her others. Slipping on a new pair of underwear she dove under the covers.

Her new outfit made her feel vulnerable and uncomfortable. There was no way she would be able to sleep in her normal clothes. But now she felt odd being barely dressed with a stranger in the room. Pierce had vouched for his character, but that did not mean she trusted him completely. It was not an ideal situation for her to be trapped in.

Caroline contemplated changing back, but the shower cut off. She knew there was no time so she would just have to deal with it. The nightgown was the longest she had, but it barely touched her knees. It may have been the longest, but she always thought of it as her sexiest. It was lacey and silky. She thought it hugged her body nicely and made her look very attractive. The more she thought the worse she felt.

When the bathroom door opened she pulled the comforter to her chin and stared at the television. With his clothes back on Ethan dried his hair. He looked over at her in the bed and gave her a smile.

"Comfortable?" He asked her as he tossed the towel back into the bathroom. She nodded as she gripped the comforter tighter as if he would rip it off. She did not want him to see she was shaking. Her nerves were getting the better of her. She felt more uncomfortable than she thought she would. She contemplated asking Ethan to step out of the room so she could change. She decided not to and cursed herself for changing at all.

Ethan noticed the stressed look on her face and sat back in the desk chair. As he stared at the television he asked her what was on her mind. She told him she was fine, but her voice said otherwise.

"Please, let me know if there is anything I can do for you? It's because of me you're here. I swear on my life I will do everything to make sure you stay safe. I am truly sorry for all of this."

She lowered the comforter from her chin and rose up on an elbow. She looked over at him and began to relax. Something in his voice calmed her. It told her he could be trusted. She believed he meant what he said. He would protect her. He was not there to hurt her. When she saw a tear roll over his cheek she sat up. The blanket fell to her waist.

"Ethan everything is going to be all right, I'm sure. It will work itself out in the end. It has to."

He placed his head in his hands and held back the tears. The memories of Sandra were strong. It was in that moment he realized the last place he had seen her alive was their hotel room. Now he was sharing one with a woman he did not know hiding to save his life. He would have given anything to be back with Sandra again.

The pain was overwhelming, but he did not cry. He had cried enough. Now it was time to face the pain. He lifted his head but continued to gaze forward as he spoke.

"I miss her so much. I was going to ask her to marry me the day she died. Everything was set up perfectly. It was going to be beautiful and she was going to remember it forever. She died not knowing I wanted to make her my wife. I can never go back and change that. Nothing I do will ever make a difference. I can't bring her back and I can never again express my love for her. These bastards will pay for what they did to her. I will do whatever it takes to find the one responsible."

Caroline felt silly now for feeling so anxious over her wardrobe. Ethan was suffering beyond belief and she was worried about her nightgown. She felt like an idiot. Pushing the blankets off her body she climbed out of bed. Ethan's head was back in his hands as she tossed her arms around him. Neither of them spoke as she stood by his side holding him. He could no longer hold back. Tears began to roll.

Her heart went out to him. There seemed to be so much pain inside of him. She felt like a fool for not realizing it before. All of the untrustworthy thoughts she had vanished as she held him tight. He did not move or return her grasp. He merely cried into his hands

"I'm sorry," he said embarrassed. He sat up and wiped the tears from his eyes. "The last place I saw her was in a hotel room. It all just kind of flooded back." Caroline gripped him tighter but said nothing. As Ethan finished wiping his tears away he started to feel vulnerable. He poured his emotions out to a woman he did not know. He was not afraid what she thought of him, but how she would respond.

Caroline knew there was nothing she could say to him in that moment. She could not relate to how he felt at all. She had only lost boyfriends through messy breakups or by being cheated on. She had never truly lost someone she had loved with all of her heart. She understood it was what happened to Ethan. He had poured his heart and soul into this woman. She was his everything and she had been ripped from him. Someone had taken that away and left a gaping hole that could never truly be filled. Caroline knew telling him it would be all right would be useless. No one on the planet Earth could promise that to him.

How could it be all right? Nothing could make it better. Bringing those responsible to justice would be a start. But in the end, she would still be dead and Ethan would feel no better. Nothing could bring the love and joy back to his life. Even one day in the future when he finally moved on it would never be the same. A normal relationship would be hard with another woman. She would have to be okay knowing there would always be a special place in his heart for Sandra. Caroline understood that because she saw firsthand what it did to him. Another woman might not.

Caroline sat on the edge of the bed and looked at Ethan. To her left, the television blared on like background noise. She ran her fingers through her hair. "Ethan, I can't imagine what you're going through. I won't tell you that everything will be okay. I will tell you that I can tell what kind of man you are. You're a good one. Don't lose who you are. Things might seem dark all around you, but don't ever become that darkness. One day, when you're ready, you will see the light again."

She was surprised with how fluid she spoke. Impressed with herself she smiled at him. He nodded as he turned towards her. "Thank-"he started as he looked up at her for the first time since she had stood up.

Now he was surprised by what she was wearing and could not help but think how beautiful she looked. The black and white nightgown flowed over her body hugging each curve tightly. It almost glimmered in the lamp light. Ethan knew it would have been soft and silky to the touch. Her light brown hair was bunched up over her face. It was messy but attractive.

He smiled at her and continued. "Thank you, Caroline. I'm really sorry. I just needed to let off a little stress I think."

"Don't apologize. You've been through a lot it seems. If I can help at all I will."

"I will let you know if there's anything you can do for me. I'd prefer to keep you out of it as much as possible. I don't want-"

"I understand. Let's not worry about that now."

As she climbed back into bed she patted the spot next to her. The invite was warm and generous and he understood it as a friendly one. Caroline knew he had been through so much. The last thing he needed was to sleep on the cold, hard floor. He needed a good night's rest in a comfortable bed.

"Why don't you sleep here?"

"Thank you, but I couldn't. You don't know me."

"I'm willing to take the chance."

"Are you sure?"

"Completely."

"All right, thank you."

He snatched up his pillow and tossed it on the opposite side of the bed. He approached the television and switched it off. "Don't get any ideas." She said half joking. Ethan gave her another smile as he pulled back the covers. Still fully clothed he slipped into bed.

"Don't worry, Caroline I wouldn't dare. Pierce would kill me if I did."

"Oh, please."

They both laughed as Caroline turned off the lamp on the nightstand. She pulled the covers up over her chest. The bed was so large they both felt as if they were sleeping alone. She could not help but feel uncomfortable though she was warming up to him. It felt as if she knew so much about him even though they had only just met. The way he had shared his feelings with her so openly said a lot about his character. Not every man would have done so. Others would try to convince her they never cried a day in their lives. She respected him for it.

"Good night Caroline," Ethan said turning away from her. "Thanks again for everything." There was a moment of silence before Ethan spoke again. "By the way, I love what you're wearing. You look amazing." Caroline turned away from him in the bed with a large toothy smile on her face. She was happy he could not see her blush in the darkness. She decided not to thank Ethan for the compliment, but it did not matter. Seconds later she could hear him breathing softly in his sleep.

Chapter 23

That night Pierce did not sleep. He was up all night scanning every folder, every subfolder, and every hidden folder for a clue that might help. Many files on the external had to do with someone named Greene. There were photos of several officers and a couple of Major Derrick White himself.

Each photo looked like they had been taken from the inside of a car. He assumed Sandra had been tailing these officers for several days at a time. It appeared all of her resources were focused on finding out the identity of the man she called Greene. There was no first name, only Greene.

He first stumbled across the name after opening a document titled Involved. There were several names on this list that Pierce did not recognize. He hoped the list did not only include police officers. Derrick White's name stuck out like a rose among weeds. He was Ethan's superior. Pierce could not believe he was a suspect. According to Sandra's notes, she did not know how he was connected. There seemed to be little proof he was even involved.

The other name he recognized was Geoffrey Hunt. According to Ethan, he was the man who gunned down Major McKinley. It was no surprise Sandra had his name on her list. He had been marked down as a key player, but not the one in charge. Someone was pulling his strings. Sandra had theorized Derrick had authority over him. Of course, Derrick was being led by Greene.

He closed the document and sifted through the photos. They were organized in a separate folder. Each was labeled with the name of the person shown. There was several of Derrick White, but nothing out of the ordinary. Almost all were of him getting into his car at the police station or coming home from work. Not a single compromising situation. Pierce was starting to doubt he was even involved.

He doubled clicked the next folder labeled Geoffrey Hunt and nearly fell out of his chair. Immediately he recognized the man. He had been in his home recently when Derrick White had stopped by to question them. It was clear to him why he had had a bad feeling about the officer from the moment he met him. The thought of this man stepping foot into his house sickened him.

Almost all of the photos showed him in compromising situations. In several, he was accepting money for guns, drugs, and all sorts of other confiscated items. There was a document in his file stating he was stealing from the evidence room and selling the items on the street. That was where Derrick came in. He would have been able to alter the itinerary of the lock up. Sandra had theorized Geoffrey had been giving him a cut of the profits for the privilege, though she could not prove it.

He looked at the clock and rubbed his eyes. To his bewilderment, it was already three in the morning. Valerie had gone to bed hours ago, but there was no way he could sleep. He refused to sleep until he scoured through every bit of evidence. He would not be satisfied until he found something that would help Ethan. Ethan's life depended on it.

With a large gulp of coffee, he turned back towards the computer and continued to dig. There were hundreds of documents and thousands of photos. None of it seemed to help narrow anything down. He was not even sure all of it pertained to the same case.

He came across a file entitled budget cuts and opened it. It was a bill that described essential budget cuts to the Miami Police Department in order to save the city money. There was to be a vote in the next few days regarding the matter. It went on to list exactly what would be cut from their budget. Certain positions would have a pay decrease and other luxuries would be removed.

Several names were listed below the bill with the word opposed typed next to them. On top of the list was Derrick White. He was openly against the bill. Many officers were opposed to it. Naturally, a lot of them would. So it was not surprising to see Derrick was against it. Sandra's notes explained he was mounting campaigns that would help educate everyone on the jobs done by the police department. There were charts and graphs explaining what might happen if certain budgets were cut. It had seemed to become a passion.

Under all of these notes were big red letters that spelled out motive. Pierce was not sure what she meant. How could the potential cuts have been a motive for Derrick? A dirty cop, especially one in a position of power, would not help their case. It seemed to be the only thing that connected him to the others.

There was an abundance of notes regarding her investigation, but no hard evidence. Much of it would prove useless. He needed to find something more concrete. Something had to be there, he knew there had to be. She must have hidden it for a reason. Sandra had not been killed for nothing.

Pierce decided to take a break and got up from his desk. The coffee had grown cold so he headed to the kitchen to fill it up. The coffee pot was empty. As he prepared a new batch he stood staring out the front living room window. Outside the world was dark. The moon was high in the sky casting a white glimmer over the front yard. The dew shimmered in the moonlight like diamonds in the grass. He found himself wishing he was somewhere far away. He did not care where. The situation was taking its toll on him and his wife. If there was a solution he would find it, for her. She needed him now more than ever.

The rich aroma of coffee filled his nostrils and he headed back into the kitchen. Steam billowed from the mug as he poured. Deciding against cream and sugar he took the mug with him back into the study. The computer sat in the corner of the room beckoning for him to sit. The little LED light on the side of the external flashed softly as if to tease him. Somewhere on that drive was what he needed.

He sat down at the desk with only the light from the monitor to fill the room. Outside the bushes rustled against the window as the wind gusted. He stopped and looked over his shoulder. The encounter with the man from earlier had left him feeling paranoid. When he was satisfied it had only been the wind he turned towards the computer and got back to work.

Double clicking the first file he scrolled through every document and searched every folder. He found nothing helpful. He backed out to the main screen and started with the second file. It was full of several other folders. He checked each folder being careful not to miss a single detail. No stone would be left unturned. No piece of data would be left unseen.

He continued this for each folder he came across. He opened the folders and checked each subfolder. Some of the subfolders had subfolders. He dove straight into those as well. After an hour of searching through every single file, he began to give up. His wrist was cramping and his finger was getting sore. There was so much information stored on the hard drive. Sadly none of seemed as if it would help Ethan.

As he was about to give up he stumbled across an unmarked subfolder. When he clicked on it, he noticed several other folders. Each folder was labeled for a letter of the alphabet. He started with A but found nothing inside. B was the same. C had several folders, but they were all empty. He continued through the letters. Every once in a while, there would be folders, but they were always empty. Sandra had gone to great lengths to set it all up, but he was not sure why. He began to fear she had lost her mind. Maybe, in the end, it really had been a suicide. A fear began to boil in the pit of his stomach when he opened up the last folder labeled Z.

Like the others, there were several subfolders. The third he opened had a few more inside. The middle folder led to even more folders. This went on two more times before he found a folder labeled plan. He double clicked the folder but was asked for a password. He swore loudly and nearly knocked over his coffee. Sandra had done her best to hide this particular folder. No one would have stumbled across it by accident. Pierce would have commended her for being careful if it was not hindering him.

He looked over at the clock. It was well past four in the morning. He thought about calling Ethan to ask about possible passwords but decided not to. With everything he had ahead of him, he would need his rest. If the news was to be believed police in every major city would be conducting full-scale manhunts. Then there was the small fact of someone hunting Ethan down. There was a lot on Ethan's plate. Pierce knew he could figure it out alone. He would just have to think.

For ten minutes he sat motionless and stared at the screen. The password request still hung over the document. He tried to think of something Sandra would have used. There was no chance it would have been something obvious like her birthday or Ethan's. Sandra was smarter than that. Regardless Pierce tried both. He had to check Sandra's Facebook for her birthday. He did his best to ignore all the photos and posts she had made before she died. It was too depressing.

Exactly as he had expected neither birthdays worked. Ethan's name did not work nor did their street number. Pierce did not know their social security numbers but decided she would never have used them anyway. He feared Sandra had used a random combination of numbers and letters. If that were the case he would never be able to open the file alone. He would need to find someone to crack the file open.

He continued to type in any word he thought would work. Any date that may have been important to her he used. He tried all kinds of words. He tried every combination of words and numbers he could think of, but none worked. Hope escaped him. He realized it would be impossible to guess her password.

A thought occurred to him. Perhaps it was simpler than it seemed. Maybe the password was something she was looking for, not something she already knew. Sandra may have used Greene as the password. He pounded on the keys and held his breath. Again he received the familiar password rejected message and he slumped back in his chair. Now he knew he had to face defeat. He had no choice but to wait until morning. If Ethan could not help the information would not be recovered in time.

Pierce disconnected the external and powered down the computer. After stretching he stood up and took his empty mug to the kitchen sink. Outside the wind howled fiercely. He knew a storm was approaching.

He walked into his bedroom and peeled off his shirt. He climbed into bed next to Valerie and cuddled up next to her. She barely moved as he kissed her on the cheek. Before closing his eyes he took a moment to look at her. She looked so beautiful and peaceful. He pushed his body close to hers and closed his eyes.

For a while, his mind raced wildly. He still tried to figure out the password. His mind was not going to let him sleep. Eventually, a headache formed and he forced himself to forget about the external drive. Finally, he began to drift to sleep as his mind began to wander. His body relaxed as the darkness closed in all around him.

On the brink of sleep before the final plunge towards unconsciousness, he bolted up and stared into the darkness around him. An idea had found its way in. He leaped out of bed he ran through the doorway and out into the hall. Seconds later he was in the study once again.

He booted up the computer and waited anxiously as it flashed to life. When his desktop appeared he reconnected the external hard drive. It took a few seconds to read the drive before Pierce could access it. Again he began to pour through the documents. What he was looking for would most likely be in the earliest document. Eventually, he found exactly what he needed. A document labeled Start of Investigation.

His heart skipped a beat as he double clicked the icon. A document appeared littered with notes and dates. He scanned the virtual sheet until he found exactly what he needed. It had to be it, he just knew it. Sandra Delano had marked the exact date to the start of her investigation. It had been nothing more than a footnote in the document. But something about it gave him hope. He wrote the date on a scratch piece of paper next to the keyboard. He was still a little groggy and did not want to forget it.

Once he relocated the hidden file he tried to access it. The familiar password pop-up generated. Slowly he typed one number at a time. He contemplated using a dash between each number but decided against it. Finally, the whole date had been entered. He stared at the screen for a few seconds. If this did not work he would be crushed and out of ideas. This was truly his last hope.

With his index finger on the enter button, he took a deep breath. The button clicked loudly in the silent room. For a moment nothing seemed to happen. The window advised it was authenticating the password. It had done this several times before rejecting all the others. He could only hope this one would be different. He resisted the urge to jump out of his chair in excitement when the password finally accepted. Instead, he celebrated quietly to himself.

Pierce was overwhelmed with the amount of information stored in this one document alone. There were notes, photos, locations, and several other items. He started from the beginning and began to read everything.

After a while, he realized what he was looking at. Sandra Delano had uncovered some sort of conspiracy within the police department. A few members of the police force were working together to fight the budget cuts. This particular group of officers was planning what could only be thought of as a large-scale attack of some kind. Sandra had marked down several locations as possible targets. She clearly was not sure what kind of weapon would be used. There were casualty estimates, but the ranges were wide. She was uncertain if it would be a small assassination or a terrorist sized attack.

Several videos were embedded in the document of interrogations run by Sandra. Each video contained a different person in the same isolated room. No one-way mirror was present in the room like most police stations. Instead, there were two chairs, no table, and only white walls. Other than the door and the ceiling light the room was bare. Pierce found himself wondering where these interrogations were held.

In each of the videos, Sandra asked the same questions. She asked who Greene was. Some people seemed to know him, just never seen him, others had no clue. She also asked where they obtained the weapons or drugs they had been caught with. Many times they described Geoffrey Hunt in full detail. Other times they would describe someone else. Sandra would always hold up three photos. All seemed to be officers dressed in full uniform. Pierce could not make out the officers faces, but he knew one was Geoffrey. Sandra named the other two as Thomas Sheeder and Fidel Sanchez.

Each officer had been labeled a criminal at least once by these people. All three had knowingly sold them stolen police property. Pierce remembered the photos he had seen earlier on the drive. Other officers had appeared in them. He now knew that they were Thomas Sheeder and Fidel Sanchez. Sandra must have taken these confessions and followed the guilty officers to obtain proof. She had done an excellent job as each officer had been photographed with stolen items and known criminals.

She would go on to ask them about the upcoming votes and what they knew about them. Most of them had no idea what she was talking about. Only two people had a response. The first told her Geoffrey Hunt had mentioned something about budget cuts and needing more money. It was why he was selling the drugs and weapons. And the second only seemed to have the same story.

He scrolled down and found a transcript of an email conversation. It was between Geoffrey and Derrick. Nothing in the email seemed to prove they were dirty, but it sounded suspicious.

> Derrick: These cuts are going to ruin this place!
> Geoffrey: I know, I agree.
> Derrick: Something has to be done.
> Geoffrey: Like what?
> Derrick: I don't know, anything. We have to do something. We'll do whatever it takes.

Geoffrey: Just let me know what you need.

Derrick: Will do. Tell the others to proceed as planned for now. If something changes I will let you know. Remember they can't know I am with you on this.

Geoffrey: Of course. No problem.

Derrick: And delete your inbox for fuck's sake!

Geoffrey: K

Pierce was certain Derrick White was involved in something, but it was not exactly proof. For all he knew, those two were planning to organize a protest or try to create a counter bill to stop the vote. He knew it was not the truth, but what he knew was not good enough. There would have to be solid evidence that Derrick White was involved in illegal activity to bring him down. The other officers would be arrested with little trouble. There was plenty of evidence to go on.

Pierce wondered why Sandra did not move on Thomas, Fidel, and Geoffrey. All three of them were guilty and she could prove it. Why was she trying so hard to implicate Derrick White? Why was she so sure he was up to something? There must have been a bigger picture. He remembered the satellite images of locations around Miami labeled possible targets. He assumed these four men must have been a part of it all. It was the only explanation as to why she had not arrested them. If she had taken them down too early she would not have been able to stop what was being planned.

He continued to search through the file until he came across an audio file. It was labeled wiretap. He clicked the icon and sat back. He listened to several seconds of silence before a voice boomed through the speakers. It was the unmistakable voice of Derrick White.

It sounded as if Sandra had bugged a part of his office at work. Pierce wondered if she had to get a warrant for it, then decided he did not care. He listened to the soft whisper of Derrick White to another man in the room. His mouth dropped open in shock at the conversation. He could barely believe what he was hearing.

Chapter 24

Ethan slowly opened his eyes as the morning sunlight breached the hotel curtains. Outside he could hear birds chirping and cars driving by. Several people began to stir in the hall as they left their rooms for the day. A few rooms away housekeeping started working on their rounds. Soon they would be in their room. He decided he would get up and put the do not disturb sign on the knob.

Before he got up he looked over at Caroline. She slept peacefully with her back towards him. He scanned over her body and admired her figure. She was thin and curvy like an hour glass. Her hair barely touched her shoulders and looked as soft as silk. As he watched her breathe softly in her sleep he realized he was aroused by her. She was a beautiful woman who had allowed him to sleep in bed with her. She had also trusted him where most people would not.

He stretched and threw the covers off his body. Before heading to the door he made a trip to the bathroom to relieve his bladder. When he was finished he stepped into the hall and slapped the do not disturb sign on the door. As he shut it and locked the dead bolt Caroline began to stir.

She rolled over in bed and stared at Ethan with a smile on her face. The covers were rolled completely around her now like a cocoon. Her silk hair fell over her face and she brushed it away. As she smiled at him she said, "Thanks for last night. That was wonderful." Ethan tripped over his own feet as his heart raced. He had no idea what she was talking about. Quickly he started to search his mind for a memory of the night before. From what he could remember they had a long conversation before she let him sleep in the bed. Afterward, they had gone to sleep. Could it have been possible that they had awakened in the middle of the night and fooled around? Had he been too drowsy to remember? How could this have happened? He attempted to respond but only stuttered.

Caroline started to giggle as she watched him stammer. "Just kidding, you got really nervous though didn't you?" Ethan clutched his chest pretending to have a heart attack. He took a deep breath and laughed.

"You scared me to death. I couldn't remember anything other than falling asleep last night. You had me wondering."

She smiled as she climbed out of bed. Her short nightgown flowed over her body hugging her features nicely. When she made her way into the bathroom he sat on the bed and rubbed his eyes. He felt awful for how he felt about her. He was still miserable over Sandra's death and still loved her deeply. He was worried his attraction to Caroline made him a horrible person, but he assured himself it was only physical. There would be no chance he would ever act upon them anyway.

Moments later Caroline emerged from the bathroom still dressed in her nightgown. She walked over to the dresser and pulled out a pair of jeans and a blouse. Ethan watched her every step of the way. Her hips swayed gently back and forth as she walked. Each step she took was like a taunt. He shook the feeling away as she changed in the bathroom. He took the moment to open the bag of complimentary coffee. Coffee was not his normal choice of beverage, but he decided to make an exception. Anything to get his mind off of Caroline's body.

She returned from the bathroom as the pot started to fill. She looked over at him and smiled. "Smells good," she said as she dropped her dirty clothes in a small pile next to the dresser. She sat down at the desk fully clothed staring at him. Ethan began to serve them both a cup.

As she blew on hers she asked, "So what's the plan?" From the moment he had poured the drinks he had been asking himself the same question. He had no answer, but before he could say so his cell phone began to ring.

He looked down at it and recognized the number as Pierce. With excitement, he took the call. "Pierce," he asked. "Have any news?" He heard Pierce take a large breath as if he had a lot to say.

"I do. You're not going to believe this, Ethan."

"What is it?"

"You might want to sit down if you aren't."

Ethan sat down on the bed.

"What's going on?"

"Valerie and I went to your place yesterday. We were looking for anything that might help."

"You find anything?"

"Well, the police really scoured that place. There wasn't much."

"Oh?"

"But we found something. Are you aware that there's a false book on your bookshelf?"

"A what?"

"A false book. You know, a book that's been carved out so you can hide something inside?"

"There was? I had no idea. What was in it?"

"We found an external hard drive. It belonged to Sandra."

"What?"

"It had all kinds of notes on it regarding Sandra's investigation. There's photos of cops involved, videos of her interrogating several criminals, and a couple audio files."

"What have you learned?"

"It's not good Ethan."

"What?"

Caroline still sat at the desk watching Ethan as he talked to Pierce. She was engulfed in confusion. From her position, she could not hear Pierce on the other end. She could only hear Ethan's responses. There was not much she understood.

"Derrick White is involved."

"McKinley told me he might be."

"No, Ethan, it's worse than that."

"What do you mean?"

"There was a hidden file that was password protected. I was able to get through it. There's all sorts of information on it. Something big is going to happen. Unfortunately, Sandra did not know what it was exactly. It has to do with the upcoming budget votes. Derrick's openly against the cuts and he's willing to do whatever it takes to prove it's a bad idea. There was a sound clip in that file. It sounds like Sandra bugged Derrick's office. I don't think she had a warrant for it since she never busted him."

"What was on it?"

"Derrick speaking with Geoffrey Hunt, the officer you said killed Major McKinley. They are openly discussing a plan. They don't give many specifics, but it sounds bad. Geoffrey's been selling weapons and drugs that he's stolen from the evidence lockup. Derrick has been falsifying documents to cover his trail. It seems as if they are selling them to specific criminals. Derrick is collecting the money for something. Geoffrey and several other officers take a large cut. Derrick has been using his to slowly collect what he referred to as the supplies. He said once the vote passes there will be a major event that could have been avoided if they were fully funded. Ethan, it sounds like Derrick and several other officers are funding crime in order to fund their own scheme. If that vote passes I think Derrick is willing to hurt a lot of people to prove his point about that bill."

Ethan was stunned. For nearly a minute he sat on the bed and stared at the wall. Pierce remained quiet. He could tell Ethan was processing it all. Finally, he cleared his throat and said, "Do you think Derrick killed Sandra?"

"I'm not sure, Ethan. She didn't have anything on him except for this conversation. I'm not even sure what he's planning. For all we know it's a strike."

"A strike with stolen weapons and dirty cops?"

Pierce laughed uncomfortably.

"All right, well obviously not a strike, but we don't know what is all I'm saying. There hasn't been any evidence to prove that Derrick is a murderer. Sandra believed he may have been a pawn in all of this, like Geoffrey. There's mention of a man named Greene."

"Yeah, I've heard the name."

"Who is it?"

"I have no idea."

"Yeah, neither did Sandra. But he must be a key player. She seemed to think finding his identity was important."

"I agree."

"Ethan, I think you should be careful with this. I think looking for Greene is what got her killed. It seems like he's a man who doesn't want to be found."

"Why do you say that?"

"In all of her interrogations she mentioned his name. Not all of them had heard it before, but the ones that did got scared. They didn't want to talk about him and when they did they didn't say much. This guy is bad news, Ethan. I have a feeling he's the one who killed Sandra."

Ethan was quiet again. It was a lot to take in. If this mystery man had killed Sandra he would figure out his identity right before putting a bullet between his eyes. He was no longer an officer of the law. He was wanted for murder. If he discovered Greene's identity before this was all over he would kill him. There was no doubt in his mind he could do it.

"Thanks for everything, Pierce. I should get moving."

"Of course, Ethan, call me if you need anything at all. I will keep looking over the drive, see if there was anything I missed."

"Have you heard anything about your home intruder?"

"Not yet, hopefully, we do soon."

"I think I know who it was."

"Geoffrey Hunt?"

"Yeah."

"I was thinking that too. Which means he's out there looking for you. Watch your back, Ethan."

"Will do."

With that, Ethan hung up and slipped the phone into his pocket. He looked over at Caroline sitting at the desk. Her expression was one of concern, but her body language gave her away. She was nervous. Ethan wished there was something he could have said to make her feel better, but there was nothing. She had been dragged into all of this and it was not fair. He wished he could send her away, but it was too late for that. Geoffrey knew where she lived, which means he probably knew who she was. He would kill her to get to Ethan if he had to. There was no doubt about it. Now it was his duty to keep her safe. Where he had failed Sandra he would succeed with her. He owed Caroline that much.

"So, now what Ethan?"

There still was not a single idea in his mind. So much raced through he almost felt dizzy. If he did not come up with something she might lose all hope in him. He had to think of something fast. Geoffrey Hunt was out there looking for him as he sat idle. It would not take him long. If he knew Caroline's identity it would only be a matter of time before he found the hotel.

He looked into her eyes and held back a smile. Her eyes were beautiful and big. They reminded him of Sandra's and the way he used to get lost in them. He shook off the feeling and stood up.

"All right," he said. "Here's what we do."

***

"Caroline, are you home?" The woman called out from the hallway. The door to her condo stood wide open. All the lights were turned off. She wondered if there had been a break-in. As long as she had lived in the building there had never been a single break-in. It was shocking to think one may have happened the night before.

She stepped inside and flipped on the light. In front of the bar, a large heap was slumped over. It almost looked like a body. She wondered what she was looking at as she approached. When she was close enough she screamed and nearly toppled over. Collapsed on the ground was her elderly neighbor, Tom. A pool of now drying blood had formed around his body. The back of his head was matted with it. Holding in the urge to vomit she ran out of the condo and collapsed in the hall.

For nearly a minute she cried on the floor. She did not understand why her neighbor's body was in Caroline's apartment. Caroline had been a sweet and quiet woman. She would not believe Caroline had done it. She was not even sure Caroline had been there. The only scenario that made sense to her was a burglar had shot Tom dead when he stumbled inside asking what was going on.

It had been Tom's personality. He was the elderly man in the building always sticking his nose in other's business. It never bothered anyone because he was a sweet old man. When others needed it he was always there to help. Several of them had been to his place for drinks on many occasions. It was a running joke that one day he would get himself killed by getting involved in someone's issues.

Caroline had been the exact opposite. She had always been friendly, but usually kept to herself when she was there. Enjoying a drink with her neighbors was never high on her to-do list. Tom had tried to break the ice with her, but never quite got her out of her shell. He had always said one day he would convince her to come to one of his parties.

The woman gained her composure and ran back down the hall. From her condominium, she would call the police. She had planned to sleep on the beach all day and work on her tan. She had left her cell phone in the condo hoping to get some peace and quiet from it. Now she wished she had brought it with her.

***

Geoffrey sat behind the wheel of his jet-black Hummer. Despite his windows being cracked to stop from overheating, he was drenched in a pool of sweat. The night had been hot and sticky. Many times through the night he had questioned his decision to sleep in the Hummer. The police scanner was switched on waiting for a confirmation the body had been found.

He planned to have the local authorities do part of the work for him. First, they would identify the owner of the condominium. Once they did they would be on the lookout for them. He would listen for their possible location and get there before they could. Ethan was most likely with them, but if not he would get them to tell him where he was. Eventually, they would talk. He would make sure of it. He knew the drill. There could be no loose ends. It added to his list of reasons why Greene would have to die. Greene had made a killer out of him.

The more he did Greene's dirty work the deeper his hands got in blood. There was only one way to be free from his clutches and soon he would have his chance.

A voice broke over the scanner and mentioned a body found in the condominium. Excitement coursed through his veins as he turned up the volume. It was definitely his. The address was rattled off and several cars were dispatched to the location. He had high hopes he would have their location within the hour.

He watched as the police cruisers pulled in the parking lot a few blocks down the street. They were there for quite some time before anything was said. Finally one of the officers reported a name, Caroline West. She was labeled as the owner of the condo. Her current location had been requested.

Now some officer sitting at a desk would run her name through their system. They would get her photo identification pulled up. Shortly after that her credit information as well. A trace would be run in the surrounding areas to see if she had made any purchases. If so they would be able to narrow down her location. All Geoffrey had to do was wait.

When the call finally came through as to her possible location Geoffrey started his engine. Within seconds he had pulled out of the parking lot and was cruising down the road. If he was going to get to her before the police he would need to move quickly. If they picked her up before he did the chance to find Ethan might be gone. And if Ethan was caught everything would be ruined. Ethan needed to die. Even if he could not prove his own innocence he would be able to take Geoffrey down with him. He could not take that chance. He could not fail. Geoffrey hoped the local police would put him down when they found him. He was an accused cop killer, it was possible. If they did his dirty work for him it would be wonderful.

It was a short ten-minute drive to the hotel her card had been reported at. He knew he would beat the police for sure. The officers at the condo would not be leaving. Others would be dispatched. If he was lucky they would not be close by. He was certain he would be safe.

When he arrived at the hotel he parked his Hummer across the street. If he needed to leave in a hurry it would be easier on foot. He rushed across the street and into the hotel parking lot. None of the vehicles stood out, but he did not expect they would.

The real challenge would be to get the room number. Quickly he thought up a plan and headed for the lobby. The woman standing behind the counter greeted him with a toothy smile. She was round and pretty with long black hair that framed her face. The black jacket hugged her body tightly as if it were one size too small.

"Hello," he said flashing his Miami Police badge quickly. "I'm looking for a woman by the name of Caroline West. I believe she is staying at this hotel." The woman hesitated for a moment before typing the name into her computer. With a nervous smile, she said, "Yeah she checked in late last night. Room four ten." Geoffrey thanked her with a smile and headed for the elevator.

When he was safely concealed by the elevator doors he pulled out his pistol. The suppressor had been tucked away in his pocket so he could conceal the gun better. Now he reattached it with a solid click. Moments later the doors slid open and he was in the hall. Room four hundred ten was only a few doors away from the elevator. When he arrived he found the do not disturb sign on the door. He wondered if Ethan was having sex with this woman. He hoped that he was. The kill would be a lot easier that way.

The cleaning lady was busy in the room next door, but her cart was positioned against the outside wall. Geoffrey knocked on the door as he stared at the cart. No one answered. No sound stirred from inside. He knocked one more time with no luck.

As he pushed the pistol into the back of his pants he approached the open room. The cleaning lady was busy changing the comforters with a disgusted look on her face. He could only imagine some of the nasty things she had seen as she cleaned.

"Excuse me, I need your assistance." Again he flashed his badge quickly and the lady nodded. "I need you to open the room next door for me. After I want you to go back to your room and don't say a word." The lady nodded again. Now she looked terrified.

She followed him next door and slid her key card in the reader. When the light turned green she propped open the door. Geoffrey placed his hand on the top of the door and pushed it open. The cleaning lady took off back to her room at a quick sprint. As the door swung shut behind him he grew worried. The room was dark and no one was there. He darted into the bathroom but found it empty. There was no luggage or clothes left behind. The woman at the front desk had not said they checked out.

He walked to the window and peered outside. Several police cruisers were screeching to a halt in the parking lot. He was out of time and had to leave. There was no way he could be trapped in this building while Caroline and Ethan were out there. Geoffrey detached the suppressor and slid it back into his pocket. The gun went back into his waistband. Seconds later he was in the hallway. Instead of going back the same way he took the stairs at the opposite end of the hall. Once on the first floor, he took a second door which led to the back of the parking lot. As the police rushed inside he turned the corner back into the parking lot.

Picking up the pace he made it back across the street and into his hummer. Now he had no way of knowing where they had gone. He did not know what car they were driving. Not what Caroline looked like. Not where they would be heading. He was unsure what to do next. Going back to the condo was no longer an option. Neither was hanging around the hotel. Somehow they knew they had been compromised. From now on they would only use cash, he was sure of it. Geoffrey was afraid their trail had gone cold.

He tried to put himself in their position. What would I do if I were them? He thought. His first thought drifted to a cheap motel. Somewhere that would accept cash without a card on file. There had to be one of those somewhere. He pulled up the browser on his phone and searched for nearby motels. There were a few in the area that looked particularly run down. They must have been staying at one. He decided he would check them all if he had to. It would only be a matter of time before they were found. He just preferred it was by him.

***

They sat in the front seat of Caroline's rental car staring out the windshield. They were parked on a side street a few blocks down from a small marina. Ethan was busy scoping it out trying to plan his next moves carefully. When he was satisfied he looked over at Caroline.

"All right, here's the plan. Park the car somewhere in the back of the lot. Make sure to back up to conceal the plate. Eventually, the police will be looking for this car, but we can't ditch it just yet. We may need it soon."

"Okay, then what?"

"After that, we go yacht shopping."

Caroline looked confused, but Ethan did not elaborate. Instead, he told her to drive. She did as she was told and reversed into a spot near the back. As she shut off the engine Ethan climbed out. Moments later she was right on his heels. They walked side by side down the marina. Ethan looked left to right at each boat. Near the end of the dock, he found a larger boat with a large cabin. It was a decent boat, large enough to live on. It did not stand out as something special which is exactly what they needed. He told her to wait while he checked it out.

He hoped up on the deck and scanned it over. It looked like the boat had not been taken out in at least a couple weeks. Whoever it belonged to was probably very busy. It seemed like a good choice. He tried the cabin door and was surprised to find it unlocked. He examined the inside and liked what he saw. Moments later he was back on the deck helping Caroline climb aboard.

They stowed away in the cabin as the waves rocked it gently. Ethan sat down at the table and stared out the window. He could see the ocean stretching on for almost a mile before land intervened. Off to the right, the water jutted out into the Gulf of Mexico. He was tempted to take the boat out and never return. Just sail into the wind and find a new home. Start a new life with Caroline by his side. He shook the feeling from his mind and turned to face Caroline.

"Well, it isn't much, but we can be safe here for a while."

"What if the owner decides to take it out?"

"With the amount of dust that's settled in here, I don't think he will. It's probably been a while since she's been out to sea."

"But we don't know."

"That's true, we don't know. I do know we don't want to be caught by the man looking for me. Compared to him some random boat owner will be a breeze."

She shrugged as if to say whatever as she made her way towards the end of the cabin. Behind another door in the front of the boat sat a queen size bed with maroon colored sheets. Overall the boat was nice. It was not quite a floating mansion, but it was not a trash heap either. It was something Caroline could see herself owning. She had always wanted to own a boat but had never found the time. There was a lot of responsibility and a lot of hard work. She decided when it was all over she would look into finding herself a nice one.

"How do you know the police won't look for us here?"

"Would you?"

"I guess not."

"What they'll do when they don't find us at the hotel is send our descriptions out to each officer in the city. Everyone will be on the lookout for us. After that, they will check all of the obvious places like cheap motels. If they still don't find us they will leave the case open until something new comes up. Not many people would think to look for us here. Let's just hope that our luck holds out long enough to get out of this mess."

"And how do you plan to do that?"

"Honestly, I don't know."

Caroline sighed deep.

"I wish I could tell you how all of this will end, Caroline, but I can't. All I know is someone killed my fiancé and now they are coming after me. It has something to do with a vote happening in the next couple days."

"A vote about what?"

"Budget cuts to the police department. One of the high ranking officers is conspiring with others to put a stop to the bill. From what it sounds like they are willing to hurt people to do so. I don't know their full plan, but I will figure it out. I will find out who killed Sandra and then I'm going to kill him."

He spoke matter of factly with hardly any emotion. It made Caroline nervous. He did not seem like the same man he had been only hours before. Now he seemed full of anger and hatred. She could not blame him for feeling that way. Caroline only hoped it would not be his downfall.

"Ethan, what are we going to do about food and supplies? We don't know how long we'll be trapped here."

"Yeah, you're right. I guess we'll have to take a trip out to the store. I might want to pick up an extra pair of clothes too."

Ethan stood up and headed for the door.

"Come on, we shouldn't split up. Let's get out and back as quickly as we can. The longer we are out the more risk we take."

Caroline rose from the bed and followed Ethan out of the boat and back into the rental car. She climbed behind the wheel as he relaxed in the passenger seat. Her hands shook as she shifted into drive. She was terrified.

"Take as many back streets as you can. We don't want someone to recognize us."

Chapter 25

Detective Jackson waited at the front desk in the hotel lobby. The woman behind the counter had confirmed Caroline had been there. She even identified her in a photograph. She had not seen the man with her. The woman had also told him an officer had already visited a few moments before asking for the same people. At first, he was confused, but quickly let it go. He thought one of the officers had been overzealous and asked about them before he arrived.

Jackson was furious they had missed Ethan. After receiving the report from the condo stating a body had been found he had been ready to jump into action. Ethan McCormick's prints had been found all over the condo as well as Caroline's. It was presumed that Ethan killed the old man when he discovered he was there. Afterward, he got nervous and fled forcing Caroline to go with him. Most likely Ethan did not have a dime to spend which is why he forced her to put them up in a hotel for the night, but in the morning realized his mistake. Now he was out there looking for a place to lie low. Next, they would be checking cheap motels. Most likely he would be looking for a place to pay in cash. When the press learned he had slipped through their fingers they would run with the story like a forest ablaze.

Jackson was eager to find Ethan and put him in handcuffs. The reports had told him that at least one officer had died at his hands. Now an innocent bystander had been found dead. Jackson would not see it happen again if he could help it. Ethan McCormick would be stopped by any means necessary. If he had to shoot him then so be it.

The crimes scene investigation unit stumbled down the stairs with all of the equipment in hand. The man in charge walked over to Jackson and began to explain what they had found.

"The room was lousy with prints. One set belonged to McCormick the other belonging to Ms. West. It's my opinion they spent the night but left sometime this morning. Had to have been extremely early."

Jackson thanked him as he carried about his business. He walked back over to the woman behind the counter. "Are there camera's on the outside of the building?" The woman nodded. "I need access to the footage." She motioned for him to follow and led him back behind the counter. There was a small office with one monitor propped up on an old wooden desk. She motioned for him to sit. She explained how to scroll through the footage and folded her arms as she watched him work.

Jackson moved the footage back to the previous night. Several cars came and went. He had no way of knowing which car they would arrive in. He only hoped to see Ethan or Caroline. From there they could get the car. For about fifteen minutes he watched vehicles pull in as people checked in to the hotel.

"Exactly what time did they check in last night," Jackson asked.

"Let me check," she said as she left the room.

He was just about to fast forward to the morning when something caught his eye. A car pulled in and parked just out of the frame. A woman climbed out alone and headed into the lobby. After she disappeared

Detective Jackson confirmed the check-in time with the woman now standing over him. It seemed to match the stamp on the video. He knew it was Caroline. He rewound the video in the attempt to make out the car she had driven in, but it was too dark to tell.

He decided to move the footage to the morning. He watched Ethan and Caroline leave the hotel and back towards the vehicle. Finally, he caught a break. The vehicle came into focus and lit up by the sun in a magnificent sparkle. He was not able to see the plate, but it did not matter. The description was a start. He smiled and slapped the desk.

He jumped up and walked back out into the lobby. After thanking the employees for their time he headed back to his car. Gripping the radio in his hand he said, "All units we're looking for a Silver Chevrolet Impala. Again, Ethan McCormick and Caroline West last seen in a Silver Chevrolet Impala." With that, he started his engine and headed off. As he drove he checked every vehicle. If it matched the description he would pull up next to the car and profile the people inside. It was tedious, but eventually, it had to pay off.

Jackson had been shocked when he heard a manhunt was underway for a Miami police officer. He had been labeled a murderer. Not just a murderer, but a cop killer. It was crazy to think he was hiding out here. Why would someone trying to get away from the police stay in the same state? It would have been in his best interest to skip town and keep driving until he hit Alaska. Nobody would look for him there. Jackson had read Ethan's file, he was a smart man. He had been a good cop up until the moment he snapped. The decision to stay in the same state had been a poor one. Now the law was right on his tail. It would only be a matter of time before he was caught. Jackson would see it through personally. He could not allow a cop killer to stay at large.

***

A red light forced Geoffrey to come to a stop. He sat idle at the intersection staring straight ahead. There were several cheap motels in the area he planned to investigate. Ethan and his new friend were bound to be at one of them. It would only be a matter of time before he found them. The key was figuring out which motel before the police did.

They had more resources and a lot more manpower. It would be quick and easy for them to check more than one at a time. If he was going to find them first he knew he would have to pick the right motel the first time. Luck had to be on his side.

He tried to think what Ethan would do. If he were trying to get away from the condo he might choose the farthest motel. However, he may have thought ahead and chosen one about half the distance. In reality, every option would be a guess. Ethan may have left town and was sleeping under a bridge in Georgia for all he knew. If he was smart he was on a boat to Mexico.

The light blinked green and he rolled through the intersection. It was about a mile to the motel he had decided on. If Ethan was not there he might fail. Failure was not possible. Geoffrey knew he was a dead man if he failed. The stories he had heard about Greene were terrible. He was capable of killing people in the darkest ways. The worst part, he always had someone do it for him. He never got his hands dirty. Leverage was his secret. Anyone with something to hide could become a pawn in his game.

Up ahead he could see the motel sign. It was a faded red sign with dingy yellow lettering. The grass on the property had not been cut in weeks and trash littered the parking lot. If there was ever a place that only accepted cash, this was it. They for sure had to be there.

He pulled his monstrosity into the parking lot and killed the engine. It did not fit in with all the rusted junkers in the lot. As he walked towards the main office he started to wonder if he had made the wrong choice. Would Ethan really have stayed in this dump? Would anyone with even a small bit of brain power?

The door swung open and the smell of mildew wafted from the office. The man sitting behind the desk was reading a book with the cover torn clean off. He placed it down and looked up at Geoffrey with disgust. "Whadya want?" He asked staring hard at Geoffrey. He wondered why the man seemed to dislike him. Quickly he realized it was obvious he was not there for a room. The vehicle he drove in, the nice clothes he was wearing, and the lack of smell gave it away. This man knew Geoffrey needed something and he took it as a waste of time.

Geoffrey flashed his badge quickly and said, "I'm looking for a man and a woman who might be staying here. Their names are Ethan and Caroline. Did anyone by those names check in recently?"

"I ain't give a shit about names here. Long as they has cash we fine."

Geoffrey gave him Ethan's description but was quickly told no one like that was staying there. In fact, no one had checked in at all the through the week. There was no chance of finding Ethan or Caroline there. He did not bother to thank the man for his time. Instead, he turned around and headed back towards his Hummer. Climbed in the cab and drove off.

He was angry with himself. It had been his one chance and he blew it. The local police were definitely checking other motels by now. The chance of getting to Ethan before them was nearly gone. Ethan and Caroline were as good as caught. His best chance now would be to get back to Miami. Maybe he could bargain with Greene to have another officer kill him once he was transferred back. Perhaps Greene would spare his life. He wondered if there was still enough time to learn Greene's identity before everything went wrong.

Another light switched to red and he slammed on the break. Tires screeched to a halt. He craned his neck to look around to make sure no cops had been alerted. The last thing he needed was the attention. He spotted a beautiful woman looking up at him from her car on his passenger side. Quickly she looked away when their eyes met. Geoffrey looked over at her and admired the part of her body he could see. Her chest was the perfect size and lifted up high. The tips or her silky hair barely touched the tops of her shoulders. He ached to see the rest of her.

Shaking the thought from his mind he sat back in his seat. Then something occurred to him. The description of Caroline's car had come over the radio hours earlier. Slowly he turned his head to the right and stared at the silver Chevrolet Impala sitting idle beside him. He knew it could not be them. It would have been impossible to be so lucky.

With pure anticipation, he waited for the light to turn green. He purposely let the Impala pull ahead. Without signaling, he darted behind them and followed as close as he dared. There was a passenger sunk down low. It seemed as if they were trying their best not to be seen. It was them, it had to be. He could not believe his luck. Somehow he had run into them out on the road. How could they have been so stupid? Why would they risk being out on the street? The police would have found them sooner or later. They must have been desperate. Or maybe they were looking for a place to ditch the car.

Whatever their reason he was happy he found them. Now it would be a matter of following them until the right moment. When they pulled over somewhere quiet he would kill them both. The pistol and suppressor rested on the passenger seat ready to be assembled. He could not believe it was almost over. Soon they would be dead. The police would find their bodies. He would do his best to make it look like a murder-suicide. Again Ethan would take the fall.

The Impala's blinker came to life as the vehicle pulled into a parking lot. Geoffrey followed but drove around the perimeter of the lot as they drove through the aisles. There was no sense keeping right on them if he could still see them. The Impala pulled to a stop in a spot and sat for a moment. Geoffrey nearly laughed when he realized what was going on. They were going grocery shopping. How could Ethan have been so stupid? Why did Greene think he was such a threat? Clearly, he was a moron. Hiding from the police was not his specialty. Then he realized that every cop in the area was busy searching the obvious locations. At that moment they were at a huge advantage. Every available police officer was checking the nearby motels and hotels. It would be hours before they widened their search. He started to wonder if

Ethan was aware of this or if he had been taking a huge risk. He decided he did not care.

He watched as the woman climbed out of the car and walked towards the building. Her hips swayed slightly as she did. Ethan was alone in the car still sunk down low. Now was his time to strike. Silently taking them out one at a time would be easier than trying to kill them together. He grabbed the Berretta and clasped the suppressor back on. With it tucked back in his waistband he jumped out of the Hummer.

Slowly he snuck up on the Impala. He kept his head low and surveyed his surroundings making sure no one was around. The parking lot was mostly devoid of people. Cars littered the lot giving him plenty of cover. When he was only two car lengths from Ethan he crouched down low. Ethan stared in the opposite direction probably watching for Caroline to come back out.

Now Geoffrey removed his sidearm and crouch-walked towards the passenger window. When he was close enough he tapped the suppressor on the window making sure to keep it pointed directly at Ethan's head. He turned and stared up at Geoffrey in horror. His eyes grew wide with fear. Geoffrey felt the familiar rush in the pit of his stomach. He was beginning to enjoy himself.

"Out of the car quietly," He ordered. Ethan nodded and slowly emerged from the car. As soon as he was standing Geoffrey grabbed him by the shoulder and spun him around. Geoffrey stuck the barrel in the small of his back as they walked back towards the Hummer. The idea was to capture both quietly and tie them up. Then he could take them somewhere and take his time. He thought he might take them to the beach in the cover of night and let the bodies drift out to sea. The salt water would destroy all evidence of murder. In the end, no one would care. Ethan was a cop killer. The people would rejoice when his body washed ashore.

"Geoffrey, you don't have to do this."

"Shut up."

"There's still time for you to walk away."

"I said shut up."

"You don't want any more blood on your hands."

"I swear to God I will shoot you in the throat and let you choke on blood! Now shut the hell up!"

He resisted the urge to pull the trigger right then, though it was strong. It was insulting that Ethan was trying to reason with him. There was no going back now. He had watched him kill McKinley. Did he really think he would just let him go? This had to be done and they both knew it.

They were a few steps away from the Hummer when a woman's voice broke through the still air. "Ethan?" She cried out. Geoffrey glanced over his shoulder for only a moment. Ethan wasted no time. He swung his left elbow back striking him square in the face. In the same moment, he dove to the side avoiding the shot Geoffrey took on impulse.

While Geoffrey recovered from the blow Ethan spun around and charged him. He rammed into Geoffrey with tremendous force and they both tumbled to the concrete. "Get in the car!" Ethan yelled at Caroline. She let the cart of groceries go and they rolled across the lot denting a random car.

As the engine started Ethan was thrown away from Geoffrey. He slid across the ground landing hard. Both men climbed to their feet simultaneously. They stared each other down. Geoffrey's gun had slid from his hand and landed behind the tire of a parked car. Ethan knew his next move would be to go for the gun.

Ethan darted forward toward Geoffrey as he sprinted towards the gun. Geoffrey bent under the car and reached for it, but Ethan rammed him into the back bumper. He cried out in pain as he collapsed. Caroline pulled out of the parking space and positioned the vehicle just behind the two of them. Ethan pulled himself to his feet and spun on his heel. Caroline motioned for him to climb in, but Geoffrey was already on his feet.

He grabbed Ethan by the back of the neck and flung him across the hood. It dented under his back and the air was forced from his lungs. Geoffrey turned back towards the handgun as Ethan rolled off of the hood. He landed hard scraping the skin on his palms. Still gasping for air he crawled to the passenger door and pulled himself inside. As Caroline peeled away Geoffrey retrieved the gun and open fired. Its muted puff echoed through the parking lot as bullets buried into Caroline's trunk.

He bolted to the driver side of his Hummer and tossed the Berretta across the cab. The engine roared to life like an angry lion. Moments later he was in pursuit of the silver car. He knew he had to end this fast before the police caught on. Firing his weapon in the parking lot had been a mistake and he knew it.

Chapter 26

Caroline whipped through the busy streets trying her best to avoid bringing any attention. It was not working as well as she hoped. Several cars blared their horns as she cut them off. Others tossed their middle fingers out the window. As long as she did not hit any other cars the police would most likely not be called. She continued to swerve around traffic while Geoffrey floored his Hummer trying to catch up.

He decided not to move as gracefully as her. He slammed on his horn. When the car ahead did not move he rammed the rear end and watched them spiral out of the way. Adrenaline was coursing through his entire body. The hunt was close to being up and he was not going to let the opportunity slip through his fingers.

In the passenger seat of the Impala Ethan spun his head around wildly. He tried to keep Geoffrey in his sights as much as possible. Meanwhile, he was on the lookout for police. It would only be a matter of time before someone called them. When they did they would be in more trouble. He knew Geoffrey was there to kill him, but the local police was not a better alternative. They had to get off the main street fast.

Ethan yelled for Caroline to take a right turn as sharp as she could. She fishtailed around the corner nearly clipping another car. Once she was straight again she pressed the accelerator to the floor and sped off. A short time later Geoffrey tried to slide his Hummer but lost control. His back end smashed the headlight on an oncoming car which spun him around in the opposite direction. Ethan watched it all happen and refrained from showing his excitement. They needed to get somewhere and hide the car. Soon there would be too much heat to keep going.

Geoffrey spun around quickly and sped off towards Caroline and Ethan. He knew it would not take him long to catch up with them. Her Impala was small and maneuverable, but it was no match for the horsepower under his hood. Within seconds he would be back on their tail.

Caroline weaved through traffic once again being careful not to clip anyone. The traffic light ahead burned bright red and she knew she could not stop. And running it was a terrible option. Most likely they would end up a twisted wreck on the side of the road if she tried. Instead, she let off the gas. Slowing down to a reasonable speed she was about to attempt another turn. Before she could Geoffrey rammed into her back bumper. She lost control of her car and started to slide towards the intersection. At first she tried to correct it but eventually gave up. She pulled her arms into her chest and let the car slide.

It came to a stop in the middle of the intersection. To her surprise not a single car hit them. Everyone had come to a complete stop on all four sides. It was then she realized the light had just changed. She would have made it through the light after all. She cursed herself as she stepped on the gas once again.

Geoffrey was quickly approaching their side as she moved forward. He missed by inches. He was able to correct himself and was back on their tail. Several times he bumped them, but she remained in control.

As she swerved around another car Ethan said, "We need to end this Caroline. The cops will be on us any second." She nodded as she dodged another car. With Geoffrey right on her tail, she sped up towards another vehicle. At the last second, she jerked the wheel to the left and pressed hard on the gas. Immediately after she was pulling back to the right and cutting the driver off. The driver swerved to dodge Caroline as she pulled down a side street. Geoffrey rammed the back end of the other car. Both were sent into a short spin.

In the distance, Geoffrey could hear sirens. They were headed their way. He knew his time was up. There was no way he could keep after them like he was. He slid around and drove down the same road as Caroline, but saw no sign of her. He drove slowly through the neighborhood streets checking the houses. If they were attempting to hide in someone's driveway he would find them. But after three blocks he still did not see them. Finally, he gave in and accepted he had lost them.

He drove to the end of the street and slid to a stop in front of a stop sign. The sirens still blared in the distance so he kept moving. He would have to stash the dented Hummer somewhere for the time being. Whoever had called the cops most likely mentioned it. He could not risk the cops identifying him on his mission.

A for sale sign hung in the yard a few house away. He pulled into the driveway and climbed out while leaving the engine running. He picked the lock. Less than thirty-five seconds. Moments later he was opening the garage door. Once his hummer was secure inside he walked out and shut it behind him. He hoped no one would stumble across it. If he was lucky he would be back later that night to pick it up when his job was finished. He only hoped Ethan and Caroline were able to outrun the police. It felt funny rooting for his enemy.

***

Once Caroline had broken the line of sight she pressed the pedal to the floor. The Impala's engine whined as she tore through the neighborhood. Without a second thought, she slid around the first right turn she spotted. Disappointingly it led to a cul-de-sac. Before she had the chance to curse herself she noticed a dirt path running off to the left behind several houses. The tires gripped the loose gravel creating a cloud of smoke as she drove on. She could only hope it would settle down before Geoffrey spotted it.

Now they drove at a normal speed through the neighborhood. Ethan kept his eyes glued behind them. He never saw Geoffrey's hummer. Nearby police sirens wailed. He figured Geoffrey had ditched the pursuit once the sirens approached. He wanted to avoid the police as much as Ethan. Now there was a new danger ahead. It would only be a matter of time before they were caught.

Soon roadblocks would be set up on all major roads. If they kept to side streets they had a chance of missing them. Ethan was unfamiliar with the area. His navigation would suffer tremendously. He decided not to ask Caroline how familiar she was. Instead, he instructed her to stop the car. She pulled over in front of a driveway and looked over at him.

"We can't keep driving around like this, it's too dangerous."

"So, what do we do?"

Ethan was quiet for a moment as he formulated an idea. He did not want her running from the police. It would make her as guilty as they thought he was. He thought splitting up would be the best option, but thought about Geoffrey. He was out there somewhere and there was no way to know where. If he let her go by herself she could be vulnerable. Ethan could not allow her to get hurt. Nor could he risk her giving away his position.

"We need to change places."

"What?"

"Get out, let me drive."

"I think I can handle driving."

"It's not that. I don't want you running from the cops. If we get caught you can claim that I kidnapped you and kept you with me."

"That's not true. I won't say that."

"If you admit you've been helping me they will charge you on aiding and abetting. I'm wanted for murder. You don't want to go down that road."

Caroline was silent for a moment. The engine rumbled lightly. In the distance, Ethan could still hear the sirens wailing. He was starting to get nervous. They needed to leave the area as soon as possible. "Fine," she said as she climbed out of the car. Quickly they changed places and Ethan moved the car slowly down the street.

They skipped several major roads on the back streets until they came to a dead end. They had no choice. Ethan doubled back towards the main road and turned right on Court Street. Up ahead a large green sign told him the beaches were straight ahead. He hoped they could get back to the marina without incident. Ahead the road seemed clear of police. It seemed as if everything would work out.

Court Street curved sharply to the right. When it straightened out Ethan's heart thudded so hard in his chest he thought he was having a heart attack. At the next intersection two police cruisers were parked blocking the road. One officer stood by his cruiser while the other stopped each car checking it thoroughly. Caroline looked at Ethan with a sick and worried look on her face. She said something, but Ethan did not hear it. He was deep in thought.

There was no turning around. It would draw attention and the officers would be on his tail. More than likely they were aware of the make and model of the car, and maybe even the license plate number. If they drove through the checkpoint he would be stopped. Most likely the officer would draw his weapon. If he tried to run there was high chance either of being shot. There was no turn offs, no side roads, only one way through. They were left with no choice.

The oncoming lane was clear. After they moved forward towards the barricade Ethan whipped the wheel to the left and accelerated. At first, the officers were caught off guard. They spun around to stare at the Impala barreling towards them. When they were within just a few yards both officers drew their weapons. Ethan heard one of them yell to stop the vehicle.

Just as he reached the checkpoint they opened fire. Several rounds dug into the hood. One bounced off the street just missing a tire. One more broke through the windshield and buried into the dashboard. Caroline let out a scream and Ethan flinched as they rushed past the officers. He knew luck had been on their side when neither of them was shot. He could only hope they were aiming to disable the vehicle and not to kill.

The two officers bolted into their vehicles and chased after Ethan. The chase had to end fast. If the chase lasted too long a police helicopter would be dispatched. Once it was in the air their chances of escape would be slim.

He veered around several cars, but the cruisers stayed right on his tail. No doubt they were radioing for backup. By now they would have run his plates. They knew exactly who they were chasing. Within minutes they would be pulling out all the stops. Ethan struggled to think quickly.

Another cruiser was racing towards him in the oncoming lane. Ethan knew the officers' next move would be to stop his car in the center of the road making it harder for him to pass. Before the officer could create the blockade Ethan zipped by. The two cruisers negotiated the maneuver with the same amount of grace.

"How can we get off this road? I need to get closer to the beach." He yelled.

"Keep going straight. The bridge ahead will lead to Clearwater Beach."

"OK."

He pushed the car as fast as it would go. Only a handful of cars traveled on the same road and Ethan navigated through them with ease. Unfortunately, the cruisers never left his tail. His palms began to sweat and his heart beat faster. A lone cruiser began to sneak up behind him. Any moment he would ram Ethan's bumper. They would try the same P.I.T. maneuver Ethan had done several days ago. To him, it felt like months.

Ethan darted into oncoming traffic to avoid the cruiser and none of them followed. They stayed close and followed from the right lane. He dodged several cars before cutting back across to the right. Caroline pointed out the bridge just ahead. His foot was already touching the floor. He pressed harder as if it would help. He needed more horsepower. There was no way of outrunning the police in his car. He needed a plan.

"Caroline, check for helicopters."

She craned her neck to look out every possible window.

"I don't see anything."

"Not yet, but they'll be here soon. We need to end this!"

They barreled across the bridge. Red and blue lights flashed across shortly behind him. The vehicles ahead began to pull over to the side of the road to give room. From the top of the bridge, Ethan could see for several yards. Ahead to the left sat the marina they had been earlier that day. Across the water, he spotted a neighborhood. Each home sat on the edge of the bay. Docks jutted from every one. He decided to head for them.

They hurdled towards a roundabout and Caroline seemed to tense up with a look of worry on her face. Ethan cracked a slight grin. He would use it his advantage. Letting off the gas as he approached he flung the wheel to the left. The back tires slid out, but he quickly regained control. With a minor correction of the wheel, he was straight again. The cruiser on his tail slowed down to a safe speed in order to make the turn. They were not going to risk injuring themselves to make it. They could also not risk hitting any of the other vehicles still using the roundabout.

Ethan had done well, but his work was not over. The first left turn was a road called Frist Street. He jutted left and took it. Up ahead sat the cluster of homes he had seen from the bridge. The yards were small and there was not enough distance between them to drive through. Before he abandoned his plan he noticed a small parking lot just before the row of houses. It was clear enough to see the bay and the marina was far in the background. He gripped the wheel tighter as he powered straight for it.

"Pull your arms in, don't brace," he yelled as they entered the parking lot. She pulled her arms into her chest. If she braced against the dashboard the impact could snap her arms like toothpicks. Seconds later the silver Impala slipped over the grass and crashed through the low concrete wall. Water exploded around the Impala covering all the windows. They could no longer see. Caroline began to panic as water pooled around their ankles.

"Listen to me Caroline," he said as he unbuckled her seat belt followed by his. She reached for the door, but he gripped her hand. "Just relax. Take slow, deep breaths. Trust me." With a panicked look, she took deep, sharp breaths. As the water rose to her knees she seemed to panic more, but never stopped breathing.

Ethan continued to breathe as he held her hand. He watched as the ocean slipped over the windshield and they made their way towards the bottom. Water rose up to their abdomen. Seconds later it was up to their shoulders. Still, they continued to breathe. Ethan could see the fear in Caroline's eyes. He said nothing.

Instinctively they both took one last large breath as the water slipped over their heads. The car landed with a thud on the ocean floor. Ethan gripped her hand and pointed to his door. She watched as Ethan calmly opened it. He then turned back to her and pointed at hers. Quickly she pushed open her door. Before she could swim to the surface he swam around the hood of the car and gripped her hand again. He pointed towards the empty abyss motioning for her to follow. She looked confused but followed closely behind him.

***

The two cruisers which had been close on Ethan's tail pulled to a stop in the parking lot. Both climbed out as two more cruisers arrived. They stared at the broken bit of wall where the Impala had crashed through. In astonishment, they called for backup.

Several minutes later a helicopter was in the air hovering directly over the area. More officers showed up and locked the area down. Barricades were set up on the neighborhood street. A dive crew was called along with a crane. While they waited a large unit of officers started working their way down the line of houses.

They pounded on the doors and explained a fugitive was in the area. Their homes needed to be searched. Not a single person protested. The officers checked the homes from top to bottom. No stone was left unturned. When nothing was found they moved to the next. The street ended in a dead end. If they had somehow climbed back onto land and made a run for it there was nowhere for them to go. If they doubled back the checkpoint would catch them. If they were taking shelter in one of the homes they would be caught. It was only a matter of time.

Forty-five minutes later the dive crew and crane arrived. The four-man team sank to the bottom of the ocean and investigated the vehicle. The doors were wide open, but the car was empty. The driver and passenger had survived the crash. When they surfaced they helped connect the cables from the crane to the chassis. The crane lifted the car from the depth with ease. As it broke the surface water rushed from every crack. Each officer stood in disbelief at the empty vehicle. Moments later the search team returned empty-handed.

Detective Jackson arrived on the scene in time to see the empty Impala placed on dry land. He was quickly brought up to speed. Glancing around he could not tell where they had gone. He began to instruct the officers to start searching every neighborhood and every house.

"If they're here you're damn sure we'll find them." He said as the officers split into groups. Detective Jackson stared out at the water wondering where Ethan and Caroline had gone.

Chapter 27

Before the helicopter arrived on scene Ethan and Caroline had kicked and stroked beneath the surface heading away from the wreck. Their lungs burned as they finally reached their destination. A large white hull appeared above their heads and they began to rise. Ethan placed his hand on it and pushed towards the back end. Both Caroline and Ethan breached the surface gasping wildly for air. As quick as they could manage they caught their breath. Caroline could now see they were back at the stern of the boat. Ethan looked over at her and gave a smile.

"We're home," he said as he pulled himself up. Water poured off his body. Once he had hoisted Caroline aboard the police helicopter swooped across the bay. The blades cut noisily through the air as it hovered over the ocean where they had been. A spray of water spread out in a large circle under the downdraft. Without a moment's thought, they burst through the cabin door and shut it. With their clothes dripping over the carpet they took a seat at the table exhausted.

Ethan pushed apart the blinds and stared across the bay. He could see the officers splitting off into small units and searching the homes. Exactly as he thought they would. Any moment a crane and dive team would arrive to retrieve the wreckage. Most of the officers were probably hoping for a body. He could only hope they would not think to check the marina. For the next few hours, the whole area would be on lockdown giving them nowhere to go. He could not help but feel trapped, though he refrained from telling Caroline. There was no telling which direction they would search. All it would take was one witted officer to point out the marina was a good hiding spot. The distance between the wreck site and the boat seemed incredible. He hoped they would believe it was too far.

He sat back and stared across the table. Caroline's hair was matted against her face and her clothes were soaked. She crossed her arms across her body and shivered. Droplets of water ran from her hair and down her cheeks like tears. Ethan could not help but feel sorry for her.

"Your luggage was in the trunk wasn't it?"

She nodded.

"Sorry."

"Now we're even."

"What?"

"You didn't have a change of clothes either. Now we're even."

She laughed quietly as she shivered. Ethan stood and walked over to her side of the table. She slid over exposing the wet bench. He sat down next to her and wrapped his arm around her. It was not much, but he hoped it would help warm her up. Then Ethan realized she might not have been cold, but rather in shock. She just ran from the police, was shot at, crashed into the ocean, and felt as if she would drown. It was a lot for someone to take in. Now she was probably afraid the police would bust down the door at any moment. The thought was definitely on his mind.

"Are you OK?"

"I'm fine."

"Are you cold?"

"I don't think so."

"I think you might be in shock. Try and take deep breaths and relax."

Caroline started to breathe short, quick breaths. At first, it seemed as if she would hyperventilate. Eventually, it evened out and she started to breathe normally again. Moments later tears rolled down her cheeks and she buried her face in Ethan's chest. He held her tight.

He felt awful. All of this was his fault. Every emotion she was feeling was because of him. He dragged her into this. There was nothing he could do to take it all back. In that moment he started to think about turning himself in. If it would save Caroline from more pain it would be worth it. Valerie and Pierce slid back into his mind and he realized he could not risk their safety. Although Geoffrey was away from Miami he could not guarantee there was not another person back home watching them. For all, Ethan knew he had a backup waiting for the order.

Caroline pulled her head away and wiped off her tears. She looked up at Ethan and smiled. "I'm sorry," she said as she lifted her head. He told her not to worry about it. "I'm going to go lay down on the bed for a bit. Do you mind?"

"Of course not."

She excused herself and walked towards the room. Once she stepped inside she slid closed the accordion door. He listened as she rustled around for a moment. There was a loud plop as she dropped her wet clothes to the floor. Ethan sat there staring at the door imagining her wet and naked just beyond the threshold. Again he felt the familiar mixture of arousal and shame.

Pushing the thought from his mind he slid to the window and peered out again. The officers were still hard at work checking from house to house. Finally, the dive team showed up followed by the crane. He watched as the divers prepped and fell into the ocean. Within seconds everyone would know they survived the crash.

Ethan stared as the crane hoisted the dented Impala from the depths. Water gushed from the hood. Both doors hung open flapping as the crane pulled the car back to shore. A small team of crime scene investigators picked the car apart once it was on the ground. He thought they looked like vultures in lab coats.

A plain clothes detective moved about barking orders. When the search teams came back he threw his arms up in the air. He then turned back and motioned towards the streets farther away. Ethan smiled wide. It seemed they thought Ethan and Caroline had doubled back towards the neighborhood. Several cruisers blasted down the street to create a barricade. Now he knew they were safe, at least for the moment. With each passing minute, the police drifted farther and farther away from their location. They would search as long as they could, but eventually they would give up and declare them still at large.

Now he was able to relax a bit. No one showed any interest in the marina just across the bay. Not that he could blame them. Looking at the distance they had swum underwater it seemed impossible.

The helicopter pulled away and headed off back towards the heliport. He was relieved to see it go. He stood up and walked to the bedroom door. With his ear pressed against it, he could hear her breathing quietly. He smiled and walked back to the table.

A brief moment of panic took him as he reached into his pocket. The pay by the minute phone was soaked. The screen did not light up and it would not power on. He cursed himself for not leaving it behind. The back came off easy enough and he pried the battery out. There was no way of knowing if it would be all right, but he thought he would try. He left the components on the table hoping for it to dry out. It was his only line back to Valerie and Pierce. If something new developed he would have no way of knowing.

Once more he dared a glance out the window. The police cruisers were all but gone. He started to pace in the cabin, his clothes dripped as he walked. He assumed Caroline was fast asleep. He decided it was time to slip out of his clothes and try to dry off.

He kicked off his shoes first then peeled off his socks. His pants were dropped next. Followed by his shirt. He now stood in the cabin in only his boxers. He fought the vulnerable feeling and dropped his clothes on the counter. It would be better than wearing soggy clothes the rest of the day.

He lay down on the floor and closed his eyes. The police were moving slowly away from them. His clothes were drying and Caroline was fast asleep in the bedroom. Now it seemed like there was only one thing left to do. Ethan let his body relax as he drifted slowly to sleep. A few minutes later the bedroom door creaked slowly open an inch. Caroline stared at Ethan for a moment. When she was sure he was asleep she slid the door shut and lay back on the bed.

***

"He's not picking up," Pierce said as he hung up the phone. He turned back to Valerie who was sitting in front of the large, flat screen television. Breaking News flashed in the bottom left-hand corner in bold, red letters. A news anchor with perfectly combed, jet black hair sat at his desk. He was in the middle of explaining the events on the coast of western Florida. He explained Ethan's involvement in a high-speed chase which ended with his vehicle wrecked at the bottom of the bay.

"When authorities removed the wreckage from the ocean Ethan was nowhere to be found. It isn't clear at this time whether Ethan and his unidentified passenger survived the crash. There is speculation that he is still at large. Police are locking down-"

Valerie muted the television as she looked back at Pierce. "They think he might still be alive," she said with tears in her eyes. Pierce did not know what to say. He sat down next to his wife and put an arm around her.

"I'm sure he is. Your brother is a smart man. And he's very resourceful."

Valerie said nothing.

"I can't reach him, though. I don't know what to do. I can't figure any of this out without him."

"Why not?" She said rubbing her eyes.

"I'm not a cop. I can't go around investigating anything. One of the suspects is Ethan's boss. What am I supposed to do with that?"

"If only there was another cop who could help us."

Pierce smiled wide and kissed Valerie hard. "That's a great idea," he said as he stood up and pulled his cell phone from his pocket. He dialed Brad Forester's number and waited. A few short seconds later he heard Brad answer.

"Brad it's Pierce."

"Hey, Pierce. I was just watching the news. How's Valerie?"

"About as good as she can be. Listen, we need to talk."

"What can I do for you?"

"What if I told you that I have evidence that might help prove Ethan's innocence and implicates somebody in the department?"

"I would be very interested to see something like that."

"Ethan did not do what they say he did. I think I can figure out who did."

"All right, we need to meet in person."

"Head here as soon as you can."

"I will be there in less than twenty minutes."

Pierce hung up the phone and looked over at Valerie. He was smiling wide. She did not seem to share in his excitement. A scowl formed on her face. For the first time since he had known her, he was nervous.

"What are you doing?"

"We need help."

"From him? He's trying to arrest Ethan!"

"He's also the only ally we have right now."

"So what, you're just going to hand over Sandra's external to him? What if he's part of all this?"

"I'm not going to just let him have it and he's not part of this. Whether we like it or not we have to trust him. I think he's the only other person on the planet that believes Ethan is innocent. We need his help."

Valerie did not respond. She stormed out of the room and up the stairs. Pierce let her go. It was better to let her vent. As fragile as the situation was they could not risk a fight. Pierce could only hope he was not wrong about Brad.

Exactly sixteen minutes later Brad Forester arrived at their front door and he rang the doorbell. It chimed a cheery tune in the otherwise dismal home and Pierce ushered Brad inside. Brad spotted the television in the background noting they were still talking about Ethan.

"What a mess."

"It is. Before we get started, Brad, did the DNA test come back yet?"

"Actually, I am expecting that sometime today. They will call my cell when the results are in. Now, about this evidence."

"I have an external hard drive that belonged to Sandra Delano. On the drive is all kinds of information about a few officers. All of them are implicated in theft and illegal distribution of weapons and narcotics. It also mentions a man named Greene."

Brad seemed to perk up at the mention of the name.

"Did Sandra know who he was?"

Pierce shook his head.

"No, she didn't. There were two men on the list that might surprise you."

"Let me guess, Geoffrey Hunt and Derrick White?"

Pierce was shocked, his mouth hung open in surprise. He did not expect Brad to already know. He watched as Brad reached into his pocket and pulled something out. He held it out in front of him offering it to Pierce. It was Ethan's badge with a small piece of paper tucked under the clip. He removed the slip of paper and unfolded it. Three names were listed. Greene, Hunt, and White.

"Ethan wrote it and left it with his badge."

"Where did you get this?"

"The night he ran. I found this in the airport restroom. He had thrown it away. With it was that note. He was trying to tell somebody something. I'm glad I found it. Do you have evidence implicating Derrick White?"

"Not exactly, but I can show you what we have. We need your help. We can't hand this evidence over to the police. We aren't sure who can be trusted. You're about the only person we can."

"I swear to you I will do whatever I can to help."

Pierce led Brad to his computer and pulled up the external drive. They began to go through the data. He showed him everything. Sandra's interrogations. Her trying to learn Greene's identity. The photos, the notes, and the audio files. Pierce showed him it all. When they were finished Brad sat back in disbelief.

"Well, it proves Derrick is guilty of aiding Geoffrey with the sale of weapons. I might be able to make a case out of it."

"I don't think Sandra had a warrant. I don't think you'd be able to use any of it against him."

Brad rubbed his temples and shook his head. It was clear Derrick was behind something. The way he spoke about the budget vote with Geoffrey certainly sounded as if he had something planned.

"Sandra didn't know what his plan was?"

Pierce shook his head.

"I think she was close to figuring that out when she was killed. Unfortunately, she didn't note anything else here. I'm not sure what to do next."

"We need to figure out what he's planning and stop him."

"What about Ethan?"

"We help Ethan by stopping Derrick. If we can prove he is behind any of this it gives Ethan a shot."

"If we can prove Derrick set Ethan up then he's free."

"If Derrick is behind Sandra's death or he forced Ethan into this I will make sure he spends the rest of his life in the deepest, darkest hole I can find."

Pierce nodded his head in approval. He knew he could trust Brad. It was clear in his eyes. There was an anger there that burned like embers. There was no doubt he would be true to his word. Now all they needed was proof against Derrick. Pierce did not know where they could find it.

Moments later Brad's phone rang. He answered it quickly as he stood from the desk. As he listened to the other end he paced back and forth behind Pierce. When he was finished he hung up and cleared his throat. Pierce spun around and stared at him.

"They positively identified your intruder."

"Who was it?"

"Geoffrey Hunt."

"We need to find him as fast as possible."

"I'm heading back to the station. All officers will be on the lookout. If he's still in Miami we'll find him. Once we do we can see what he knows."

"Brad, he asked where Ethan was."

"Did you tell him?"
"I had no choice."
"Shit."
"I warned Ethan he was on his way to him."
"You have contact with Ethan?"
"Well I did, but not anymore."
Brad looked at him, concerned.
"What happened?"
"I have no idea."

Chapter 28

Since they were not searching for him slipping from the police had been simple. The majority of their efforts were focused on finding Ethan McCormick. Geoffrey had heard the sirens grow louder, then race in the other direction. It was clear Ethan had been spotted.

At first, he had been angry. He had let Ethan get away and he would probably be captured. If they did there would be no chance of getting near him. Geoffrey sulked to the nearest bar. It was a dark and smoked filled room with very few patrons. It was the perfect place to lay low.

As he ordered a drink he spotted the flat screen on the far wall. The news silently flashed. With the Closed Caption on he had read about a police chase which had concluded. Then he had seen something that made him grin. The chase had been with suspect Ethan McCormick of the Miami Police Department. His current status was still at large.

When his drink had finally come he sipped at it while staring at the television. Eventually, they had given the exact location where Ethan had driven into the bay. He downed the rest of his rum and coke. As he felt the warmth slip down his throat he slapped a twenty down on the bar counter. With haste, he rushed from the bar. He headed towards the neighborhood where he had left his Hummer.

Less than an hour later he was scoping the area where Ethan had last been seen. He decided to play it safe and stayed on the opposite side of the bay from where Ethan had crashed. The search units had long since moved on and the reporters had all dispersed. Several blocks away the streets were still being blocked off. It would only be a matter of time before they admitted defeat and called off the search.

Geoffrey went over the details of the crash in his mind. Ethan's vehicle had crashed over the wall and sank to the bottom of the bay. He could see the damaged wall from where he was. He remembered the doors were wide open as the car was hoisted from the water. Obviously, no bodies had been recovered. Somehow Ethan and his new friend had slipped away. He was cleverer than Geoffrey had given him credit for. He decided he got lucky. He could not bear the thought of giving Ethan credit for something.

From his current position, he could see the whole bay. A few yards in front of him sat a small marina where several large boats rocked with the waves. Beyond the marina was the large body of water Ethan had crashed into. He tried to imagine Ethan and Caroline swimming away from the wrecked vehicle. There were only a couple places they could have reached in one breath. The most likely place was the neighborhood. It could not be the direction they had gone if the police were still coming up empty handed.

Other than the marina in front of him there was a small bridge that separated the bay from the Gulf of Mexico. It was close enough. They may have reached it in one breathe. However, there was not much cover. It would have left them entirely exposed. From there they would have had to climb the bridge to get to the mainland. At the time of the crash, everything beyond the bridge had been blocked off. If an officer did not spot them the helicopter would have.

Beyond the bridge was Clearwater Beach. The water from the bridge sliced between the two islands like a knife. It was possible they had come up under the bridge then continued to the beach. Geoffrey did not think this was very likely. Again it would have left them too exposed. Again the helicopter would have spotted them for sure.

The only location left was the marina in front of him. He looked at the distance from the crash site. The distance seemed incredible. There was a possibility they made it, but it was slim. Without conditioning and only one breathe it seemed impossible they could have made it. He decided the best option was the neighborhoods like the police had thought. It was the only possible location. Somehow they had climbed ashore and moved through the neighborhoods, dodging detection. By now they could be anywhere.

Still sitting behind the wheel of his Hummer he leaned forward. The police searches were several blocks away now. It was obvious they would not find anything. The day was getting late. The sun was starting to droop towards the horizon. Soon the store, whose parking lot he was currently using, would close. He would have to leave or risk suspicion.

He needed a place to stay for the night. There would be no hunting for Ethan while the police were all stirred up. He could not chance brining any attention to himself. The marina seemed a perfect place to store his car among all the others. People had parked their cars and set sail on their yachts for the weekend. Another one sitting silently in the lot would draw no attention.

Geoffrey fired up the engine. As it rumbled he slowly pulled away from the store and made his way to the marina. He made sure to park facing towards the water. The windows were tinted well enough to keep him hidden, but the windshield would not. He wanted to be cautious.

As he sat staring at the calm ocean the police lights in the distance practically disappeared. He pulled out his phone and searched for any news stories about Ethan. The car crash was still the top story. No news about Ethan being found. He was out there somewhere and Geoffrey knew he would find him.

The phone buzzed once and went still. He glanced at the number. It was Greene. Is Ethan dead? The text read. Geoffrey rolled his eyes as he replied back not yet. Before he could put the phone down the reply came through. Finish this now. Ignoring it he slipped the phone back in his pocket.

Greene was getting anxious. Ethan had been on the run for three days now. By now he should have been dead. He did not know why Greene was so worried. Ethan had no clue who he was and probably knew nothing about him. So why was he in such a panic? If anyone should have been worried it should be Geoffrey. Ethan had watched him kill McKinley in cold blood. Geoffrey would go to prison for life if Ethan was not stopped. It was clear the issue was not a main concern for Greene. None of it could be traced back to him. They had never met in person and he did not know his identity. There was nothing Geoffrey could do to bring him down. Not yet.

His mind wandered at the thought of confronting Greene. Once he was dead there would be no one left to blackmail him. He could finally live in peace. Whatever evidence Greene had he would see to it that it was destroyed. When it was taken care of he would take a long vacation. Maybe go down to Brazil. He always had a weakness for dark skinned women.

The sun started to sink fast as Geoffrey shut his eyes. He figured he would pass the time with a short nap to regain his strength. He thought about Brazil, relaxing on the beach with a cocktail in one hand and a woman on his arm. Together they would watch the sunset. When it was dark they would head back to his penthouse and spend the evening together. In his dream, the woman wore the smallest bikini he had ever seen. Just as they began to climb into bed he sat up.

He looked around, dazed for a moment. Then he remembered he was still inside his Hummer. The humidity was almost unbearable. His body was drenched in sweat and it was getting harder to breathe. The sun was still above the horizon, but sinking fast. When darkness finally fell he would continue with his search.

For the moment he needed air. He climbed out of his vehicle and started down the docks. The cool sea breeze felt good on his warm skin. He could hear the soft slap of the water against the boats. All around him they rose and fell softly. At the end of the short pier, he sat on the edge with his feet just above the water. Looking down at his reflection he could see he was noticeably tired. Not just sleepy, but exhausted. He wanted the whole ordeal behind him. It had pushed him to the brink of pure exhaustion chasing Ethan across the state. The stress was almost too much to handle. As he sat on the deck trying to relax his mind raced with the thought of

Ethan's location. He hoped the end was near. He could not take much more.

A small wave rose up and engulfed his shoes. He pulled up his feet and stood back up. He continued to walk down the boardwalk looking at each boat. Many were small fishing boats. Only a few were large enough to be called a yacht. None looked entirely fancy. They were locked up in a smaller, private marina. Most of the expensive yachts would be kept on people's personal docks or at the large marina at Clearwater beach. Still, these were nice enough. He found himself wishing he owned one. Sailing the ocean for days on end would bring him peace. When everything was done he would buy a yacht. The weapons and narcotics he had sold had made him a small fortune. Since he had not spent a dime he would have plenty to spare. There was enough money to buy a rather large one and leave Miami behind for a few days.

He smiled as he walked by the boats. The thought of owning one glistened in his mind. Something in the corner of his eye caught his attention. One of the boats on the farthest stretch of dock floated quietly in the water like the rest, but something was different. There was a small window near the bow. Curtains had been drawn across, but there was the distinct glow of a light from between the slight crack. Someone was there. He looked around and noticed it was the only one in use. It roused his curiosity. It seemed strange a person would stay onboard while tied to the dock. Maybe if it was a houseboat. It seemed very suspicious. He decided to investigate.

***

Ethan woke up on the floor of the boat. His clothes were still draped over the counter. They looked slightly damp, but for the most part dry. He could handle damp clothes.

He stood up tall and stretched his limbs. Forgetting he was only in his underwear he walked back to the table and peered out the window. The sun hung just above the horizon. He had slept longer than he thought. The flashing red and blue lights were hardly visible. For the moment they seemed safe.

He pulled away from the window and headed towards his clothes. It was then he noticed the door to the bedroom was pulled back. The overhead light was beaming out. Caroline cleared her throat as she stared at him from the bed. Now he was fully aware how naked he felt and his hand bolted for his clothes.

He could hear her giggle as he pulled on his pants and shirt. With a nervous smile, he looked over at her. She sat on the bed with her clothes back on. They looked dry enough. She motioned for him to come sit on the bed with her. Hiding his embarrassment he walked over to her and sat on the end of the bed. For a moment they said nothing. They sat in silence and stared into each other's eyes. Ethan fought the urge to lean in and kiss her. She had been dragged into a stressful situation. The last thing he wanted to do was take advantage of her.

She smiled as if reading his mind. Ethan returned it. It calmed him down and took his stress away. Somehow sitting on the bed just sharing a moment with another person made him feel much better. He could not imagine how he would have felt had he been alone. The image of the gun in the end table crept up on his mind and he realized she had saved him. To what extent he was not sure, but she had given him reason to live. There was a reason to not be reckless. There was another life in his hands. If he flew off the handle it would endanger her. She was keeping him grounded. He started to wonder if Sandra had somehow sent her as a way to protect him. The thought was enough to comfort him.

Caroline finally broke the silence. "I tried to come out of the room earlier, but you were sleeping. I didn't want to wake you."

"I'm sorry. I didn't mean to make you stay in the room all alone. You should have woken me."

"I think you needed the rest. Especially after everything you've been through."

"Well then thank you."

"Of course," she said giving him a coy smile. For a moment it looked as if her eyes darted across his body. He was not sure if he should say anything or not. Was she flirting with him? Was she just being friendly? He could not tell. He did not dare risk it. Instead, he smiled back at her. When she looked over at the window with the curtain drawn he chanced a look at her body. Another smiled formed on her lips as she turned her head back.

"I saw that."

"Saw what?"

"Oh, please Ethan. Men are terrible at hiding it. You have no idea how to subtly check out a woman."

"No, I wasn't...I mean...I was...but not-"

"It's all right Ethan. Look all you want. It won't hurt me."

With that, she got up from the bed and walked towards the table. Her hips swayed back and forth as she did. She looked back at him over her shoulder and smiled.

They both laughed as Ethan stood up. Now he understood she was trying to keep him relaxed. She had no idea how relaxed he had become.

He joined her at the table letting out a sigh. She looked up at him with a troubled expression. "What is it?" She asked with genuine concern in her voice.

"We were supposed to pick up supplies and we left them behind."

"We would have lost them any way I think."

"Good point."

"I know."

Again she smiled.

"Well, it's all right, Ethan. I'm not really hungry. Besides now's as good a time as any to start a diet."

They both laughed and Ethan said, "I think you are fine the way you are." Caroline smiled but did not respond. Now she glanced out the window. The sun was almost ready to slip behind the horizon. Off in the distance, she caught a faint strobe of red and blue lights. They seemed so distant now. In the short amount of time, they had been laying low they had moved far. It put her mind at ease.

Just outside the boat, they heard the dock creak quietly followed by the soft sound of a footstep. They both froze in horror as they listened. Ethan's first thought ran to Geoffrey. He wondered if somehow he had found them. It seemed impossible. The police did not even think to check the marina. Why would he? If it was Geoffrey he must have stumbled across them by accident. There was the chance the police found them which scared him just as much.

He motioned for Caroline to stay seated while he investigated. The sound had stopped, but it had been clear. Someone had been there. Ethan looked out the window facing the dock. He saw nothing, but there was something just as unsettling. Wet footprints led to the side of the boat. Just short of the deck they vanished. Someone was onboard with them.

Ethan turned back towards Caroline and told her to go in the room and lock the door. She sat motionless at first. Ethan said it again. This time she could see the seriousness in his eyes. At once she stood up and silently walked to the room. When the accordion door had slid shut Ethan spun on his heel and headed for the cabin door. He needed to know who was out there. There was no chance it was the owner. They would not sneak onboard their own boat.

He pressed his back against the wall next to the cabin door. It was the same accordion style as the bedroom. It would be noisy to open, but Ethan had no choice. With his left arm, he slid the door open and stood there still pressed against the wall. For three minutes nothing happened. With his hands balled into fists and his heart racing he spun around and stepped out onto the deck.

In the darkness, he saw nothing. He wondered if someone had only walked by, though he knew that was not right. The footprint had ended right at the deck and someone had climbed aboard. Ethan could see the whole stern from his location. There was nowhere for someone to hide, not in front of him. Then he realized next to the cabin was a narrow walkway that led to the bow. There was a second deck where the pilot drove the craft. He was sure no one was up there. They would have most likely heard them walking around. The only option was next to the cabin.

He began to spin around, but it was too late. Something hit him hard from behind. He sprawled out across the deck, barely keeping himself from sliding off the back and into the water. He rolled over to see Geoffrey tower over him. In his hand was a suppressed Berretta and it was pointed right at him. There was anger in Geoffrey's eyes and Ethan knew his time was almost up. In a matter of seconds, he would squeeze the trigger.

Geoffrey did pull the trigger, but the shot went high splashing into the ocean. Caroline had flung herself against his back and they both tumbled to the deck. The gun slid from his hand towards the edge of the boat. Ethan scrambled to grab it but missed. It slipped into the dark ocean and sank quickly to the bottom.

With great force, Geoffrey flung Caroline from his back and she landed with a hard thud on the deck. The air was forced from her lungs and she began to gasp. Now Ethan and Geoffrey stood eye to eye. Ethan raised his fists in defense. There was not much room on the deck to properly block an attack. It had to end quickly before Geoffrey could get the upper hand. He cursed himself for missing the gun.

Geoffrey lunged at him and Ethan leaped forward. They collided nearly knocking each other over and Caroline coughed on the deck behind them. Geoffrey grasped Ethan by the throat and landed three punches to his cheek before he was able to slip free. With his jaw on fire, he threw his elbow directly into the middle of his chest. Geoffrey yelled out in pain as he stumbled backward. Ethan attempted a right hook to the side of his face, but Geoffrey dodged it in time.

With Ethan off balance Geoffrey tackled him to the deck. Ethan blocked several shots before one slipped through pounding him in the shoulder. He was able to hook his knee up under Geoffrey's leg and thrust up with all of his force. His knee landed in the center of his groin and Geoffrey tumbled forward off of him. In one swift move, Ethan was back on his feet followed shortly by Geoffrey. Behind Ethan, Caroline was finally breathing normal again. As she slowly climbed to her feet Ethan stepped in front of her like a shield.

Geoffrey lunged forward grabbing Ethan at the midsection. The two men flew backward into the cabin. Caroline barely dodged them as they went. They rolled around on the floor each trying to gain the upper hand. They exchanged blows until they wrestled free of one another. Back on his feet, Ethan delivered his knee to Geoffrey's stomach. As he bent over in pain, crying out, Ethan slammed his head against the table. The skin just above his eyebrow broke and a thin stream of blood ran down to his lip.

It only seemed to fill Geoffrey with rage. He swung wildly at Ethan, but he dodged each strike. Ethan tried to hit back, but Geoffrey blocked every blow. A rope appeared from behind Geoffrey and wrapped tightly around his throat. Caroline pressed her foot in the small of his back and pulled the two ends together as tight as she could. He began to choke and grasp wildly at the rope. Before Ethan could help Geoffrey had twisted his lower body causing Caroline to lose balance. Her foot slipped out of his back and the rope slackened. He tore it free from his neck and grasped it tight in his right hand. He threw his left hand out for a jab. She tried to parry, but it was too late. The hit caught her in the chest and she stumbled backward. The table was just behind her and she toppled over slamming her head on the edge. Ethan yelled out as he rushed Geoffrey.

A punch to Geoffrey's cheek threw him off balance. The next hit landed below the rib cage. Before he recovered Ethan wrapped both arms over his right shoulder and pulled him into his knee. It connected with the center of his chest. Ethan repeated this two more times before Geoffrey began to stumble backward.

Ethan followed him out on the deck. With a kick in the stomach, he gripped the rope and pulled it free from Geoffrey's hand. He had not toppled over despite the beating he had taken from Ethan, but he looked weakened. He took advantage of this and grasped Geoffrey's right arm wrapping the rope around it. He was about to force him to the floor and tie the other hand when Geoffrey flung his head forward. His forehead connected with Ethan's. White hot pain shot through Ethan's skull as he fell backward dizzy.

Before he could see straight again Geoffrey had wrapped the rope tight around his neck. The other end he tied to the side rail of the boat. "Goodbye, Ethan." He said as he tossed him over the side. Splashing down in the water the rope tightened. The rope squeezed his neck holding him just below the surface. In sheer panic, Ethan grabbed at the rope trying to pry himself free.

On the deck, Geoffrey caught his breath and turned back towards the cabin. The woman inside was just beginning to stir. If he moved quickly he could choke the life from her before she got up. Caroline slowly lifted her head as Geoffrey approached. He could not help but feel pleased. Ethan would strangle or drown and soon the woman would be dead too. Finally, things were starting to look up. Soon he would be on his way home to finally take down Greene and be free.

With a knee on either side of her body he reached down and grasped her neck. As he squeezed he wondered if he should have some fun with her first. She was a gorgeous woman. He thought about removing her clothes before killing her. Perhaps killing her in the nude would be fun. He decided against it and continued to choke Caroline.

Under the water, Ethan was in a fierce panic. It felt as if needles were protruding through his lungs as he struggled for air. The rope felt as if it would collapse his esophagus at any moment. Desperately he tried to pry the rope from his throat. It was tied to the boat keeping it secure around his neck. He knew his only chance would be to climb back onboard.

He could feel darkness closing around him as he thrashed his arms out of the water reaching for the banister. His first attempt missed. On the second try, he gripped it, but his fingers slipped. With one last thrust using all of his energy he wrapped his hand around the banister and pulled. His head was lifted from the water and the rope loosened. Immediately air choked into his lungs and he began to cough. With his last bit of strength, he rolled over the side and back on the deck. He lay on his back staring at the sky and coughed violently.

Geoffrey rolled his eyes and let go of Caroline. She too began to choke as she inhaled. She had been so close to death. He had seen it in her eyes. But Ethan posed the biggest threat. The woman was easy enough, but not Ethan. He needed to kill him before he gained the upper hand again. He marched outside to see Ethan on his hands and knees struggling to stand. He flailed out his foot and kicked him in the ribs. The force sent him onto his back and he groaned in pain. There was no energy left in him to fight. Pulling himself from the abyss had drained what little he had left. Now he could barely move.

As Geoffrey roughed Ethan up in anger Caroline began to stand. Adrenaline pumped through her veins. Almost instantly she forgot about the pain in her lungs and her throat. Fight or flight had kicked in and she could feel the strong urge to fight. She had never felt the urge so strong in her life. The painful cries from Ethan only encouraged her.

Desperately she searched the cabin for anything she could use as a weapon. She flung open cabinets and found nothing useful. The first two drawers she pulled open were useless. When her hands gripped a third drawer she ripped it open. Sitting in the center of the drawer shining like treasure rested a gutting knife. She held back the urge to celebrate as she snatched it up. Outside she found Geoffrey's back turned to her with Ethan facing towards her in a headlock. She leaped forward and sliced the back of his thigh. Geoffrey screamed in pain as the knife tore open his flesh. Blood oozed over the deck.

He dropped Ethan and turned around limping as he did. She swung the knife at his face, but he caught her arm and bent it back. The knife fell from her grasp and fluttered across the deck. He paid no attention to it as he grabbed her by the throat. He slammed her body to the deck and flung a fist into her chest. She cried out in pain, but he held his hand over her mouth. Again he slammed his fist into her chest. He listened to her muffled cries soaking them in with glee. Tears streamed out of her eyes as he delivered the next blow to her midsection.

Before Geoffrey had time to react something cold pressed against the right side of his throat just under the chin. It was yanked backward with great force. The pronged tip dug into his throat and severed the artery. A large chunk of flesh came off with the knife as blood poured freely down his side. He choked and grasped at his neck. Geoffrey collapsed on the deck and held his wound as blood spurted from it.

Ethan was aware he had only minutes to live. He did not have long to get the information he needed. There was no use saving him. He was already gone. Before he wanted to see Geoffrey rot in prison for everything he had done. But seeing Geoffrey ruthlessly beat Caroline had sparked hatred inside him. He had grabbed the knife and went straight for the throat.

Ethan crouched down directly in Geoffrey's face. He could smell the sick coppery smell of his blood. "It was you wasn't it you son of a bitch? You killed Sandra just like you killed McKinley?" Geoffrey did not respond, but Ethan knew it was true. "You deserve to die for what you did, but if you tell me what I need to know I will call for help." Now Geoffrey nodded furiously, blood still pouring.

"Who is Greene?"

"I...don't....know..." He choked trying to speak.

"Did he send you to kill me? Did he have you kill Sandra and McKinley?"

He only nodded.

"What is Derrick planning?"

"He...he...bayside..."

He choked on the last word before his eyes shut. He was not dead, not yet. Shock had taken over his body. It would not be long before he was dead. Ethan took a step back and turned to face Caroline. "Are you OK?" He asked as he put his hands on her shoulders. She wiped tears from her eyes as she nodded slowly. "Good. We need to move him."

"Are you going to call an ambulance?"

"No."

"I thought you said you would call for help."

She spoke as if she did not care if Geoffrey died. There was a look of disgust on her face as she looked over at him. Ethan could not tell if it was because of the blood or the person.

"I said I was calling for help, not an ambulance. I will tell them where they can find the body."

With that, he searched Geoffrey's pockets. He found a small touch screen phone. When he unlocked the screen he was greeted by a text message. "Perfect," he said as he stood back up.

Chapter 29

With a firm grip on the phone, he scrolled through the text messages. There was only one text conversation open. Within it were only three messages, two from Greene and one from Geoffrey. He had been asked if Ethan had been killed. Geoffrey responded not yet. The last message told him to finish it.

I'm coming for you next, he typed. He grinned as he hit send. Slipping the phone in his pocket he turned to Caroline. "Help me bring his body into the cabin." Ethan grasped his fingers around Geoffrey's wrists. Reluctantly Caroline grabbed his feet. Together they carried the body into the cabin. They plopped the body down just before the bedroom door. Ethan found the gutting knife and tossed it on his chest.

The phone buzzed in his pocket as he closed the cabin doors behind him. Caroline stood on the deck with the moonlight reflecting off her soft skin. He took a moment to admire her beauty before pulling out the phone. Geoffrey? The response said. Furiously Ethan typed He's dead. You're next. He waited a minute but there was no response. He could only hope Greene was terrified and would be looking over his shoulder. Maybe it would make him careless. Maybe he would inadvertently give up his identity. Maybe he would call off his plans altogether.

Ethan instructed Caroline to find something to write with and some paper. After several minutes of searching, she finally found a worn-down pencil and an old receipt. Ethan quickly scratched down Greene's number. It might prove useful. Then Ethan dialed Pierce's number and waited impatiently as it rang. "Hello?" The familiar voice said.

"Hey, Pierce, it's Ethan."

"Ethan, thank God! Are you OK?"

"I'm fine."

"Listen, we know who broke into our home. It was Geoffrey Hunt."

"Yeah I know that already."

"Be careful. He's looking for you."

"Well, not anymore."

"What do you mean?"

Ethan explained what had happened only moments before. He told him he had no option but to kill him. He was not going to stop until they were dead. There was no chance of apprehending him. There was a long moment of silence on the other end.

Finally, Pierce said, "I'm sorry Ethan. I'm glad you and Caroline are all right. We were starting to worry. We could not get a hold of you. What happened to your phone?"

"Lost it in the wreck. I'm using Geoffrey's now. I won't be able to keep it. I'll have to leave it with the body."

"I understand."

"Have you learned anything else?"

"Actually," Pierce said as he switched the phone over to speaker. "Brad Forester is here with me."

Ethan's blood felt as if it turned to ice. Brad Forester was there probably trying to get information regarding his whereabouts. Ethan did not understand what Pierce was doing. He began to wonder if he was giving him up. Maybe Pierce no longer believed he was innocent. Maybe he was growing tired of it all. Ethan wondered if Pierce would do something so horrible to him.

"Ethan, it's OK," Brad said recognizing his silence as a sign of concern. "Pierce has shown me some evidence that might help absolve you. The FBI has been coming down on us to produce some results. I should advise you to turn yourself over to the authorities so we can let the courts sort the rest of this out."

"I'm not going to do that."

"Why not?"

"I still don't know who I can trust. I don't know if I should trust you. Either way, Greene is still out there. We don't know who he is. As long as he's still alive my family is in danger. Until we put a stop to all of this I can't come home. It's too dangerous."

"Ok Ethan," Brad said. "We are still trying to figure out what Derrick is up to. So far we have no leads. If he left a trail he covered it up well."

"Bayside."

"What?"

"That's what Geoffrey said before he died. I think he meant Bayside Marketplace."

"We'll look into it. Did he say what his plan was?"

"He didn't have the chance."

The cold manner in which Ethan spoke sent a chill over Pierce's spine. It did not sound like the same Ethan he knew. It was emotionless and dark. He could only hope this whole experience had not changed him for the worst.

"Don't worry. We will scope it out. If he's up to something we'll stop him."

"And Ethan," Pierce said softly. "We hope to see you soon. It's been three days. Valerie misses you. We all do."

With that, Ethan hung up. The last thing Pierce said still buzzed in his ears. He turned back to Caroline. She had been standing there listening to his conversation. He gazed into her sparkling eyes. She stared back at him with a question on her face. He knew right away she wanted to know what was next.

Without saying a word he stepped back into the cabin and rooted around in Geoffrey's pocket one last time. He pulled a wallet from his back pocket. A few bills stuck out and he snatched them up. It was not much, but it was enough to get them a place to stay and some food. He realized he was starving as he stuffed the wallet back in Geoffrey's pocket.

When he returned to the deck Caroline looked back at him still puzzled. Finally, he said, "This is almost over. I need to make a phone call." He dialed and listened as the operator picked up.

"Hello, can I please be transferred to whoever is in charge of the Ethan McCormick case...never mind who this is. I would like to remain anonymous. I have a tip that he would be very interested to hear...Of course, I will hold."

He looked at Caroline and smiled as the phone rang in his ear. She gave him a confused smile back as she waited.

"This is Detective Jackson," the voice on the other end boomed.

"Detective Jackson, nice to speak with you."
"Who is this?"
"The man you're looking for."

"Ethan McCormick? What the hell do you want?"

"First I wanted to tell you you're wasting your time trying to catch me. I'm innocent and I'm going to prove that."

"Then why are you running?"

"Long story."

"Let me bring you in. There will be plenty of time to tell it."

"I can't, my family is in danger. If I'm caught they might be killed. I need just a little more time. I promise I will make everything right."

"You didn't call just to tell me this."

"There was a man who's been trying to kill me, Geoffrey Hunt. Call the Miami Police Department and talk to a man named Brad Forester. He will tell you all about him."

"And why does any of this matter to me."

"He's dead. I wanted to tell you where the body was. Check Geoffrey's phone when you find the body. And please make that call."

With that, he hung up and looked back at Caroline. Now she looked worried. Ethan put a hand on her shoulder with a firm grip. "Everything is going to be fine. We have one thing off our back now." He said as he motioned toward Geoffrey's body in the cabin. "We're getting closer to sorting all of this out."

"But why report the body? Won't that be evidence against you?"

"It might, but it was worth the risk."

"What was?"

"I know the lead detectives name. That might come in handy. And if he makes that call he might believe me."

Caroline nodded as Ethan looked down at the phone. He wished he could keep it, but knew it was not worth the risk. Jackson would have the phone traced. There would be no safety with it around. There still had been no reply from Greene. So Ethan tossed the phone into the cabin. It bounced and skid across the floor resting at the foot of the body. Blood seeped across the floor like a small river heading straight for it. Ethan slid the cabin door shut for the last time. He turned back towards Caroline and grabbed her by the hand. "We need to move. They will be here soon."

***

They walked for several hours using side streets and avoiding major intersections. It was mainly uneventful. Every so often they heard sirens in the distance being carried by the wind, but they never spotted a squad car. Eventually, they left the city of Clearwater and found themselves in the neighboring city of Largo. It was as far as Ethan dared go. It was too much of a risk to stay on the streets while the police searched for them. It was a miracle they had not been spotted. After a couple miles, they spotted a hotel towering over a city park. He motioned for Caroline to follow him as he headed inside.

Ethan approached the front desk and explained they were on a road trip and their car had broken down. They only had cash on them and hoped they could still get a room. The woman behind the counter told him they preferred to have a card on file. Luckily they decided to accept cash under the circumstances. They were put down for one night. Check out was at eleven in the morning. The clerk asked for his driver's license and his heart nearly stopped.

"I only need to copy down your information in case there are damages to the room. Since you don't have a card on file we will mail you the bill."

He looked over at Caroline. She shrugged. Her wallet had been lost in the accident. She hoped she would be able to retrieve it once everything was over. Otherwise, it would be a pain to get all of her cards renewed, especially the license.

"Of course," he said. "But we'll be extra careful." He handed over his card and the woman made a photocopy. She gave him a smile as she returned it.

"Enjoy your stay," she said as they walked away. Ethan tried to keep the worry from his mind. The woman hardly looked at his I.D. and had tucked the paper in a file as they left. Hopefully, she did not look it over in detail and recognize the name.

As they climbed the stairs to the fifth floor Ethan began to calm his nerves. Geoffrey was dead which was a huge relief. There was no longer the overbearing threat of death looming over his head. However, the threat of arrest still plagued him. With almost every officer in the state believing he was a cop killer it would only get worse when they discovered Geoffrey's body. He hoped Jackson would make the phone call.

They found their room on the fifth floor and Ethan stepped in and looked around. It was a decent sized room with a queen sized bed stuck directly in the center. He smiled at the thought of sharing the bed again. Two windows framed a small flat screen television which faced towards the bed. The bathroom was on the left wall opposite the door. Everything was perfectly clean and almost seemed to shine.

Ethan walked to the window and peered out the curtain. Below he could see they were facing the park he spotted earlier. Later he would learn it was called Largo Central Park. From what he could see it was a beautiful park, mostly grass and sidewalks. In the distance, there was a large playground surrounded by a large black metal fence. Just ahead he could see a small pond surrounded by small trees and flowers. It seemed to be man-made. A track for a small train crossed the pond and veered away. He assumed it was a sort of child's ride.

He turned back around and watched Caroline climb into the bed. She slipped under the sheets and tossed and turned as if to rub the soft sheets over her body. She looked up at him and smiled. "It feels good to relax."

"How about something to eat? Geoffrey's treat."

She gave a half-hearted laugh as she nodded. Ethan grabbed the in room phone and dialed the front desk asking for the number to the nearest pizza delivery service. Within the hour the driver had dropped off the pizza and they were sitting on the bed together devouring the two large pizzas.

They finished both and tossed the boxes across the room. "I think I need to shower," Caroline said. "I feel gross and I probably smell." Ethan shook his head.

"You smell fine, but feel free. I think I will do the same when you're finished. Maybe we should wash our clothes tonight? They could probably use it."

"Not a bad idea. There might be a couple robes in the closet. Could you fish them out while I shower?"

Ethan said he would as she disappeared into the bathroom. Forty minutes later she came out wrapped in a towel. He left her robe on the bed and made his way into the bathroom. She had left her clothes in a pile on the tile floor. He added his clothes to it and climbed in the shower. He scrubbed his scalp with a handful of shampoo. He did this twice before grabbing the small bottle of body wash. When he was done he used the last bit of shampoo to clean their clothes. When they were rinsed out completely he left them to dry on the shower rod and threw on his robe.

With nothing but a robe, he walked out of the bathroom and sat on the end of the bed. Caroline was already under the sheet and she looked comfortable. He desperately wanted to climb under with her but refrained. He knew what was on his mind and could not act upon those feelings.

For what seemed an eternity they sat in silence as they stared into each other's eyes. Finally, she motioned for him to lay down with her. With his heart racing, he lay on top of the sheets at her side. Keeping under the covers she rolled on her side and looked at him. A hand came from under the sheets and brushed his hair out of his eyes. He smiled and she smiled back.

"You saved my life today, Ethan."

"You saved mine too, you know."

"Yeah, I guess I did didn't I?"

Her hand slipped down towards the tie on his robe and pulled. It loosened, but Ethan grabbed at it. Caroline pushed the sheets off of her body and rolled over on top of him. She was no longer wearing the robe. Her breasts swung free in front of him as she pinned him down. She brought her lips close to his and stopped.

"Either way, thank you." With that, she pressed her lips hard against his. Ethan kissed her back then quickly pulled back his head.

"Caroline, we should stop."

"Why?"

"You don't need to thank me like this. You don't owe it to me."

Caroline rolled her eyes.

"Shut up and kiss me."

Without a second thought, he wrapped his arms around her back and pulled her closer. His robe slid open and their naked bodies pressed against each other. Ethan ran his fingers across her silky smooth skin as she began to kiss his neck softly. She sat back and straddled Ethan smiling down at him. He was at a loss for words. He swept his eyes over her body and pulled her closer. They tangled themselves in the sheets sweating and panting. Together they forgot about everything they had been through. And for the first time that night they did not worry about what was to come.

***

The body had been where Ethan said it would. Detective Jackson watched as the coroner loaded it into a large black bag. When it was fully zipped it was carried to the back of a gray colored van. The bag was flung onto a metal table fastened to the wall. The gutting knife had been collected by one of the crime scene investigators and placed in a clear plastic bag. Anything else that seemed like evidence was also bagged.

He instructed the investigators not to bother searching the cabin for prints. Ethan had confessed to the crime and his prints would be found on the murder weapon. He was sure of it. Standing on the deck he looked down at a long piece of rope. It was swollen with water as if it had been pulled from the ocean. He could not help but be curious.

As the investigation wrapped up he instructed everyone to keep him informed with everything regarding the scene. If Ethan's prints were found on the knife, like he knew they would be, he wanted to hear about it right away. The identification in the man's wallet had named him as Geoffrey Hunt. The name did not sound familiar, but Ethan had told him to get in touch with a man named Brad Forester. He said he would explain everything.

Jackson climbed behind the wheel of his white unmarked cruiser and stared out the windshield. He was unsure if he should trust Ethan and make the call. Maybe there was some useful information he could gain. And it was probably time to consult with them about their fugitive anyway. He shook his head and questioned himself. He's a cop killer, why would I trust him? He thought.

Earlier the news had made a statement regarding previously unheard information. A forensic unit had recovered Ethan's personal computer from his home. A document had come to light with some disturbing evidence. Ethan had written a suicide note and it proved he was unstable and unpredictable. Maybe he was on the run hoping another officer would put him down. Maybe it was his way of ending it all. Maybe he could not do it himself. Now he was looking to force someone's hand.

According to the official statements his girlfriend had committed suicide while the two of them were on vacation. She had thrown herself from their hotel balcony. The media described it as a severe mental breakdown. The stress of work finally caught up with her. Her job in internal affairs pulled her in multiple directions. They speculated Ethan blamed her superior, Major McKinley. It explained why Ethan gunned him down in the street. The man had to be stopped. He had lost all touch with reality. For all Jackson knew the body now being hauled away belonged to the owner of the boat. He may have come out to check on his boat and found Ethan stashed away. Ethan panicked and grabbed the knife. Now they were hauling a body away and like an idiot, Jackson was on the verge of trusting him.

Then he started to think about the suicide note. If he truly wanted to die why was he running? Why not get into a firefight with the police and force them to kill you? Why try and stay alive? Why run? It did not make sense. As far as Jackson knew there had been no reports of Ethan taking a shot at pursuing officers. But the two bodies Ethan had left in his wake only proved he was a killer. Ethan's prints had been found all over the condo. And they would be found here as well. But why would he kill innocent bystanders, but not shoot at the police?

Jackson struggled to figure out the motive. There had to be one. Nothing he could think of made sense. Maybe he was not trying to kill himself. Perhaps he was still convinced he had done nothing wrong. In his eyes, Killing McKinley had been justified. It had been his fault his girlfriend took her own life. Perhaps Ethan thought he was delivering justice.

But that poked a hole in everything. If Ethan was merely seeking justice why gun down an innocent old man and whoever the newest John Doe was? Justice was not what Ethan wanted. It must have been revenge. Although it still left the question of the innocent bystanders open. People had a motive for the things they did. Money, power, revenge, and so on. Jackson could not believe Ethan was merely psychotic. Speaking to him on the phone he sounded completely rational. If he had lost his mind he would have been spewing all sorts of nonsense, but there had been nothing. He had sounded normal. He could not have lost touch with reality.

He looked around to make sure he was alone. The crime scene unit had left leaving him by himself. Quickly he pulled a cell phone out of his pocket. He had been the first to arrive on the scene. The phone sat at the body's feet with a trail of blood heading towards it. Without thinking, he had snatched it up. For reasons he could not explain he had decided to pocket the phone. Now he decided to take a look at the contents. There was only one contact labeled Greene. He backed out and checked the recent calls and found nothing. Once more he backed out and checked the recent text messages. There he found a short conversation with Greene. He had asked if Ethan was dead. The response had said not yet. Jackson was disturbed. He began to wonder who Greene was and what was going on. He wondered if Ethan had been telling the truth.

Jackson struggled with the thought before firing up the engine. A minor headache was beginning to form just behind his eyes and he decided to clear his head. Maybe he would give Brad Forester a call, but it could wait until morning. He wanted to wait for the results of the crime scene first. He shifted into drive and pulled his car out into the street. The question about Ethan still nagged silently at him.

***

Ethan stared at the ceiling and panted like a dog. His heart still raced from excitement. The sheets had long been kicked from the bed. Now he and Caroline lay naked together in each other's embrace. Her chest was pressed tight against his side with her left arm draped across him. Her face was nestled into his neck. She breathed softly tickling him slightly. Little beads of sweat formed across her face and down her neck. Her hair flailed in every direction with parts matted with sweat.

"That was incredible," she said as she draped her leg over his. Ethan smiled and squeezed her hand. She pulled away from him and stood next to the bed. Bending over she began to pick up the sheets from the floor. Ethan watched her as she did.

She was very beautiful and he enjoyed every bit of what they had done. But he could not shake the little voice in the back of his head. He felt as if he had betrayed Sandra. He had slept with another woman and Sandra had been the love of his life. He tried to tell himself Sandra was dead and it was not a betrayal, but it did not matter. The thought still persisted. He felt horrible and ashamed all at once. It was too early to move on. He was disgusted with himself. He could not help but feel as if he were a terrible human being.

Caroline jumped in bed next to him and pulled the sheets just below her breasts. He stopped himself from looking and tried to think of something else. She took notice of his strange behavior and started to struggle with her own feelings. She wondered if she had not been as good as she had hoped. Then she realized it was a selfish thought. His actions were not because of her.

She recalled the story he had told her while they were in the first hotel. His fiancé had been killed and he was tormented over it. He wanted to bring those who did it to justice. It was obvious he had loved her. Now here he was in bed with another woman. The pain and resentment he must have been feeling at that exact moment must have been tremendous.

Reaching out she rubbed her fingers through his hair. "Ethan, I know this is hard for you and if I made you do something that you regret I am truly sorry."

He turned towards her and stared into her eyes. She looked back at him with a soft and understanding expression. Now she wrapped the sheets around her body covering her breasts. He could still feel her warmth under the blanket.

"I don't regret any of it. It was wonderful. I just...I don't know. I can't exactly describe how I feel. I still love her and I shouldn't be moving on so quickly."

"Of course you still love her. Being intimate with another woman doesn't change that. I know she is still in your heart and I understand that. There will always be a special place for her there."

He gave her a smile.

"That spot will always be reserved for her no matter what. When you are finally ready to move on emotionally your partner is going to have to accept that."

He leaned forward and kissed her on the lips. The nagging thought was still there, but it had quieted. She smiled at him and he smiled back. "Thank you, Caroline. That helps, it really does."

"I'm glad."

"And for the record you really were amazing."

Caroline blushed and gave him a playful push. They kissed again and Caroline turned over. Ethan put his hands behind his head and stared at the ceiling. He ignored the nagging feeling and began to concentrate on the real issue. Caroline said, "You don't mind if I don't put clothes back on do you?" Ethan smiled.

"You can get dressed in the morning."

He could not see it, but Caroline smiled wide as she closed her eyes. He continued to stare at the ceiling as he thought.

There was another issue on his mind. He could not help but wonder if Detective Jackson had made the phone call. He decided there was only one way to find out. Once he was sure Caroline was asleep he sat up and grabbed the phone. From memory, he dialed Brad's personal number.

He answered on the third ring.

"It's Ethan."

"What's going on?"

"Did a man named Detective Jackson give you a call earlier?"

"I don't believe he did."

"Damnit."

"Who is he?"

"He's the detective in charge of finding me. I called him and told him where to find Geoffrey's body. I hoped he would call you so you could explain things to him. I thought maybe it would give me a chance."

"Unfortunately he didn't."

"Shit."

"Hold on, let me look at something."

"All right."

The phone was silent for several minutes. He could hear Brad typing on his computer. Finally, he said, "Well this is interesting."

"What?"

"I think you might be able to talk this guy into trusting you."

"Why do you say that?"

"Well, he's got himself a history with dirty cops it would seem."

"What do you mean?"

"Says here that a couple years ago Jackson was accused of taking bribes along with a few other officers. Jesus Christ-"

"What?"

"The three other officers involved kidnapped the accuser and tried to take the evidence from him and kill him. Jackson saved the man's life and they all went to trial, even Jackson. The others were found guilty of a thousand different crimes, but Jackson was found innocent. Doesn't really say exactly why."

"Well that might just prove useful, thank you, Brad."

"Be careful, Ethan. It might backfire on you. He's had a run in with dirty cops before and right now he thinks you're one. It might make him hesitant to trust you."

"I'll see what I can do."

"All right, Ethan. And first thing tomorrow morning I will give him a call and try and vouch for you. My word will have to mean something."

"Don't forget the vote is tomorrow. We still need to know what Derrick is up to."

"Got it covered. Tomorrow I will be sending three of my guys to Bayside Marketplace. They will be on the lookout for anything suspicious."

"Thanks again for everything Brad. I owe you."

"Just come home safe, Ethan. We will get all of this sorted out, I promise."

Ethan dropped the phone in the cradle and rolled back into bed. Beside him, Caroline's soft breath put him at ease. He cuddled close behind her pressing his lower body tight against her. Right now she made him feel safe and grounded. He wrapped and arm around her and kissed the back of her head.

He closed his eyes and quickly drifted off to sleep. In his dream he heard the faint voice of Pierce say it's been three days, Valerie misses you. Then the image of Sandra flooded into his mind. She was sprawled across the ground in a pool of blood. He reeled back in horror and started to cry. Her arm was reaching out slowly with three fingers extended. She had pressed them hard against the ground leaving a bloody imprint. He struggled to understand what it meant. Why did Sandra leave him this message? What was the significance of the number three? Then his heart nearly stopped. It was not a three. It was obvious and he cursed for not thinking of it before. It was not a three. Instead, her fingers had come together to form a W. She was trying to tell him who had killed her. Though that could not be right. Geoffrey had killed her. He confessed to it as he lay dying. Then he realized it was not about the killer. Surely she would have been thinking of the big picture. She wanted Ethan to know something more important. It was the only message she could have left him.

He woke with a start and shot up in bed. Caroline jumped and sat up next to him. Ethan was covered in sweat and breathing heavy. She wrapped her arms around him. "What's wrong?" She asked.

Ethan stared straight ahead and smiled. "I know who Greene is."

Chapter 30

Derrick White lay in bed and stared up at the ceiling. Sleep was not going to happen. The whole Ethan McCormick situation drove him crazy. The entire Miami Police Department had been looking for him and failed. Half the state of Florida was looking for him, but still, he was not caught. The police on the other coast had come close. His face was plastered on every news station across the country. There was no place for him to hide. He could not possibly find sanctuary anywhere. He could not understand what was taking them so long to bring him down.

He sat up and rubbed his eyes. The clock read four fifty-five in the morning. Getting up he headed to the kitchen to get a drink. First, he thought about a glass of water but decided on something a little stronger. He grabbed a bottle of Whiskey. Skipping the cup he gulped it straight from the bottle. He wanted to drink until he passed out. Unfortunately for him, he did not have enough alcohol.

As he pulled his robe tighter around his body he sat on the couch. After another swig, he placed the bottle on the floor. The wind was gusting outside as if a storm was approaching. It was summer which for Florida meant large storms were common. He almost wished it would rain. He wanted the clouds to be as black as night and the rain to fall for hours. Lighting would crack across the sky followed by the loud rumble of thunder. Somehow he thought it would bring him peace.

Snatching up the bottle he gulped down another drink cursing Ethan as he did. Because of him, he had been put in a terrible spot. He had slipped right through their fingers and now the country knew it. It would be hard to argue the effectiveness of the department if they could not catch one officer on a full budget. He had made them all look like fools, incompetent, idiotic fools. He stood up and drank more whiskey. It ran warm down his throat.

Then he fell to his knees nearly dropping the bottle. After a moment of staring at nothing, he let the bottle slip from his hands. It did not shatter. It only toppled over and rolled across the floor spilling whiskey as it went. He put his face in his hands and yelled out in frustration. It seemed to him that everything was falling apart. All he had worked so hard on would be for nothing. This had all started out as a simple plan but had quickly become a nightmare. Now he was struggling to pick up the pieces and salvage whatever was left.

"God damn you for getting involved in this Ethan!" He yelled out into the darkness. He knew it had not been Ethan's fault. It had been Sandra's. Her investigation had made her a target. Being associated with her had become dangerous.

Lying on the living room carpet he rolled to his side and began to cry. The wind picked up outside whipping the tree branches against the window. The constant scratching of the leaves gave him a headache. His hands began to tremble as stress took over his body. The bottle of whiskey had stopped rolling and now pooled in the corner of the room. The stench of alcohol was pungent.

Sandra's death had been a terrible one. It was a true loss to the police department. She had been a fine officer and a wonderful person. Her death had spared Derrick and his future plans. Although it had been tragic he also saw it as necessary. Sandra needed to be taken care of. For months Derrick had been hard at work on his plan. It was all supposed to be so easy. Sandra should never have been involved.

The deaths of officers had not been in the plan, not at first. There would have been some casualties along the way, but all would have been necessary. They certainly would not have been officers. When Sandra started to poke around he got nervous. After months of careful planning, she threatened to pull it apart at the seams. He did what he thought had to be done. Derrick White ordered Geoffrey Hunt to kill her.

Geoffrey was unaware that the order had come from him. He had adopted an alter ego with the name of Greene. This name was used with several of his criminal contacts on the streets. He never met with them in person as to conceal his identity. Nothing could be traced back to him. He only contacted his associates via text message under the alias. He had a pay by the minute phone tucked away in his desk at home. It was how he contacted those who were part of his plan. He used this method to contact Geoffrey shortly after he learned Sandra was investigating him. He blackmailed him and forced him to do his dirty work. By not using his real name he was being extra cautious. He already had a hand in helping Geoffrey steal from the lock-up, but he could not let him know he was behind the murder of fellow officers. If Geoffrey was caught he would have sold him out in a heartbeat. This way he could operate quietly and in secret.

Shortly after Geoffrey silenced Sandra he realized he could still be useful. Soon Derrick learned Major McKinley was growing suspicious. After Sandra's death, he started going through her files. Derrick was unsure of what he had uncovered, but he knew he could not take the risk. Derrick gained access to his computer and began to read his emails. He saw he had set up a meeting with Ethan McCormick. It had made his blood run cold. Things were getting out of hand.

That was when an idea had formed. He ordered Geoffrey to kill Major McKinley and frame Ethan. It was the perfect set up. McKinley was Sandra's superior. The story could be manipulated without much effort. Ethan had gone crazy over the death of his girlfriend. He even blamed her boss for her death. Derrick was ecstatic with how perfect the plan was. Now he had a scapegoat for everything. All of his plans could be blamed on Ethan. In order for it to be believable Ethan would have to run. Once again Geoffrey did as he was instructed. Ethan looked guilty by running and Derrick was free to move forward with his plans. Everything was back on schedule. Soon after he would have Geoffrey clean up his last mess by killing McCormick and then he could finally relax.

Derrick had regretted what he had done. Ethan McCormick was one of the best officers to ever serve. He had struggled through some hardships himself. In his early years with the force, a man had taken his sister hostage on the roof of an apartment complex. He planned to kill Valerie for revenge. Ethan had arrested several of his partners effectively destroying his drug traffic ring. When he had been able to start back up again he found he was no longer trusted. He had blamed Ethan. It was only a matter of time before he was caught and placed in jail. He decided he would destroy Ethan's life before that happened.

In the end, Ethan had killed the man and saved his sister. He was awarded several medals for his efforts and quickly became a legend among the other officers. He created several friends within the force including several high-ranking officials. Derrick had been one of them. It was heart wrenching when he finally made the decision to bring Ethan down. Derrick had not done it with a smile. He lost days of sleep over the matter. Eventually, he had accepted it and moved forward. He told himself Ethan's sacrifice was part of something bigger. But now Ethan was making it complicated again.

The plan had been to pin the death of Sandra and Major McKinley on Ethan, effectively keeping Derrick safe from any further investigations. While leaving the scene of McKinley's death he was supposed to have been caught. He was never supposed to leave the city. Either he would have been killed while running or arrested and killed in jail. He had people who could do it for him. If his plan to eliminate Ethan in custody failed he was ready. He would falsify the evidence to ensure Ethan was convicted. Geoffrey may have been pulled down in the process, but Derrick did not care. He needed to make sure he stayed free to continue with his work. The budget vote was approaching fast and he needed to combat it with everything he had. One way or another he would make sure it failed. He would show them what Miami would be like with a less effective police force.

Slowly he rose from the floor and collapsed on the couch. His head still pounded and the wind outside still gusted. Ethan still haunted his thoughts and no matter how hard he tried he could not shake it. The longer he was free the higher the chance of everything coming undone. Derrick could not allow that to happen. Geoffrey Hunt had been instructed to kill him, but Derrick was worried he had failed. The text message he had received was unsettling.

He decided he was not going to worry about it anymore. As far as he was concerned he was free. Sandra could not possibly have any hard evidence to convict him and nobody knew the real identity of Greene. In the end, his plan would work, that was all that mattered. All of the pieces would fall into place. Ethan McCormick would be taken care of either way. He reassured himself that no plan had ever worked perfectly. Surely there had been mistakes made during D-day. Operation Neptune Spear had several things go wrong yet Osama Bin Laden was still killed. If these operations had worked even with mistakes and issues he was confident his would too.

Finally, Derrick shut his eyes as he lay on the couch. The first drops of rain started to pelt against the windows. It relaxed his body and calmed his mind. Within a few moments, Derrick White was fast asleep and he dreamt of climbing Mont Everest. Just when he reached the summit the storm in the real world worsened.

Chapter 31

The rain pelted the roof of the metal shed creating metallic pings that began to hurt Greg's ears. He stood in the center of the shed staring at the location of the hidden bag. Water dripped from his clothes and pooled across the wooden floor. After waiting a minute he snatched up the bag and slung it over his shoulder. He was not looking forward to heading back out into the rain.

Greg had decided to take the week off of work, but his wife was at hers. He had claimed to feel terrible and needed some time to himself. Greene had instructed him to be available at any given time through the week. He did not want to disappoint the man who was capable of destroying his life. So when the text message came through telling him to get the device ready he ran to the shed.

The metal doors screeched open and he took off running through the mud and rain. By the time he reached the back door and clambered inside his pants were caked in mud. He slipped out of his shoes so he would not track it over the carpet. He dropped the backpack next to the door and went to the bedroom to change.

When he was in new, dry clothes the phone chimed again. Leave it at the drop spot tomorrow. Do not be late. Greg was glad the whole ordeal was almost behind him. The stress of it all was becoming too much to bear. One mistake and Greene would break his life down. His wife would know everything he had done. Once the device was planted he hoped the texts would stop.

Several miles away a woman received a similar text. She was told to get her pack ready and to leave it at her designated point. With tears in her eyes, she slid her backpack under the bed. Tomorrow she would leave the house with it over her shoulder and drop it where she had been instructed to. She tried to tell herself it was not her fault. She wanted to believe the victims would not be on her. She had been forced to build the device but was not responsible for it. She knew better than to believe it. All of the deaths would be because of her. Their blood would be on her hands. She wished she could stop. Greene had left her no choice.

Unlike Greg, she had not been blackmailed. Her son was an attorney. Thanks to him dangerous criminals had been pulled off the streets. He was truly making the world a better place. He was always honest in his work and only defended the victims of horrible acts of violence.

One day she received a text from a man named Greene. He told her he could make life very difficult for her if she did not comply with him. Greene sent her photos of her son at work and on his lunch break. Then he sent her photos of him heading home after work. Then a text that sent a chill over her spine. I know his every move. Alexis had no idea what this man was going to do so she told him she was calling the police. She was stopped by another message. Call the cops and your son is a dead man. Fail to follow my instructions and he's dead. Eventually, he explained he knew several people that had been put away by her son. Those people would have loved the opportunity to have him killed. Greene was willing to make that happen. If Alexis did not obey him Greene would kill her son. With this threat, she broke down and did exactly as he had asked.

At first, it seemed so harmless. She was sent to several different department stores and a few pharmacies. She picked up all the items she had been instructed to. It was not until she was assembling it on her kitchen table that she began to realize what it was. The bomb that was now stuffed under her bed tormented her every waking moment. She could not wait to have it out of her home and off her mind for good. Only she knew it would never truly be off of her mind. When the bomb was used for its intended purpose she would take all of the blame. She thought her son could take her case and keep her from going to jail. In the end, she decided she would not fight it. For what she was doing she deserved to be punished and she would make sure it happened.

Somewhere across the city a third and final bomb had been built. Unlike the other two, this man was a police officer. His name was Thomas Sheeder. He had worked alongside Geoffrey Hunt to steal weapons and sell them on the streets. Geoffrey had hooked him up with the job. He had no clue how Geoffrey was able to get away with it, but he did not ask. Instead, he enjoyed the extra cash flowing into his wallet. Then he too received a text message from Greene. Eventually, he was forced to build a device identical to the others. In less than five hours he would be following his instructions and leaving the backpack in the center of the courtyard at bayside marketplace.

Late into the morning the storm still had not let up. The clouds overhead were as dark as night and lightning flashed every few seconds. Thunder shook the air as the wind forced the falling rain to the side. Puddles formed on the street and quickly turned to large pools. Vehicles on the roads drove slowly, many with their hazard lights flashing.

Three officers in yellow ponchos walked back and forth around the shops at the Bayside Marketplace. It was an outdoor shopping plaza with several stores, bars, and restaurants. A very popular place year round, but even more so during summer. It was roughly the shape of a U sitting next to the ocean with a marina in the bay. There were two floors each lined with shops as well as a courtyard overlooking the bay. Boat owners would sail into the marina and tie up to the docks. Tourists frequented the area dining at several of the restaurants and enjoyed the live music that sometimes performed on a stage in the courtyard.

The three officers watched as store owners showed up to open their shops. Despite the rain, a few tourists still arrived to enjoy the day. If anything was going to happen it would be easy to spot with how few people were there. But the summer rains could vanish at any moment. When it did the marketplace would flood with people. Then the real danger would begin.

They had been instructed to keep their eyes open for suspicious activity. Any unattended packages would be searched immediately. If anyone acted strangely or seemed as if they were avoiding the officers they were to watch them. And if necessary approach them.

Over the next few hours, the rain began to die down to a mere sprinkle. The sun was finally peeking out from behind the clouds. When the storm finally subsided the officers stuck to their same search patterns and scrutinized every person they spotted. Every so often a drunken man would draw too much attention and the closest officer would approach him. When they were sure he was not a threat he was escorted off the property and told to go home.

Derrick sat in his office with the blinds pulled shut and a bottle of Jack Daniels on his desk. He had received the news the vote had passed less than ten minutes before. He had expected it to pass. He had prepared for it. His whole plan had been centered on the vote passing. Ethan had been the unfortunate result of cleanup. Had Sandra not put her nose in his business she would still be alive.

It had been harder than he thought to kill Ethan. He was out there somewhere waiting to bring everything down. Derrick took out his pay by the minute phone and pulled up the last message from Geoffrey. I'm coming for you next was still sharply displayed. It was like a knife in his side. He was not sure if Geoffrey was dead or in handcuffs. Either way, it did not bode well for him.

Derrick began to smile. He had made a contingency plan in case Geoffrey had failed. After the text had come through he sent one of his own, but not to Geoffrey. Fidel Sanchez had been ordered to leave town immediately and find Ethan McCormick.

After his work a couple days ago with the prisoner, Derrick knew he could be trusted. Derrick had ordered him to take care of the man Ethan had arrested. Fidel had found his way inside his cell and hung him with his own sheets. Several hours later it looked like a suicide and no one bothered to look into it any further. His friend had killed himself to escape the clutches of Greene. It was not a stretch to imagine he would too.

Fidel had left a few hours after he received Derrick's text. He made it to the other coast before the sun rose. Soon he would find Ethan McCormick and put an end to everything. Fidel was his last chance. If he failed there would be no choice but to kill him. He would do anything to keep his plan from being destroyed. The ever increasing body count disturbed him.

***

Detective Jackson got an early start at work. The information regarding the body they found the night before was sitting on his desk. With a cup of coffee in hand, he began to go over the details. The body had been identified as Geoffrey Hunt of the Miami Police Department. He was a fellow officer of Ethan's. Ethan's prints had been found on the knife just as he knew they would.

According to the forensic report, there had been a struggle. Both Ethan and his companion had fought with the man. It was unclear who had started the fight and why. Jackson thought Geoffrey may have been acting alone to stop Ethan. Maybe he wanted to be seen as a hero. It did not really matter. Ethan had murdered another officer and this time it was in Jackson's city. He would not allow him to get away with it.

He thought about the phone call he had received from Ethan and picked up his desk phone. After listening to the dial tone for several minutes he punched in Brad Forester's number. He was not sure what to expect.

On the fourth ring, Brad picked up sounding exhausted and stressed. "Hello, Mr. Forester. This is Detective Jackson of the Clearwater police department."

"Jackson, what can I do for you?"

"Well, I received an interesting phone call from Ethan McCormick last night."

"Oh?"

"It seems he left the body of fellow officer Geoffrey Hunt at the marina. He claimed it was self-defense. It's hard to believe that since he is still hiding. He told me to call you and said you might be able to fill me in on some details. So, what is it you need to explain to me?"

"Geoffrey Hunt was a dirty cop with a vendetta against Ethan. I can't give you all of the details unfortunately as it is part of an ongoing investigation. I can tell you that I personally believe Ethan to be innocent and I might have evidence to prove it."

"Where is this evidence?"

"I'm working on getting it."

"Well, then you can see why I might be a little skeptical."

"I can't say that I blame you."

"If he is innocent we can let the courts decide. It isn't our job to judge who is guilty or innocent. He needs to be proven so in a court of law. If he's innocent then he has nothing to worry about."

"It's a bit more complicated than that."

"How's that?"

"Someone set him up and we don't know their identity. On top of that, his superior is corrupt. He's planning something for tomorrow. We think he's prepared to hurt innocent people to prove a point."

"What point?"

Brad explained the budget cuts and told him everything he knew about it all. He knew it sounded ridiculous to someone who had not seen the evidence for himself. If they could produce evidence against Derrick and learn the identity of Greene everything would fall into place. If they could get to Greene they could get Ethan's name cleared.

"It doesn't matter if it's true or not, Mr. Forester. If I catch Ethan I will be putting him in handcuffs. You guys can sort all of this out back in Miami. None of it is my problem."

"Fair enough Detective."

With that Jackson hung up and sipped on his coffee. Everything Brad had told him swam in his head. Still, he stuck to his statement. If Ethan was out there he would bring him in, innocent or not. That was the way it needed to be.

***

Together Caroline and Ethan gathered up food from the continental breakfast and returned to their room. Now they sat on the bed together eating yogurt and bagels. Caroline was starving. It felt as if she had not eaten in days.

They sat in silence and ate. When Ethan was finished he stood up, brushed the crumbs from his lap, and headed to the window. It was covered in morning dew. Soon the early morning sun would evaporate it away. Below the window, he could see the park sparkle in the sun. Small groups of people gathered at the park for early morning walks. A couple people brought along their dogs. They seemed to go about their day as happy as could be.

He knew that one way or another everything had to come to an end. He could not stay on the run for much longer. It was going to get him, or someone he cared about, killed. There was no chance of turning himself in yet. Not enough evidence had been collected to prove Derrick White was behind anything. In order to do that, they would have to successfully stop whatever he was planning. Ethan knew Greene's identity, but he needed to prove it. He refused to tell Brad until he had some sort of proof.

Caroline stood and brushed the crumbs off of her pants and joined Ethan at the window. She rested her head on his shoulder. Together they soaked in the morning sun. For a moment they were both completely at peace in each other's presence. In less than two hours they would be checking out of the hotel and back into the unknown. For now, they were together.

After they checked out they headed to Largo Central Park and walked around. They were careful to keep their distance from people walking by. Children played on the playground and couples walked happily. Ethan envied all of them.

"We need a car." He said.

"What are we supposed to do, steal one?"

He knew it was not the best option. Not only would he feel wrong for doing it, but the police might be called. It caused his mind to wander. He began to wonder how to prove who Greene really was.

Derrick was obviously smart. There would not be a trail leading back to him. So far it seemed Geoffrey had done all of his dirty work. Finding evidence against him would be impossible. Instead, he had to get a confession from the man himself. Ethan figured that would also be impossible. He could not imagine Derrick giving up all of his secrets. At least not if he believed he was still winning.

Then Ethan thought of something. If Derrick's plan failed he would be desperate. He could play off that desperation and draw him out. Desperation would make him foolish. He thought for a moment and knew exactly what he had to do. He turned to Caroline. "I need to make a phone call."

Chapter 32

He wished he had brushed the seat off before sitting in the car. The broken glass from the window littered the inside and was uncomfortable. He felt bad for stealing another car, but it was necessary. He remembered the woman's car he had stolen from the airport back in Miami. The Chevrolet Volt was still sitting at the Clearwater airport as far as he knew. When everything was over he would make sure it was returned to her.

As he drove through the intersection he noticed a police cruiser following close behind him. His heart pounded wildly in his chest when the lights flashed to life. As calm as he could, he pulled to the shoulder and switched the car into park. He watched as the officer stepped out of the vehicle and approached.

Before he reached the driver side door Ethan shifted into drive and slammed on the gas. The tires squealed as he pulled away. The officer ran back to his cruiser and was on Ethan's tail before he got too far. In his mirror, Ethan could see him radio for backup. He knew minutes later the entire force would come down on him. They were not going to let him get away this time. If he was not careful it could end badly. He had to play it safe.

He screeched around a corner and pressed the pedal hard. The officer was glued to his bumper. Up ahead he could see two more sets of flashing lights. More officers eager to bring the chase to an end. The more the merrier, Ethan thought trying not to smile.

When they were close enough the two cruisers spun around and fell in line with the first. He dodged several vehicles and darted down another street. The cruisers stuck behind him. Ethan knew he had to move the chase to less occupied streets. No innocent bystanders could be put in harm's way because of him.

A few minutes after the chase started an unmarked car pulled in behind him with flashing lights on the dashboard and behind the grill. Ethan looked in his mirror and smiled. It was Jackson, there was no doubt in his mind. His plan was coming together perfectly.

With another sharp turn, he was back on the main street. Again he weaved around the slow moving traffic. The officers gave him plenty of space to make sure there were no accidents. Up ahead Ethan spotted the on-ramp to the main highway. He jerked the wheel left and sailed up the ramp. Two officers, including Jackson, followed. The remainder kept to the surface streets.

Jackson came up on his bumper and gave him a light tap. It nearly sent him into the wall. He increased his speed to stay out ahead of him. Ethan did not want to end his day with a trip to the hospital.

The road was surprisingly clear on the highway. He was able to race through the traffic with ease. Ethan decided to go on for just a bit longer before putting his plan into place. Then out of nowhere a car flew up the next ramp and scraped against the passenger side of his car. At first, he thought it was another police cruiser. When he looked over he saw a regular vehicle with a man in plain clothes behind the wheel. He wondered if it was another detective. That theory was quickly dropped when he watched the police cruisers back off slightly. It was a sign they did not recognize the car either.

He shot a glance at the driver as they stayed side by side. The driver had a scowl on his face and was taking quick glances over at Ethan. He thought he recognized the man, but could not place it. Then it hit him like a semi. The man was a fellow officer named Fidel Sanchez. Ethan could not believe he was there. Had Derrick blackmailed him too? It seemed impossible that he could have his thumb on so many officers.

Fidel pulled the wheel right and quickly jerked it left. The car slammed into Ethan's and almost sent him into the opposite barrier. Ethan let out a startled yell as he pulled back into his lane. His plan had not involved another person. He had to do his best to improvise.

Ethan prepared himself for another hit, as Fidel pulled away. He slammed hard on the brake and watched as Fidel sailed past him. Fidel was able to correct himself before he plowed into the barrier. Ethan accelerated to keep ahead of Fidel. The officers behind him split into groups. Jackson stayed on Ethan while the other two cruisers pulled behind Fidel.

Several shots rang out from Fidel's back window and the officers fell back. Luckily none of them had been hit. Now he turned his sights towards Ethan. With his passenger window down he began to fire at Ethan. Bullets struck the car in random locations. Two smashed into the trunk, one just above the front tire, and the last one broke the rear driver side window.

The chase had become too dangerous to keep on the highway. A stray bullet could strike another driver. He snapped the wheel to the left and crashed into Fidel hard. The passenger door dented in and Ethan pulled back for another. They rammed each other for several minutes before Ethan darted off towards an exit. Jackson was able to follow, but Fidel and the other officers remained on the highway.

A helicopter began to buzz overhead and Ethan was anxious to see who it would follow. Fidel had open fired on the police so they should go for him, but Ethan was the man they all wanted to catch. He watched in the mirror as the helicopter left and headed for the highway. Clearly, they wanted to get Fidel under control before he killed someone.

It did not take long for Fidel to catch up. He had taken the next exit and doubled back flying through several red lights. Two vehicles swerved to avoid him and ended up smashing each other head on. Twice the officers on his tail tried to P.I.T. him, but it did not work. Eventually, he was right back behind Ethan, but Jackson stayed in the way.

Ethan was surprised to see Jackson pull out in front of Fidel to block him from Ethan. No matter how he tried to get around him Jackson blocked. Moments later more shots ripped through the air only this time they were aimed at Jackson. Several shots embedded in the trunk while others burrowed into the backseat.

Fidel was more forceful and extreme than Geoffrey. He was deliberately attacking officers to get to Ethan. It told him something. Derrick was getting desperate to shut him up. He wanted everything cleaned up before his plan was put into effect. He did not care how. Fidel would be taken care of just like everyone else. But it gave Ethan the advantage. Derrick was being reckless and now he knew it.

***

Caroline looked around at her condo as if she did not recognize it. It seemed like weeks since she had last seen it. There was a small stain on the floor just in front of the bar. It looked like blood. She stared at it in confusion and decided it did not matter. It was important she followed Ethan's instructions correctly.

She picked up her phone and dialed the number he had rattled off. After several rings, Pierce picked up the phone. It was nice to hear a familiar voice again. In that same moment, she realized how much she missed Ethan. She wondered if he was all right.

"Pierce, is Valerie nearby?"

"She's sitting right next to me. We are watching the news. What's going on?"

"Are they talking about the car chase yet?"

"Yes, it's all they're talking about. Is Ethan OK?"

"He's fine, he has a plan."

"What might that be?"

Caroline smiled wide.

"It's a pretty good one."

***

Fidel had stopped firing but was still right on Ethan's tail. He had rammed the back of Jackson's cruiser several times leaving it dented and scratched. Now they drove side by side. Jackson did his best to keep his attention focused on him, but it was obvious he would stop at nothing to get to Ethan.

The helicopter cut through the air directly over them. There was no chance to get away now. Fidel would have to kill Ethan in front of the entire police department. If Fidel succeeded he would most likely be shot on site. More than likely it was exactly what Derrick hoped for. Ethan was not about to let himself become a victim.

In fact, Fidel presented him an opportunity. Geoffrey could have provided information against Derrick. Now that Geoffrey was dead Ethan would need something else. Fidel could possibly fill that role. There had to be something he knew about Derrick. Geoffrey had been a conspirator with Derrick and Ethan was willing to bet Fidel was one too. When it was all over Fidel would tell them everything he knew.

Fidel scraped his way ahead of Jackson and began to ram Ethan's bumper. His taillight busted and Fidel's headlight cracked. Up ahead Ethan could see a line of traffic starting to form heading in the direction of the beaches. Trying to avoid the traffic he pulled off to the right and spun the car around. Fidel followed close behind. When they were close together several shots burst out again. They ricocheted off the ground and nearly popped his tire. Jackson and the other cruisers pulled around and closed the gap behind them.

He remembered the park from earlier and headed off in that direction. Slowly he had learned to navigate the city streets. The roads were simple enough to learn. Not like Miami. The streets back home were crazy and always busy.

The chase needed to come to an end, but some place where no one could get hurt. Off the top of his head, he could not think of a place to go. There were too many stores, too many parks, too many places for bystanders to get hurt. He knew that once his car finally stopped the bullets would start again.

He slid around a left turn and pressed the pedal harder. Cars whipped past him as he dodged the traffic. The sound of the helicopter and the sirens behind him was incredible. He wondered how much longer before road blocks were formed.

Several blocks ahead he spotted and old gas station. It no longer looked as if it were in use. There were large rugs hung around the fence as if on display. The paint peeled from the building and the windows were clogged with dirt and grime. It was the perfect place to corner Fidel and keep everyone else safe.

He slowed just a little as he headed towards the old gas station. At the last moment, he smashed the brake pedal and it went to the floor. The smell of burning rubber hung in the air while a trail of smoke bellowed from his back tires. He came to a halt just outside of the main doors which were covered in grime.

Before Fidel could pull to a stop Ethan smashed the glass and tumbled inside. Inside empty shelves sat under inches of dust. The counter was in shambles. A thin layer of dirt covered the floor proving It had been a long time since anyone had stepped foot inside.

There were no real places to hide inside the main building. There was an office and a small storage room along the back wall, but Ethan ignored it. Instead, he ducked behind one of the many dusty shelves and waited.

His wait was short. Fidel stumbled in quickly with the sound of police sirens behind him. Shortly after the helicopter buzzed wildly overhead. He heard Fidel's foot crunch on glass as he stepped to the side away from the door. He fired two shots blindly at the officers in an attempt to keep them back. Ethan wondered how many magazines he had brought.

"This is detective Jackson. Both of you come out with your hands above your head."

Neither man listened as Fidel crept farther into the abandoned space. Ethan made sure to move back quietly as Fidel advanced. He did not want to be caught in the open. He moved to the next aisle as Fidel stepped into the one he had just left.

"Ethan, this has to end. You can't run forever. Greene will find you. He finds everyone. The more you run the worse he will make it. Just give up." Ethan did not fall for his ploy and kept silent. He moved to the end of the aisle and waited.

Fidel stepped around the corner and Ethan tackled him to the ground. The gun soared across the room and crashed to the floor. A large cloud of dust sprang up from the impact. They wrestled on the floor for several seconds before Fidel was able to push free. He leaped across the room towards the gun, but Ethan was too quick. He snatched his foot and pulled him back to the ground. Before Ethan could deliver another blow Fidel had rolled over and rammed a foot into his stomach. He cried out in pain and nearly doubled over. It was not enough to stop Ethan, however. Instead, he threw his foot out and caught Fidel in the chest. Then he kicked him two more times.

The third kick Fidel deflected and rolled over. Within seconds he was back on his feet throwing punches at Ethan. He blocked as many as he could, but Fidel landed a few. One connected with his jaw, the other hit him in the side. Ethan retaliated with a few jabs of his own. The final one caught Fidel in the throat and he began to choke.

Outside Jackson yelled through the bullhorn, "Surrender now or we will be forced to come inside." Ethan wanted to end the fight before they did. If Fidel shot an officer his plan would be ruined and everything would be over.

As Ethan turned to retrieve the gun something came down on his back with great force. He tumbled to the floor in pain. Fidel tossed the piece of metal shelf aside and laughed as he approached the gun. "Sorry, Ethan," he said as he bent to pick it up. "It's either you or me. That's just how this works."

Ethan stood and put his hands in the air. He stared at Fidel for a moment before speaking. "You're a loose end, Fidel. You think he is going to let you live? He will kill you the first chance he gets. You know too much."

"I don't know shit. I'm only doing what I'm told."

"You know about me, that's enough."

"You can't trick me, Ethan. Say whatever you want, but I am going to kill you."

"If you kill me there will be no help for you. Those officers out there are going to storm in here and blow you away."

It seemed to draw his attention. Ethan could almost see the wheels turning in his mind. He was thinking about taking Ethan hostage. Then his expression changed.

"They are after you too. Taking you hostage will get me nowhere. You're a cop killer. They will give me a medal for killing you."

Ethan knew there was nothing more he could say. Fidel was going to pull the trigger. Before Fidel could react Ethan flung his body backward. He landed hard on his back as Fidel fired. He slid across the floor and rolled to the left until he was out of the line of fire.

Before he could pick himself off the floor several officers stormed in with their guns drawn. They yelled for Ethan to stay on the ground and put his hands behind his head. He did exactly as he was told and waited for the handcuffs. In the background, he heard them yell for Fidel to drop the gun. It was screamed several times before someone fired a shot. He hoped more than anything they had not killed Fidel.

As they dragged Ethan out of the gas station he heard one of the officers state they needed an ambulance right away. The suspect had been injured. He was immediately brought to Jackson's car and tossed in the backseat. He watched as Fidel was pulled out of the gas station. Blood poured from his arm, but otherwise, he seemed fine. He sat back in relief.

He watched the whole scene from the back of the car. An ambulance arrived and treated Fidel's wounds. When he was all patched up he was stuck in a squad car. He locked eyes with Ethan. A look of fear and hatred sat in his eyes. Ethan turned away and scanned the crowd of officers. Near the gas station was a man in plain clothes. He recognized him as Detective Jackson.

Nearly five minutes later Jackson finally climbed into the driver seat of his cruiser. There was a moment of silence before he turned around and looked at Ethan through the partition. "We finally meet, Mr. McCormick." Ethan nodded.

"That was a hell of a stunt McCormick. You could have gotten somebody killed out there. You're lucky the only one injured there is your friend."

"That man is not my friend. He was sent here to kill me."

"We've got some things to talk about Ethan."

"Yes, we do."

Jackson put the cruiser in drive and headed off towards the police station. Fidel had nearly uprooted his entire plan. Thankfully everything was back on schedule.

***

The breaking news banner rolled across the screen. An aerial view of what looked like an abandoned gas station appeared. The news anchor began to describe the events of the afternoon.

"We have received reports that the Clearwater police were involved in a high-speed chase that ended with an arrest. Ethan McCormick has been apprehended by local police along with an unidentified man. Several shots were fired during the chase. It is unclear at this time whether those shots were fired from Ethan or the unknown assailant."

The news continued to speculate what might be next for Ethan and the city of Miami. They assumed the Clearwater police would eventually hand him over to the Miami Police Department to be put on trial for his crimes.

Valerie turned off the television and stood up. "So this is it." She said looking over at Pierce. "It's almost over." Pierce nodded.

"He will be home soon."

Valerie nodded and wiped a single tear from her eye. For the first time in four days, it was a tear of relief.

Chapter 33

Derrick White paced back and forth in his living room. Ethan had been arrested. Fidel had failed. The reports stated an unknown assailant had been taken into custody. He knew it had to be Fidel. And now everything was falling apart. Nothing was going according to his plan. He could only hope the remainder of his plan would go by uninterrupted. If not all of his hard work would have been in vain and great officers would have given their lives for nothing.

He looked outside at the gloomy evening it had become. It fit his mood well. He had finished his bottle of Jack Daniels earlier in the day and now there was nothing left to drink. There would be no sleeping for him this night. Of that he was sure.

He snatched up his burner cell phone and sent another mass text message to three people. Have the devices ready. First thing tomorrow morning you will plant them. He wanted to crush the phone beneath his foot in case everything went wrong, but he still needed it. He only needed it for one more day then it would all be over. He could drop the name Greene forever. Once the city had seen its mistake with the budget hearings they would revote and everything would be restored.

For Derrick, it truly was not about the money. He cared about the city and the people. He wanted to make it a safer place. Everything he had done he had thought of as the greater good. All those who had sacrificed their lives had done so with purpose. Every death made Miami safer. They were not without meaning. He knew he would die believing that.

People like Ethan McCormick and Sandra Delano did not understand. Derrick did not think he was a bad guy. He wanted what was best. If only they could see that. If only he could have convinced them. So many people believed in following the system. Derrick saw it differently. Sometimes the rules had to be broken in order to create peace. There had to be blood before the bandages. He saw himself as the bandages. He was healing the city.

He sat down on the couch and turned on the television. He no longer wanted to think about what was going on. He wanted to relax. He flipped through the channels until he found a mindless reality show and watched.

***

Ethan McCormick was forced to spend the night in a cell. The bed was hard and uncomfortable. The sheets were stiff and smelled musty. The only positive was being alone. It gave him time to think. He thought about everything that had happened and everything yet to come. There was still a bit of work ahead, but he knew he was nearing the end.

He turned over on the cot and thought about Caroline. It was the first time in a few days he had been alone. He thought of the night they had shared together and relaxed. When this was over he wanted to see her one last time if nothing else.

Then his thoughts turned to his sister. It would be nice to finally put her mind at ease. The past three days her brother had been a fugitive being chased by the entire state. She was probably embarrassed to show her face in public. Reporters probably called the house all hours of the night looking for a statement.

She was a wonderful sister who had always been there for him. He was sorry to have put her in this situation. He was sorry to everyone. He wished he could take it all back. He wished Sandra was still alive. Instead of sleeping in this cell they could have been talking about their life together. They could have planned their wedding. Maybe even talked about having kids. It had all been stolen from him.

Geoffrey had taken it all away from him. He was dead and Ethan felt no better. He knew Derrick was the one who had her killed, but it did not matter. He thought it would have been satisfying to kill Geoffrey. He thought he would savor the moment forever. The thought of Geoffrey getting what he deserved had excited him. Now there was only an empty feeling. He could not explain it. It was neither a sad feeling nor an angry one. It was only empty.

Caroline had helped to fill that void. When she was around the emptiness felt full. There was something about her smile that helped him move on. He could not tell what it was. He could feel that everything would be all right when she was near.

He still loved Sandra, but she was gone and there was no getting her back. He knew that and knew he had to move on. It felt too soon to be having feelings for another woman. But he had them anyway and he could not wait to see her again.

***

Caroline lay in her bed at the condo. The thought of Ethan spending the night alone in a jail cell upset her. She wanted more than anything to be there with him. Only three days ago he had been a stranger, but now he seemed closer than anyone she had ever known.

Unable to sleep she stood up and walked out to the balcony. She sat outside and watched the dark waves break over the shore. The night air was cold and windy, but she embraced it. It was nice being home in fresh clothes. She had showered and changed right away. She kept expecting a knock on the door from the police ready to arrest her, but she knew it would not happen. They had their man now. They were never after her. The news had barely even mentioned her. It had always been about Ethan.

When everything was finished she thought about selling the condo and trying to move down to Florida. She was not sure how serious the thought was, but she thought it was serious enough. She had grown very fond of Ethan and she wanted to spend more time with him. Plus the cool ocean breeze was nice. She thought it would be a nice change of scenery.

With a deep breath, she stood up and left the balcony and headed back towards the bedroom. She trusted that everything would be all right with Ethan, but she could not shake the feeling something was going to go wrong.

***

The backpack bomb sat on the kitchen floor at the woman's feet. She sat at the kitchen table in the early hours of the morning. She held a mug of scorching hot coffee, but she was not drinking. Instead, she stared at the wall as her hands shook. She was tormented with the thought of what was going to happen when she left the bag. People were going to get hurt, that was obvious. She did not want that on her conscious.

The bomb was extremely dangerous. It had been outfitted with a wireless receiver so it could be activated remotely by a cell phone. Which meant the person with their finger on the trigger was going to detonate it at a specific time. If she ditched it anywhere there was the chance someone would get hurt.

She looked over at the door and thought about leaving. She would just drop it where she was told. Desperately she tried to convince herself that it was not her fault, but she knew better. "Can I really let others die to keep myself safe?" She said to herself starting to feel crazy. "What about my son? He said he would kill him if I didn't comply. My son's safety has to be a factor in this."

If something happened to her son because she did not do as she was told she would never forgive herself, nor would she if innocent people were killed because of her. She was stuck with an impossible choice and did not know what to do. Either option was unacceptable.

Then an idea occurred. One that she thought would fix all of her problems. Her son would be safe and no one would be harmed by the bomb, almost no one. She stood up and snatched the bag in two hands. She headed down the hallway towards her bedroom.

Tossing the bag under the bed she climbed in under the sheets. If the bomb detonated at her home and she was killed there would be no reason to kill her son to punish her for her failures. She hoped it would be enough to save his life.

She began to cry as she rolled over on her side. Her son would never understand what had happened and he would be devastated. She wished she could tell him she was doing the right thing. She wished she could tell him she was saving his life and many others. But she knew the chance would never come. There was no chance she could say goodbye. There was nothing left to do but close her eyes and wait for the end to come.

***

Brad Forester had made sure to get a good night's rest. He knew the morning would be a busy one. Now he was dressed and ready to go. He had a few officers on standby at the Bayside Marketplace. If anything out of the ordinary happened they would be ready for it.

He grabbed his keys and headed off into the early morning where the sun peeked over the horizon. A beautiful orange glow radiated across the sky. It was a calm feeling watching the sun rise. He let his mind wander as he headed towards the marketplace. There would be plenty of work to do when he arrived. Now was the time to relax.

When he did arrive he found each officer. Around them, the shop owners were starting to open their businesses. Within the hour the place would be mobbed with people like it was every summer. It was a very popular place. Bus tours for the city left just outside the mall every thirty minutes. There was even a boat tour that tourists lined up for. The Hard Rock Café rested just at the end of the marketplace drawing in its very own crowd. The place was generally packed all hours of the day. Today would be no different.

    Brad understood it would make stopping an attack difficult. They did not even know exactly what they were looking for. It did not matter. Brad knew they would stop it. He had complete faith in that.

    He instructed the officers which section of the outdoor mall they were assigned to. He told them he would be joining the search. One of the officers looked up at him and said, "Sir, why is it just us? If this is so important why aren't there more of us here?"

    "We are working off a tip from a credible source, but there is no guarantee that anything will happen. We were not able to provide every available officer based on the evidence we received."

    "So why are we wasting our time if nothing might happen?" One of the officers asked.

    "It's not a waste of time to make sure that everything is all right. We are here to make sure the threat is either false or to neutralize it. Keep your eyes open and if anything looks suspicious check it out."

    All three men nodded in agreement and broke away. They headed for their own sections of the marketplace. Brad did the same.

    Bayside consisted of two large buildings with two floors each. They were separated in the middle by a courtyard. Each officer had been tasked with watching a section. One officer had the first building, the other had the second building, and the last had the courtyard.

Brad would sweep all three constantly making sure there was no spot left unwatched. If something was going to happen they would stop it.

The first hour went by with no events. People were only just beginning to arrive. More people arrived as the morning inched closer to the afternoon. Brad searched the second story of the first building while the other officer searched the first. He did the same in the second building a few minutes later. He met up with the officer in the courtyard and asked him if he had seen anything yet. The officer merely shook his head.

Wandering around aimlessly was getting them nowhere and the place was getting busier. If something was going to happen it would be soon. Brad walked to the back of the courtyard and leaned against the railing. He watched as boats docked and left. Water slapped against the concrete wall just below his feet.

He turned around and surveyed the whole scene. He started to think about what Derrick would be planning. It was hard for him to accept that Derrick would kill innocent people to make a statement. The charges against him would be astounding. Conspiracy, murder, terrorism. When he was caught his life would be ripped apart. And for what? To prove the budget cuts were a bad idea? It was insane. Brad could not understand how he could do it.

He started to wonder what kind of attack would work best. A gunman would work. There were enough targets to spray and hope he hit some. But in the end, it would not be super effective. Maybe there were multiple gunmen? It was a possibility.

A young man walked past him with a backpack draped over one shoulder and Brad started to think.

Perhaps it was not a gunman. Perhaps it was a bomb. It could be easily assembled and carried in a bag. In a setting like Bayside, it would look completely normal. No one would be suspicious. The bag could be dropped in a corner of the building and detonated. Which meant it would have to be left somewhere with the most foot traffic. It ruled out a few sections of the top floors since they were always the least crowded. The food court was a good option. As well as the courtyard. But how many were they looking for? Was it just one? Or were there more? How would they know they found them all?

Brad tried to think how he would do it. If it were his plan what would he do? One bomb in the courtyard would do it, maybe another in the food court. So at least two. There might be more, but two seemed like a good number.

He snatched the radio off of his belt and said, "Keep your eyes open for anyone carrying a backpack or bag. Any unattended bags need to be examined immediately. I think we might be dealing with a bomb threat. We need to keep our eyes open on the food court and courtyard. Those might be the best areas. Stay vigilant."

He spotted the kid with the backpack heading out of the courtyard. With a brisk pace, he caught up to him and flashed his badge. The kid looked startled but did not resist when Brad told him he needed to check his bag. A laptop, iPod, folders, and some clothes were all he found. He let the young man go as he continued to walk around.

The tell-tale sign would be to find someone alone acting strangely. Someone trying to blend in with everyone else. They would be trying hard to not be noticed. It would be hard to spot that person, but Brad was confident they would.

Several other people walked by with bags over their shoulders. Brad searched as many as he could. In the other areas of the marketplace, the other officers did the same. So far everything seemed clear. He started to wonder if Ethan had been wrong. He wondered if Derrick was not planning anything at all.

The entrance to the courtyard passed by a restaurant. Opposite it was a large banyan tree. Long vines cascaded down from the top nearly touching the concrete below. A lone man stood looking up at the tree. On his back rested a black backpack. Both straps were secured over his shoulders. Still looking up the man swung his head from side to side as if checking his surroundings. Brad was immediately suspicious.

With a quick glance behind him, he spun around and walked away from the tree and towards the first building. Without a second thought, Brad walked quickly after him. When the man stepped out of the courtyard he began to survey his surroundings. It looked as if he were reading the store signs, but Brad thought he was looking for a good place to leave his bag.

He continued to walk until he reached a small bench in the center of the building. He removed the bag and slid it under. There was now no doubt in Brad's mind what he was doing. "Get down on the ground and put your hands behind your head," Brad screamed as he removed his weapon from its holster.

For a moment the man looked surprised and confused. Before Brad had time to react he pulled a small handgun from his waist and fired two shots. Somewhere behind Brad glass shattered. People screamed and started to run. The man bolted in the opposite direction. Brad did not think twice. He ran off after the man. As he did he snatched the radio from his belt and requested backup.

The man darted to the left down a hallway leading to the parking garage. He pushed past several people causing them to topple to the ground. Brad dodged everyone and kept close behind him. Once they reached the parking garage Brad once again yelled for him to stop. When he did not listen Brad fired a warning shot that shattered the mirror of a vehicle. The man threw himself behind the car and fired several shots in return.

Brad took cover behind another car as bullets ripped through the air. He needed to end this firefight before civilians got struck by stray bullets. Two other officers arrived in the parking garage with their guns drawn. They closed in on the shooter in an attempt to flank him. Another shot ricocheted off the concrete just beside Brad.

The two officers closed in silently moving from cover to cover. Before the shooter knew what was going on they were on top of him. He was thrown in a choke hold and his gun was tossed aside. They slammed him to the ground and wrapped handcuffs tight over his wrists. Brad rested against the nearest car and let out a sigh of relief.

***

The third officer had remained in the mall. He was currently watching someone walk through the food court. They walked around aimlessly with a backpack slung over his shoulder. He did not seem to be looking for a place to eat. His only concern seemed to be finding a table. Everyone in the food court moved around and stared in the direction of the gunshots. From their location it had merely sounded like fireworks. But the man did not seem concerned. He was focused on his current task. When he found a table he sat and dropped the bag under his chair. He then sat and surveyed the area.

The man looked familiar. He was sure he had seen him somewhere before. He thought he had seen him at the precinct, but knew that could not be right. Then it dawned on him. He had seen him at the precinct before because he was another officer. He tried to remember his name. It started with a T. Tony? Travis? Thomas? He thought Thomas sounded familiar. He decided he would roll with it.

He walked towards the table making sure not to draw attention. As he arrived at the table the man was standing up without the bag. "Excuse me, don't forget your bag," he said pointing down as he reached the table. "Thomas? Is that you?" The man stood for a moment not saying anything. He seemed nervous.

"Yeah, do I know you?"

"Well, we work together sort of. I mean we work in the precinct."

Thomas read his badge.

"Officer Grady, yeah I guess that sounds familiar. How are you? They got you on security at the mall?"

"Yeah, something like that. What are you up to?"

"Nothing, really. Just enjoying a day at the mall. I was thinking about picking up some lunch, but I might just walk around a bit."

"Well, have fun, Thomas."

"Will do."

Thomas started to walk away when Grady stopped him again. "Thomas, you're still forgetting your bag." Thomas stopped and rubbed his eyes. He looked back at Grady as if he were annoyed. Then he rolled his eyes.

"God damnit, Grady. I didn't want to have to do this."

He pulled a gun from his waist and pointed it at Officer Grady. He kept it low to keep it out of everyone's sight. "Don't even think about reaching for your gun."

Grady stayed perfectly still unsure of what to do. He watched in horror as Thomas pulled the hammer back on his handgun. It was clear he was going to shoot him. Right here in the food court around all of these people. Then he would escape in the panic and the bomb would detonate. They were going to win.

"Sorry Grady," Thomas said as he lifted the gun eye level. Before he could pull the trigger a man leaped from behind and tackled him to the ground. They wrestled for nearly a minute before Grady realized it had been Brad Forester who saved his life. Grady threw himself into the fight and helped to secure Thomas. The gun was pulled away and Thomas was in handcuffs. A large group had gathered around them as Thomas kicked his feet screaming to let him go.

"Shut the hell up," Brad said as he stood up and pushed his glasses up his nose. He turned back towards

Grady. "Call this in. Let them know we have two bombs on scene as well as two men in custody." Grady did as he was told. Within seconds he was told another bomb had been located across town.

"What?" Brad nearly yelled.

"A woman reported it," Grady said. "It's in her home. She gave them a story that someone forced her to build it and had told her to take it to the marketplace to leave it. She couldn't do it. She said something about keeping her son safe, but decided to call the police."

"She's very brave. She could have been killed. All right we need the bomb squad to split into two groups. The main priority is the marketplace. The secondary group can disable the bomb at her home. Let's start evacuating the people here."

As they evacuated the marketplace the bomb squad arrived. Less than ten minutes later another unit arrived at the woman's home. Both teams worked quickly to disarm the devices. When they were deemed safe they were safely stored in a protective case. Brad waited with the three officers while a police van arrived on scene. Thomas and the shooter were loaded in the back and hauled away. He shook all three of their hands and commended them on a job well done. With that, he headed back towards the precinct.

While he drove he pulled out his cell phone and called Derrick White. It rang several times before he answered. He sounded angry.

"Derrick, did you get any information about our situation?"

"Yeah, I heard there were some bombs at the mall?"

"That's right. Do you think this has something to do with Ethan?"

"It's possible. Maybe he set the whole thing up. He's become deranged."

"It's possible. I guess we'll know soon enough."

"What do you mean?"

"Didn't you hear? Ethan was apprehended by the Clearwater police department yesterday. It was all over the news."

"No, I must have missed that."

"Well he will be questioned and I'm sure they will get the truth out of him."

"Yeah."

"All right, I'm heading back in. I will be there soon."

With that, they hung up. Brad could not help but smile. Derrick was on edge. Everything was working exactly as Ethan had hoped it would.

Chapter 34

Detective Jackson sat at his desk and rubbed his eyes. The past few days had been stressful. It seemed everything was finally coming to a close. He would be happy when everything was over. The Ethan situation had been more than he had wanted.

The news had reported a shootout with police in Miami at some outdoor mall. No one was reported hurt and two men were in custody. Another incident had popped up in Miami as well. A bomb had been found in a woman's home. The bomb squad had been able to enter the home and disarm it before anyone was hurt. Jackson began to wonder what the hell was going on. Miami had been a popular city the past few days.

He shut off the television mounted to his office wall and pulled out his cell phone. A sticky note on his desk had a phone number scrawled across it. He knew he needed to make this call, but was nervous about it. There was no telling what might happen. He decided to just go for it and dialed it. After several rings, an unfamiliar voice answered.

"Hello? Who is this?"

"My name is Detective Jackson with the Clearwater police department."

"And?"

"I have something you might want."

"OK, and what might that be?"

"The man you have been looking for Major White, Ethan McCormick."

The line went silent. Derrick White was speechless. Jackson kept quiet and let his words sink in.

"You have been looking for Ethan, right?"

"Of course I have. The whole damn state has."

"I'm not calling you as an officer, Major."

"Then what is this?"

"I want to make you a deal."

Again Derrick was silent.

"Ethan's told me everything. What you've been up to, what you've been planning, everything."

"He's a criminal and a cop killer. Don't believe a word of what he says."

"You misunderstand."

"Yeah? How so?"

"I'm not trying to accuse you of anything. I want to commend you."

Derrick cleared his throat but did not respond.

"What you're doing is to protect the city. I can understand that. It's too bad people like Ethan can't. You're thinking about the greater good and I respect that. Ethan ruined that for you. Your plan didn't work because of him. If he gets back home he is only going to try and expose you. I don't want that to happen."

Derrick was quiet for some time before he said, "I don't know what you're talking about. I didn't plan anything."

"Derrick cut the bullshit all right. I know what you've been up to and I don't care. I'm not going to turn you in. I just want you to come collect your trash."

"Collect what trash?"

"I want you to come collect Ethan in person."

"Why?"

"You can't trust him with anyone else. If he is transferred back into police custody he will talk. If he talks he runs the chance of bringing you down. I don't want that to happen."

For a whole minute, Derrick was quiet. Jackson let him think. It was a tough decision to trust Jackson. He understood that. It was the only option he had and sooner or later Derrick would figure that out. "All right," he finally said. "How will we do this?"

"Leave right away. Get here as fast as you can. I will leave McCormick tied up in central park. Walk to the back of the park behind a small manmade lake with the small train track running across. He will be in the bushes. It's a nice secluded area where no one will be looking for him. Then take him back home with you."

"What do you want in return?"

"I don't want anything. I told you I believe in what you're doing."

"How do I know you can be trusted?"

Jackson let out a quiet laugh.

"What other options have you got?"

Derrick knew it was the truth. There were no other options. If Ethan was transferred to Miami a trial would begin. He might be able to bring him down. Even if Ethan did go to prison Derrick stood the chance of being discovered. It was a chance he could not take. He needed to mend the damage that had been done because of his recent failure. A new plan would have to be developed. Something needed to happen. He needed to prove his point. He needed to make them understand. He would not be able to do that while under investigation. Once Ethan was properly disposed of he would get to work on his next plan. This time Ethan would not be around to ruin it.

"All right, I'm leaving now."

"Ethan will be right where I told you. I think it's best if we don't see each other. Don't want to run the risk of being seen together. I will falsify some report that states Ethan managed to escape in my custody. Hurry up."

With that Jackson hung up the phone and sat back in his chair. He rubbed his temples and stood up. He slipped the phone into his pocket and made his way out of his office.

***

Ethan had been lying on his cot most of the morning. His thoughts were focused on the Bayside Marketplace. He had no way of knowing what was going on. Had Derrick been successful? Did something happen? For the first time in a few days, he wished he could have watched the news.

Moments later Detective Jackson appeared at the door. He slid open the cell and stepped inside. Without a word, he slapped another pair of handcuffs on Ethan. Jackson pulled him from the cell and pushed him towards the hall. He stopped a moment and peered out to make sure it was clear. It was an odd gesture for a man transporting a prisoner.

When the coast was presumably clear they continued on their way. Finally, they made it out of the precinct and into the parking lot. Ethan spotted Jackson's unmarked cruiser and they headed towards it.

Ethan was crammed into the back seat and the door slammed hard behind him. Ethan resisted the urge to say anything when Jackson climbed into the driver seat.

For nearly ten minutes they drove in complete silence. Finally, Ethan said, "Did anything happen today? In Miami I mean." Jackson looked back at him from the mirror and shook his head.

"Nothing that I've heard."

He sighed in relief. They had managed to stop whatever it was Derrick had been planning. Which meant now Derrick was in trouble. Now he could use this to his advantage. The truth could come out. He would expose Greene and everything he had done.

The cruiser came to a stop and Jackson turned around. "I'm going to un-cuff you. Don't do anything stupid." Ethan only smiled in response. He watched as Jackson climbed out of the car and walked around to his side. Within two minutes he was out of the backseat and free of the handcuffs. He looked around and recognized exactly where they were. It was the park he had seen from his hotel the night before.

"Get moving," Jackson ordered as he pushed him along. He walked in front of Jackson as he directed him with several pushes in the right direction. They moved along in silence. There was so much on Ethan's mind that he felt distracted.

Finally, they came to a large area with a small lake in the center. A small set of train tracks, which wound around the park, crossed over the lake. He recognized it immediately. He had stood in his hotel room and looked down on it. It seemed like days had gone by since then. He thought about the train and the tracks. He knew it was a ride for children that they must have run on the weekends. He pictured parents riding behind the children and thought how silly they must have looked.

Now the park was virtually empty. The train was not running. Aside from a few couples enjoying a stroll or a lone man walking his dog there was hardly anyone there. Jackson preferred it that way. It would make his next move easier.

They began to walk towards the lake. Ethan could only guess where they were headed and he started to worry. Jackson led him around the back of the lake and stopped. From here Ethan could see the hotel he had stayed out looming overhead just out of the park's boundaries. He thought he spotted the window he was looking out only the other night. Now the room was dark and the curtains were drawn. He would give anything to be back in that room with Caroline. The temptation to break free and find her was strong. They could run away and start a life together. He realized he was beginning to fall for her. There was no way of telling how everything would work out, but he hoped he would see her one more time.

Jackson broke his concentration as he wrapped a handcuff around his left wrist. He then pushed him forwards towards the back of the lake. There were all kinds of bushes and small trees along the back edge of the lake. Just beyond them was a small manmade hill. It had been made to block the surroundings from the front of the lake. It made the perfect spot to hide from the rest of the park.

Ethan was forced to lie down in the mulch and Jackson tightened the other handcuff around the thickest branch of a small tree. The branch seemed strong enough and would not break easily. If he worked at it long enough it might have broken.

"Really?" Ethan said. "You're handcuffing me to a tree?"

Jackson nodded.

"Shut up, Ethan."

With that, he took a step back and stared down at Ethan. He seemed to be admiring his work and making sure Ethan could not get free. When he was satisfied he turned around and started to walk away. "Wait," Ethan called out. Jackson stopped and turned back towards him. "Do you have any idea what you're doing?" Ethan asked. Jackson did not respond. He only smiled and walked away.

Now Ethan was alone handcuffed to a tree. From his location in the bushes, he could only see the hotel and a bit of the sky. He started to wonder about the small patch of mulch he was in. There was a high school nearby. He wondered how many teenagers had brought their dates to this exact spot. It was the perfect place for hormone-ridden teens to get some privacy. He shook the thought away. The thought of his newly formed prison used as a sex spot by teenagers disturbed him.

As he lay in silence the memory of Sandra flooded back. He missed her so much. He would give anything to have her back in his life. There was no doubt he still loved her. She had been murdered by Derrick White and he wanted the whole world to know it. He would make sure he was brought to justice for what he did to her. Sandra deserved nothing less.

A butterfly flew past his head and landed on a nearby flower. As it fed on the nectar Ethan found himself mesmerized by it. Somehow it reminded him of Sandra. He wondered if she was there with him in spirit watching over him, providing protection. The butterfly fluttered off into the blue sky and he let out a soft sigh.

***

Derrick White had been behind the wheel of his car for several hours. He had left moments after receiving the call from Detective Jackson. He was in a hurry to clean up the mess. Brad Forester and others might notice his absence, but it was important he took care of it immediately. He would be able to lie and tell them he had gone home sick. It did not matter. If he did not take care of Ethan they would find out the truth sooner or later. It was best to deal with the matter personally.

He was getting close to the city of Largo. Within minutes he would be there and Ethan would be dealt with. He knew exactly what he would do. If he was where Jackson had promised he would force him into his car. He would handcuff him in the back seat and head back towards Miami. It would be a long drive and Ethan would beg for his life the entire way.

Derrick did not want to kill Ethan, but it had to happen. He would stop in a remote area of the Everglades. With tape over Ethan's mouth, he would drag him into the swamp. There he would slit his throat and hold his head under water. He would make sure he was dead. There would be no doubt in his mind. No chance of escape to ruin everything again.

The gators would take care of the corpse. There would be no chance it would be found. The Florida

Everglades was a gigantic area. It would take months to find a body and if they did the cause of death would impossible to tell. There would be nothing that would point back to him. Of that he was sure.

Anything Ethan knew would die with him. If Jackson kept up his end of the bargain he might not have to have him killed. Though he thought about hiring someone to silence him anyway. Another lose end was just a mistake waiting to happen. There had already been too many.

His plan had been ruined. Everything had been going perfectly. Even after Sandra had started poking around. When she was no longer a worry everything still seemed to go smooth. The police assumed her death was a suicide just as he had planned. There had been no push back, no further investigation. He thought he had been in the clear.

McKinley had started to snoop in Sandra's work and found she had stumbled across something. Derrick had never been sure how much he knew, but even a little was too much. He had to be killed and what better way to do it than blame Ethan McCormick? The moment McKinley contacted Ethan he had signed for his own death. Kill McKinley and frame Ethan. Then after a day have Ethan killed. The investigation would have stopped with him leaving Derrick to continue with his work.

But Geoffrey Hunt had failed. How hard could it have been to kill two people? How could he have been so useless? Then there was Fidel Sanchez. He sent him to clean up Geoffrey's mess and he got himself shot. As far as Derrick knew he was still in intensive care. If he pulled through he would have another end to snuff out.

He hoped he would succumb to his injuries. Overall it would be the best turn out. With everything falling apart at the seams another cleanup operation was too much. The bodies were starting to pile. Too many more and suspicion would be aroused. If Fidel died Ethan was the final piece. He would do everything in his power to make sure it was taken care of right. Even if it meant getting his hands dirty.

A large tan sign stood in a small green clearing. It read Largo Central Park. He quickly changed into the left lane and took the first turn. He pulled into a small parking lot with only a handful of cars scattered about. He scanned the lot and the part of the park he could see. There seemed to be no police. It was an anxious feeling he could not shake. In the back of his mind the thought of the police arriving stung like a wasp. Jackson could have lied about giving Ethan up. It could have been an elaborate setup. He decided it was worth the risk. If Ethan was not where Jackson had promised he would drive and not stop until he was far away from Florida.

Derrick made his way across the large open green field. To his left children screamed with joy in a large playground surrounded by a tall iron fence. Their parents leaned against it and played on their phones.

The park was relatively empty and Derrick was grateful. It was best if everything happened as quiet as possible. And the fewer people who saw his face the better. It had been a long road and it was near the end. It was unfortunate it was all for nothing, but he knew he was not done. Once Ethan was dead his work would begin again.

***

A small pile of leaves crunched softly in the distance. Small footsteps continued around the side of the lake. From his place in the bushes, Ethan could not see who was there. He had been handcuffed to the tree for what seemed like an eternity. He tried several times to bend the branch, but it would not budge. Even twisting yielded no results.

The steps drew closer and stopped just beyond his field of vision. He wanted to call out, but he was sure he knew who was there. A figure stepped out and looked down at him. Ethan stared up at the familiar face of Derrick White.

Ethan almost did not recognize him. Now his face seemed longer and filled with stress and dark circles had formed under his eyes. His clothes were wrinkled and mashed against his body. Thin red veins snaked over the whites of his eyes.

With the barrel of a Glock pointed down at Ethan he said, "Hello Ethan." Ethan did his best to act shocked and scared. He looked up at him with what he hoped was betrayal plastered on his face.

"Major White?"

"Sorry, it has to be this way, Ethan. You really were a good cop."

"What are you talking about?"

"You've been alive longer than you were supposed to. I need to take care of that."

"You're just going to shoot me here? While I'm tied to this tree like a dog?"

"No, not here. We're going for a ride."

He searched the area for a few minutes and found the handcuff keys sitting a few feet out of Ethan's reach. He snatched them up and uncuffed Ethan. Derrick stepped back and kept the Glock trained on him.

"Don't do anything you will regret Ethan."

"Why not? You're just going to kill me anyway."

"I could kill you now. Or you could do as you're told and get a few more hours."

"You miserable bastard!" Ethan yelled.

"Is that the best you got, Ethan?"

Ethan glared at him.

"Before we go anywhere tell me why Derrick."

"Why what?"

"Why did you do it?"

"I don't know what you're talking about."

"God damnit, Derrick. You're Greene. It's obvious. You had Sandra and McKinley killed and you tried to pin it all on me. That's why you're here. You're mopping up your mess. Why did you do it?"

Derrick let out a quiet laugh.

"You really know how to push your luck. It doesn't matter anyway, you wouldn't understand. Let's go."

He pointed to the side motioning Ethan to start walking. Ethan thought for a moment and shook his head. Falling to his knees he looked up at Derrick.

"Fuck you, kill me here. I'm not going anywhere with you."

"I swear to God, Ethan, I will kill you here."

"Fine, at least they will find my body."

Derrick looked around making sure they were alone. He pointed the gun at Ethan as if he were going to shoot him, but put it to his side. He felt the familiar sting in the back of his mind. Maybe it was all a trap. He stepped forward and patted Ethan down making sure to cover every inch. "Are you wearing a wire you son of a bitch?" Ethan looked confused. "This better not be some kind of trap or I will make sure you are ripped limb from limb."

Ethan shook his head.

"I wish I was wearing a God damned wire. How much did you promise to pay Jackson for giving me to you?"

"He called me. I didn't offer a cent. He believes in what I was trying to do. Unlike you. You couldn't see why it was all necessary."

"Killing Sandra was necessary? I fail to see the connection."

"Yes, a few people got in the way. I had to have them killed. I did not enjoy it, but I had to. Sandra and McKinley were good cops. They just stuck their nose in the wrong place. Really you should blame Sandra. You wouldn't have been dragged into this if it wasn't for her."

Ethan gritted his teeth.

"They were trying to cut our budget, Ethan. Do you know what that means? Our resources would be limited. That could not be allowed to happen. How can we properly protect this city if we don't have the means? I was going to show them their mistake. They would regret the cuts. The bombs were supposed to destroy Bayside and I suppose you are to thank for stopping that."

"Thank your hitman Geoffrey Hunt. He gave you up after trying to kill me."

"I always knew he was weak. I was going to kill him once he took you out. He couldn't be trusted. Not like he would have been missed much I suppose."

"You were going to kill innocent people? All to prove the department should be well funded? You're insane!"

"I knew you wouldn't understand Ethan. It's about the greater good. When I put on this badge every morning I am making a promise to keep this city safe. When we can't function we can't protect it. It was the only way to make everyone understand. Every person who would have lost their life would have been doing so to protect the future of this city. I did what I had to do."

Ethan was shocked. Derrick was delusional. Somehow he justified killing innocent people for what he thought was the greater good. Nothing good would have come out of it. It was asinine. He wanted to see Derrick locked away in an asylum. He needed a padded room and straightjacket. Whatever punishment he received would be too good for him.

"It's time to go Ethan."

He pulled Ethan to his feet and pushed him forward. Ethan took two steps and stopped. The barrel of Derrick's gun jammed between his shoulder blades. "Get moving," he yelled, but Ethan did not listen. He turned around and stared into Derrick's eyes. The Glock now aimed at his heart.

"I'm not going anywhere with you. You're going to rot away in prison. It's more than you deserve."

Derrick took a long step back with the pistol still aimed at him. He looked around nervously not sure what to expect. Ethan seemed to be smiling now and it made him uneasy. He had checked him. There was no bug on him. He was sure of it. How could he think he was going to prison? Derrick thought he was trying to scare him.

"Ethan, if you don't get moving I will shoot you right now."

"It's too late for that Derrick."

The sound of movement from the other side of the lake echoed through the air. They would be surrounded. Instantly he knew what was about to happen. Somewhere behind him, someone screamed something, but Derrick did not hear them. Instead, he pulled the trigger.

Two shots rang out, but only one was from Derrick. The bullet screamed towards Ethan and the world seemed to slow down. He watched as Derrick's head snapped to the side in a spray of blood that splattered over the leaves and trees. The other bullet struck Ethan as Derrick toppled to the ground. He stumbled backward and fell flat on his back.

An S.W.A.T. unit sharpshooter had been positioned on the hotel outside of the park. Next to him another officer lay prone with a long range sensitive microphone. A large clear cone extended from what looked like a blue plastic gun. It jutted out covering the microphone. A pair of black headphones were plugged into the back end allowing him to hear everything that had been said. Every word of it had been recorded on a small recorder attached to the butt of the plastic gun.

Back on the ground, Detective Jackson ran to Ethan's side as three other officers pounced on Derrick's lifeless body. One of them checked his pulse for good measure. As blood gushed from his skull Ethan moaned in pain. A white hot pain burned in his shoulder. Jackson pulled up his sleeve and checked the wound. "There's no exit wound. The bullet is still inside," he said. An ambulance was called right away.

Jackson pulled Ethan to his feet and helped him walk away. The other officers were left to secure the area. Jackson's only focus was getting Ethan to the parking lot to wait for help. They stumbled across the grass as blood dripped down his arm. Finally, Ethan pulled away and said, "Thanks, Jackson, but I can walk." Jackson nodded and walked next to him.

Ethan held his shoulder as they walked in silence. When they reached the parking lot Ethan sat on the curb to rest. After a moment Jackson joined him.

"Thanks for hearing Brad out."

"I have to say, even though he sent me all the evidence he had I wasn't completely convinced. You're lucky your friend Fidel showed up. He told us everything he knew. I'm sorry for not believing you sooner."

"Don't worry about it, Detective. You were doing your job. I respect that."

"Well, with Derrick's confession there's enough to prove your innocence."

"Yeah."

"Once Fidel recovers we will be in contact with Miami to have him handed over. He needs to pay for his crimes."

"Yes, he does."

"It's a shame Geoffrey and Derrick won't be living behind bars."

"I think they got what they deserved."

"I suppose you're right Ethan."

They waited for the ambulance in silence. Ethan thought over the events that had transpired over the last twenty-four hours. Before he and Caroline had split up he called Brad Forester and asked for one last favor. He knew the only way to draw Derrick out would he would have to be bait. Calling Derrick himself would not have worked. Derrick would have immediately suspected a trap. Instead, he needed another officer to do it.

Ethan had asked Brad to contact Detective Jackson one more time. This time he would share all of the collected evidence. Brad would beg Jackson to give Ethan a shot. Over the phone, Brad explained Ethan's plan. At first, Jackson was not receptive. The more Brad spoke the more Jackson began to trust him. Finally, he caved. After receiving the evidence via email he decided to give Ethan a shot. He told Brad he would play along. Ethan would be seen driving around town and Jackson would pursue him. It was mostly for show. Back in Miami Derrick would truly believe Ethan had been arrested. From that moment on he would do anything to have Ethan silenced. Once Ethan received confirmation from Brad that everything was in place he got to work.

It had been a risky plan, but it had worked. Now with a bullet in his shoulder, he felt lucky to be alive. Derrick could just as easily have shot him where he lay and left. He may have been arrested moments later, but Ethan would still be dead. He decided not to focus on the what ifs.

Flashing red lights rounded the corner and mounted the curb. It drove across a small field of grass and came to rest in the parking lot only a few feet from where they sat. Jackson looked over at Ethan and patted him on the left shoulder. "Go get patched up

Ethan," he said. "Then get home. You have a lot of work ahead of you."

The ambulance drove him to the nearest hospital. The doctor told him he was lucky. The bullet had not struck the bone. They were able to extract the bullet and sew him back up. "There will be some pain for a few days, but you'll live," the doctor told him.

"Would you mind if I keep that?" Ethan said pointing to the blood covered piece of metal on the metal tray.

"The bullet? Uh, I guess you can."

"Thanks."

The doctor shook his head and shrugged as if to say I do not understand. He asked one of the nurses to wash it off. When it was clean Ethan slipped it in his pocket. When he got home he planned to run a wire through it and wear it around his neck. He thought it was a good reminder of his mortality. Whenever he decided to do something foolish he would remember he was not invincible.

With that, he was out of the hospital and on his way back home to Miami. On the trip home, he thought about Caroline. There had not been a chance to say good-bye.

***

Brad Forester had greeted him the moment he was back in Miami. He had thrown his arms around him giving a friendly hug. "It's nice to have you back, Ethan." He said. Ethan only nodded.

He quickly learned the Chief of Police had become involved in everything. Ethan was being absolved of all charges. The news had reported Geoffrey Hunt had been behind the death of Sandra Delano and Major McKinley. Now the whole world knew Ethan was innocent and had been framed by Geoffrey.

"What about Derrick?" Ethan asked.

Brad shook his head.

"Chief thinks it would be best if his name was kept out of the news."

"What? He can't do that! He's responsible for everything."

"I understand Ethan. If it were my call it wouldn't be this way. I think everyone should know the truth."

"Why is he doing that?"

"Derrick was a Major, your boss. Looks bad on the chief of police for something like that to happen under his watch. Publicity is all he cares about it seems."

"This isn't right."

"I know you're angry Ethan. Honestly, I am too. If there was anything I could do I would."

Ethan shrugged.

"But hey, there's a bit of good news. The Chief has promoted me to Major. I will be taking over for Derrick."

Ethan congratulated him doing his best to sound genuine. He was truly excited that Brad would be taking over Derrick's position. He knew he would do an excellent job. Brad was a great officer and an even better man. He would do the position well.

"Oh, one more thing Ethan. I found this in the airport bathroom."

In his hand was Ethan's badge. The gold shine almost seemed to glimmer in Brad's hand. The badge number was etched in the bottom. He knew those three number well, four hundred ten. He smiled for a moment but did not reach for it. Brad looked at him, puzzled.

"I can't stay here, Brad. It doesn't feel right. Sandra was killed because of Derrick. If she can't have true justice I don't think I can stay."

At first, Brad had looked upset and confused, but slowly he started to understand. Finally, he placed his hand on Ethan's shoulder and squeezed gently.

"I understand, Ethan. What are you going to do now?"

"I don't know. Maybe I will start a private detective company."

"You're going to be a private eye?"

"Sure, why not? Someone once told me I would be good at it."

Brad smiled.

"Good luck, Ethan. If you ever change your mind there's always a place for you here."

Ethan thanked him and turned around. With that, he walked out of the police department and into the summer heat. He stopped for a moment and took in a deep breath. The warm heat was sucked into his lungs, but it felt good. He smiled as he walked towards his car. Before climbing in he took one last look at the police department. A moment later he was behind the wheel of his Stratus and headed off down the road.

Epilogue

After returning home Ethan sat alone in his living room. He stared at the wall from his couch thinking quietly. He thought about everything that had happened. He wondered if his decision to leave the police department had been a wise one. Would he make a great private detective? How would he make money? How would he get business? He had nothing figured out. But for the first time since Sandra had been killed he was able to relax.

The silence started to reverberate in his ears. It was becoming too much to bear. He stood up and walked over to his phone. His socks scuffed across the carpet as he did. He picked up the phone from the kitchen table and stared at the touch screen. There were no missed calls. Not that he thought there would be. But deep down inside he was disappointed.

He began to dial a number he had memorized. His heart started to race faster with each new number displayed on screen. He stood with his finger hovering over the large green call button. More than anything he wanted to press it, but he was nervous. There was no telling what might happen. For all he knew she was no longer in Florida. Maybe calling her was pointless. What if she did not want anything to do with him? Maybe what they had shared that night was out of fear rather than affection. He hoped that was not true.

Finally, he broke down and pressed it. After several rings, a voice broke through the other end. It was familiar and soft. Just hearing it melted away all of his stress and fear. It was nice to hear her voice again. He had missed every moment away from her.

"Hello Caroline," he said and smiled.

Acknowledgements

First and foremost I would like to thank my good friend Timothy Schmit for creating the cover art for me. He is a very talented artist and put up with my constant revisions and questions. His help at bringing the look of my book together was invaluable. You can visit his website where he spends his free time as a photographer, http://www.timothymschmit.com/

Of course, I need to thank the friends and family who showed their support along the way. Especially my mother who always believed in me. It was always a great help knowing so many people supported me and truly wanted me to succeed. I was kept on track by the constant support and willingness to read my first book.

I would also like to make a special acknowledgment to my teacher from back in high school, Renee. It is because of her the character Ethan McCormick exists. It was in her class that I truly decided my goal in life would be to one day publish a novel. I started out writing short stories based on the character Ethan McCormick in her class and became very attached to him. For several years I planned to create a book based on him. If it had not been for that one assignment in her class I would not be publishing this book today.

Last, but definitely not least, I must thank my wife Melissa. She put up with my long hours of work and several requests to read and reread several parts of this very book. I could always count on her to give me an honest an unbiased opinion. Whenever I began to doubt myself she was there to push me back in the right direction. Without her, I believe I would never have had the confidence to finish this project. Her support and opinion were the best help I could have ever asked for.

About the author

Evan Bond has always had a passion for telling stories. From a young age, he was writing stories to entertain friends and family. As he grew older he continued to write. It transformed from one-page stories to short fiction. Eventually, it evolved into full-length novels. Evan currently lives Florida with his wife Melissa.

Printed in Great Britain
by Amazon